# Floating Twigs

# Floating Twigs

Charles Tabb

Gifted Time Books
Beaverdam, VA 23015

ISBN-10: 1722104392
ISBN-13: 978-1722104399

# ACKNOWLEDGMENTS

Writing itself is a strictly solitary act, but no book is ever actually written alone. Many people help along the way, sometimes inadvertently. Friends and family lend encouragement and assistance when one finds himself stuck on a point. This book, of course, is no exception.

First, thank you to my family for your undying support, especially my wife, Dee. The belief you all have in me goes further than you know. Writers are a strange lot. We doubt our ability to compose even a good sentence, and hearing from others that we can write good stories is like a healing balm. I mention here specifically family I thank who have moved on from this life and had characters, both major and minor, named in their honor: my maternal grandfather, Henry Pittman Mohead; my aunts, Mary Jane Dow and Dorothy Ledbetter, and my mother-in-law, Jane Terry.

Thank you to friends who allowed me to name characters after them: Dawn Burton, Josh Cutshaw, Bob Ebert, Scott Humphrey, Anne Kennedy, and Chris Pinnix. A special thank you to Chuck and Trisha Shelton. Your hospitality and friendship are more abundant than water and more valuable than gold.

Thank you to those who assisted by reading my manuscript, warts and all, and providing valuable feedback: Sue Schorling, Chuck and Trisha Shelton, and Laura Gariepy. You helped make this book much better than I alone could have ever made it.

Thank you to my editor, Marilyn Mercer, and my book interior designer, JoAnn Meaker. All the good work you did shows. If any errors in text remain, they are my own.

Finally, thank you to those who take the time to read this book. It was an intense labor of love and a story I'd carried around with me for years, which I believe all good literary books are. I hope you enjoy reading it even more than I enjoyed writing it.

## DEDICATION

For my family, especially Dee, Cherisse, Laura, Dan, Alex and Cameron, and to my late mother, Martha Anne Mohead Tabb, known to her grandchildren as "Moopy." She believed in me as only a mother can. Thank you all for everything.

This book is also for all the dogs who teach us how to love. Now all we need to do is listen.

These beauteous forms,
Through a long absence, have not been to
    me
As is a landscape to a blind man's eye:
But oft, in lonely rooms, and 'mid the din
Of towns and cities, I have owed to them,
In hours of weariness, sensations sweet,
Felt in the blood, and felt along the heart;
And passing even into my purer mind
With tranquil restoration:—feelings too
Of unremembered pleasure: such,
    perhaps,
As have no slight or trivial influence
On that best portion of a good man's life,
His little, nameless, unremembered, acts
Of kindness and of love.

        --William Wordsworth
        From "Lines Composed a
        Few Miles Above Tintern
        Abbey"


No act of kindness, no matter how small,
    is ever wasted.

        --Aesop
        "The Lion and the Mouse"

I had known the day would come when circumstances forced my return to Denton, Florida, where I grew up. My parents had died before I finished high school, but another funeral brought me here now.

The Denton of my childhood reminded me of an old man, settled and unchanging. However, on that sunny day back in 1990 as I drove across the bridge that spanned the inlet between Denton Bay and the Gulf of Mexico, I looked over the expanse of emerald-green water to the harbor that lay protected by Sugar Isle, a long barrier island of sugar-white sand. Instead of a harbor filled with fishing boats lazily dotting the landscape, a waterfront teeming with jet-skis and noise greeted me. New boat docks grew and twisted out of the adjoining land like cancerous growths. Beside the more expensive boats that had invaded the harbor, the older fishing boats looked like impoverished cousins. Seventeen years had scarred the town.

Beyond the bridge I turned onto the road that led away from the harbor toward the house where I'd grown up. The small, rundown place still sagged among the pines and scrub oaks. As I approached it, grief and loss struck me, and I sat alone in my car and cried for the first time since leaving Denton. The memories flooded back along with the tears, but this time I welcomed them instead of pushing them back into their dark corner.

Memory has a way of playing tricks on us. Sad memories fade into a haze that we never can be sure is honest, since we often embellish them with colorful hues to make them bearable, while good memories take on a luster they don't deserve. But my memory of the events surrounding my thirteenth birthday is good. At least I think it is.

It all began with finding Bones back in 1968 the day Roger, Lee and I swiped Dan Russell's rowboat for a quick trip out to a barge that had become stuck in the sand a few days before. Roger and Lee were my best friends. We were always finding something to do, sometimes dangerous and often slightly illegal, and on that sunny June day we were on the verge of another adventure. Lee and Roger would be in trouble if we were caught with a stolen rowboat. I wouldn't be because, well, my parents wouldn't care.

The barge sat mired on Sugar Isle's north shore, which faced the harbor about three-hundred yards across the inlet. We figured fish would be swarming all around the accidental reef, and we wanted to catch some before someone hauled the barge away.

We knew that Dan Russell, the rowboat's owner, was in jail for at least the next few days after he vandalized his ex-girlfriend's car and broke into her apartment, so he would never know we had "borrowed" his boat unless someone saw us and told, and that wasn't very likely, but we still argued the point.

"Man, what if your sister finds out and tells someone?" Roger said to Lee. "We'll get it for sure then. Not only will Dan find out we took his boat, but our parents will kill us, too."

"Maybe we could bribe her," I said.

"Naw, Jack," Lee said, his blue eyes twinkling at me from beneath his shaggy, sun-bleached bangs. "Sandra won't tell. I got something on her if she does and she knows it."

"What?" I asked.

"Caught her smoking with Greg."

Greg was Sandra's boyfriend. I knew she wouldn't tell with that hanging over her head. Her parents despised Greg. Adding smoking to being with him would only make the offense worse.

"What if they come for the barge and we're fishing from it?" asked Roger. His freckles would grow as red as his curly hair when he became agitated, and they shone brightly now.

Lee looked at Roger as if he had sprouted another nose. "So? We just leave. All they can do is yell at us."

"So, what are we waiting for?" I asked with a grin.

Lee and I clambered into the small rowboat and Roger followed, still complaining under his breath. We stored our fishing gear in the shallow hull while making bets about who would catch the most fish. Untying the rope that secured the boat to the dock, we took turns rowing across the waters of the natural harbor. Once we were on our way, Roger's apprehension faded, as we knew it would. He would always complain, but he never backed out of a plan.

Soon we were approaching the trapped barge. After we found a place to tie the boat to the abandoned craft, I climbed onto the flat, metal deck and instantly regretted it.

"Hot feet! Hot feet!" I squealed as I danced around the surface of the barge, lifting my bare feet as soon as they landed on the sun-heated metal. Laughing, Lee and Roger grabbed two of the buckets we had brought to hold the fish, filled them with water, and emptied them onto the hot surface.

I immediately hopped onto the wet area.

"More. It's better but still too hot," I said, still doing a jig.

They doused the deck a few more times before I was able to walk on it. "Man, you looked like your feet were on fire," Lee said, laughing.

"They were," I said, joining their laughter.

I was enjoying our simple camaraderie despite my home life, or maybe because of it. Although Lee and Roger knew my situation at home, we never discussed it. Everyone in town knew my parents were drunks. I had watched lots of Andy Griffith on TV and thought every town had its own drunk, and that it was my bad luck to have been born to Denton's resident "Otis" and his equally intoxicated wife. However, I never laughed at the comic character on the TV show. For me it felt too real to be funny.

We prepared to drop our lines into the water, baiting our hooks with bits of the raw bacon Lee had taken from his family's refrigerator. The emptiness of Sugar Isle stretched out behind us, with only sand dunes to witness our day. The sun hung overhead and cooked our backs, already browned to a deep, golden tan from a lifetime of exposure.

Lee's line hit the water first, and a swarm of silver trout rushed to the greasy bait. "Whoa!" Lee said as he pulled his line up as fast as it had gone into the water. A small silver trout dangled and flipped on the hook.

"Wow! They must be starving or something," said Roger, dropping his line into the water. Immediately, a fish struck the bait. "Man, I ain't never seen anything like this!" he said as he lifted the squirming fish from the water.

"You *ain't never* been to school either, huh?" I said and laughed.

Roger looked at me. "Yeah, well you better get your line in the water if you expect to catch more than I do, Poindexter."

I dropped my line into the salt water with the same result. "Cooler than grits," I said, holding up the wriggling fish.

Within fifteen minutes, each of us had crept past any reasonable limit, but we continued to fish, undaunted. Finally, Roger noticed the abundance of fish and spoke up.

"Hey, guys. I think we're past our limit."

Lee and I looked at the three buckets, which were nearly overflowing.

"Aw, man, look at that!" Lee said, amazed at how many we could catch so quickly. "We must have at least fifteen apiece!"

"If someone sees that, we're sunk. We're gonna have to put some back." Roger's tone hinted he expected disagreement.

"Are you crazy? I worked hard for those fish,"

Lee said, seeming to dare Roger to force the issue.

"Worked hard? It's only been ten minutes!" said Roger.

I watched the exchange. "More like fifteen."

"Gee, five more minutes. I'm sure the Marine Patrol will overlook the fact we've doubled what we could legally catch and keep because it took us a whole fifteen minutes to catch this many," Roger said.

Of course, it was Lee who made the pronouncement. "We'll keep the thirty biggest ones. That's ten apiece."

"But the limit is eight," reminded Roger.

Lee looked him in the eye and shrugged. "I'm keeping ten. You can throw all yours back if you want. No skin off my nose."

As we began choosing our fish, I heard a sound behind Lee. I looked toward the soft noise and my eyes bulged. "Oh, my God," I whispered.

"What?"

"Look," I said, but they had seen my frightened gaze and had already turned in its direction.

"Sweet Jesus in a chariot race," said Roger.

Hobbling toward us was a large, mixed-breed male dog, at least that was what it seemed to be. It looked more like a dog's skeleton with skin thrown over it like some threadbare rug tossed over a bush. The dog was starving. It was easy for us to see every bone beneath his hide. His fur was pale yellow with some white areas mixed in, but his most noticeable feature, other than the fact he was starving, was he was missing his right foreleg. It appeared to have been amputated at some point, and he had adjusted to getting around on his remaining legs.

"What do we do?" asked Roger, the fear straining his voice to a squeal.

At the sound of Roger's voice, the dog's tail began to wag sluggishly as his head drooped in submission. I exhaled, unaware I had been holding my breath. We didn't know where the dog came from, or how he came to be on Sugar Isle, but he appeared to be friendly at least.

"He must have smelled the fish," said Lee.

"Or the bacon," I said. With that, I reached down and picked up the remaining bacon and tossed a few small pieces of it to the dog, who caught every piece before it hit the ground and swallowed it before he knew it was in his mouth. Fascinated, we stared at the result of extreme neglect.

"What do we do?" asked Roger again, this time with pity.

"He looks like he'd be a fine-looking dog if he wasn't starving," I said.

"Yeah, and had four legs," Lee added.

"So what do we do?" asked Roger a third time.

"I'm taking him home. I'm adopting him." I was as surprised at my decision as my friends were.

"Are you nuts? Your dad won't let you keep a dog!" said Lee.

I looked at him. He looked exasperated, as if I'd suggested we bring the barge home and store it in my back yard. I could tell what Lee was thinking; it was in his eyes. Your dad and mom are drunks. They'll never go for this! Dogs cost money. You're poor, the look said. But I had made up my mind.

"Are you gonna take him home?" I asked Lee, challenging him.

"I can't. My mom's scared of big dogs, especially ones that look hungry enough to eat you."

I looked at Roger.

"No way!" said Roger without being asked. "We already have a dog. My dad would just put him down anyway, which may not be such a bad idea. He's suffering."

"Not if he gets fed," I said and began to approach the dog warily.

"Ja-a-ack," said Roger.

"It's okay. I'm the one with the food," I said, holding up the remaining bacon. When I walked closer, the dog went to its back and bared its belly. I knelt to pet him, and he wagged his tail some more and licked my face. I could smell the raw bacon on his breath. I fed him the rest of it a piece at a time and smiled down at what I was already viewing as my new dog.

"See? He's my dog." I looked at him as if he had suddenly been transformed into an award-winning show dog. "Come home with me, boy. I'll figure out a way to fatten you up."

I stood and made a kissing sound, patting my thigh as I walked to the rowboat, the fish all but forgotten. The dog struggled to his feet and followed.

I saw Lee and Roger exchange bewildered looks. "What are we gonna do?" Roger asked Lee, this time referring to me.

Lee shrugged his shoulders and continued sorting the smallest fish from his catch and throwing them back. "Help him bury the dog when his dad shoots it, I guess," Lee said, not caring if I heard. They lacked my faith, which in reality I had no right to have.

They looked at me again. I must have looked as though I had just found the pot of gold at the end of the rainbow. And in a way, I guess I had.

We climbed into the rowboat, making room for the dog, and paddled back to shore. We cleaned our catch, tossing the fish guts to the dog, who continued to swallow the offered food too fast to taste it while I wondered how I would convince my parents, especially my dad, to let me have the dog. Keeping a dog costs money. He obviously needed some veterinary care and lots of food. As we took turns rowing, we discussed how the dog ended up on the island in the first place. It was apparent from his condition he'd been abandoned for some time, probably roaming the beach and looking for food until we showed up.

"You wanna come with me?" I asked Lee and Roger.

"Where?" Lee asked.

"To talk to my dad about the dog."

For the second time that day, Lee looked at me as if I had lost my mind. "No way." I didn't even need to get an answer from Roger. His look said it all.

"How you think I should do it? I mean, you could at least try to give me some advice or something."

"You already ignored my advice," Lee said.

"Come on, Lee," I said.

He looked at me, accepting my decision with a shake of his head. "Well, I'd make sure he was in a good mood first. Other than that, I don't know."

Roger spoke up. "How will you get the money to feed him? Your dad's sure not to like that."

"I guess I could clean fish," I said.

In Denton many of the older kids would go down to the docks where the larger party boats brought the tourists in from a day of deep-sea fishing. They would stand along the edges of the dock, asking those getting off the boat if they needed their fish cleaned. The going rate was ten cents per pound of fish. A few red snapper and a couple of large grouper could net as much as three dollars. If the fishing was good and the tourists drunk enough, they might even add a tip on top of that. That was a lot of money in 1968, especially for a twelve-year-old. It would also pay for enough dog food for a week at least. One good week could pay for a veterinarian to look at the dog and take care of any minor problems. Three good weeks, and a kid my age felt like a Rockefeller.

Roger, of course, was quick to point out the problem with my plan. "They don't let kids our age clean fish. Nobody under thirteen is allowed."

"That isn't a law or anything. It's not even a rule of the party boats," I said.

"No. But it's Tommy's rule."

Roger said this as if it were worse than any law the police might enforce. Tommy Gordon was the biggest kid at the docks. He was sixteen and had quit school the day after he'd reached that milestone when the state believed a person was old enough to decide whether or not to attend. Tommy was known for being a bully, especially to the younger kids like me. He more or less ruled the docks as far as Denton's youth were concerned. Nobody my age argued with Tommy unless he wanted a severe beating. The word was his parents hadn't even argued with him when he quit school. I figured that was probably more because he was destined to work on the fishing boats instead of going to college, but it wasn't hard to imagine they were afraid of him. We were, so it was easy to think everyone was.

One thing Tommy was good at, though, was controlling his turf. The docks were his turf, and he always made sure the competition for work cleaning fish was kept at a minimum. I guess he decided denying anyone under thirteen the right to work the docks was his way of making sure he had enough fish to clean, not to mention it gave him a chance to bully the younger kids.

I wondered how I would get around that when an idea struck me with such clarity I was surprised I hadn't thought of it before. "I'll just tell Tommy I turned thirteen. He doesn't know my birthday."

I could see they were surprised they hadn't thought of this simple solution themselves. Tommy wasn't the smartest kid around by any means. I was nearly thirteen anyway and a bit tall for my age, so he might believe me. Probably would, in fact.

"You still have to convince your dad to let you have a starving dog," said Roger.

"Yeah, I know," I said. "Maybe if I hang out in town 'til he heads home from work, he might be in a better mood."

I wasn't saying it, but Lee and Roger knew what I meant. My dad worked at a local bar. He shucked oysters and served beer until around eight most evenings before he stopped by the liquor store on his way home and spent his tips on a bottle of cheap whiskey. He would drink most of it on the walk home, so he was drunk, or close to it, by the time he arrived.

Fortunately, my dad wasn't a mean drunk. He was only mean when he was sober and needed a drink. I knew if I caught him about half way home from the liquor store, he would be in a fairly good mood. I would promise him almost anything if he would let me keep the dog.

"What'll you name him if your dad lets you keep him?" Lee asked.

I looked at the dog and said the first word that came to my mind.

"Bones."

This cracked Lee and Roger up. "It fits, at least," said Lee, packing his cleaned fish into his bucket and setting off toward his house. I could hear him chuckling to himself, repeating my dog's name as he walked away. "Bones—sheesh." He stopped after taking a few steps and said, "Good luck. You're gonna need it."

Roger picked up his bucket, which held only eight fish, the legal limit. "Good luck with your dad," he said and strode off.

I stood there with my bucket of cleaned fish. I started for home to put them in the refrigerator before meeting my dad on his way home. He would be happy I'd caught some trout for dinner, and I hoped that and the whiskey would put him in a good enough mood to let me keep Bones.

When I arrived home, my mom was asleep on the couch, the TV blaring. A half-finished can of beer sat on the scarred and ring-marked table beside her. I didn't care for beer, but I took a swallow before putting the fish in the refrigerator. I took Bones to a place in the woods about a hundred feet behind our house and tied him to a tree so if he barked he wouldn't wake my mom. After that, I walked back toward town, but not before telling Bones good-bye and I would be back for him. He was starting to even act like my dog. We seemed to have some sort of communication, and he lay down in the sandy dirt as if to wait for me.

It was almost eight o'clock, and my dad would be getting off work soon. I would wait for him on the corner a few blocks up the street from our house. Over a half-hour later, I saw him strolling up the street. It was getting dark, but I could tell by his gait that he was already drunk. He held a paper sack in his right hand. In it, hidden below the lip of the bag, was the neck of the bottle. He would shuffle a couple of steps, take a swallow, and stumble along until the need for another swig hit him. As he weaved slowly up the street, I rehearsed for the thousandth time what I would say while still making small changes to my argument as I thought of his possible objections.

He stopped in front of me, a happy smile forming on his face.

"'Lo, Jack! You know? You look just like your brother when he was your age."

I had a brother who had joined the marines. His name was Rick, and he was about to ship out to Vietnam.

"So, what gives?" he asked, obviously wondering why I was meeting him, which I did sometimes but not often.

"Not a lot," I lied. I knew I would have to ease into my pitch. "I caught some trout for dinner. Eight of 'em." He wouldn't care if I went over the limit, but I didn't want him to know I had filleted and given the other two to Bones.

"That's great, boy. Where'd you catch 'em?"

"Lee, Roger and I took Dan Russell's rowboat and went across to Sugar Isle where that barge is stuck. We caught a whole bunch but threw the little ones back. The rest are in the fridge. I can cook 'em if you want."

"Sounds good to me," my dad said, taking a swig from his bottle and continuing his stroll home.

"Strangest thing happened when we were out there." My heart hammered against my ribs.

"Oh? What?" He was still concentrating on his bottle and wasn't really listening.

"This dog came along on the shore."

"Who you reckon it belonged to?"

"Don't know," I said, hoping this next part would go well.

"A stray," he said. "Gotta be careful o' strays. They got diseases. Bite sometimes, too."

"Not this one. He was gentle. He turned his belly up to me."

He looked down at me, and his face told me he'd been listening better than I thought.

"Can't keep a dog, Jack."

"Why not? He's starving, Dad. You can see all his bones under his skin. I mean all of them."

"There you go. Dogs cost too much to keep. He'll be needin' a vet and a ton o' food to get him healthy again."

"But that's the best part," I said, launching into what I hoped was my big selling point. I had once heard that a good salesman turns objections into reasons to want the product. I was going to do the best job of that I could do.

My dad looked at me, his eyes swimming slightly in their sockets. If he hadn't been drunk, the look would have been just like Lee's earlier that day.

"The best part is he costs too much?" he asked, squinting at me.

"Not really. The best part is I can earn the money to feed him and everything."

I could see that struck a chord. "How you gonna do that?" At least he was still listening.

"Clean fish at the docks."

He laughed. "You know Tommy Gordon won't let a kid your age work at the docks. He'll chew you up and spit you out."

"I'll be thirteen in October. He doesn't know when my birthday is."

"You planning to tell him you're thirteen?"

"He'll never know the difference."

My dad considered that as he swayed like a boat in choppy seas and decided it was possible. "That takes care of the summer, but what about when the boats ain't runnin'?"

"I figure I can make enough for the whole year."

He made a noise that said he doubted it.

"If not, I could work during the winter washing people's cars and running errands. Please, Dad. I'll make enough. I promise you won't have to pay a dime for the dog."

"Promises are cheap. 'Specially from a boy who wants a dog."

We had reached our house. I stopped and stood in the moonlight, facing him. I think he was surprised at my determination.

"This promise isn't cheap. If I don't make the money to keep him, I'll put him down myself."

He paused, nodding. "I don't want to have to do nothin' for this dog, you hear me?"

"Yessir." I was winning!

Then he dropped the bomb. "But a person who makes money pays rent. What doesn't go for the dog goes to me and your mama for your room and board."

This was completely unexpected. Pay rent? "Why do I have to do that?"

"Because. If you start gettin' the idea all the money you make is yours, you get the wrong idea. All your money ain't never yours, just as all mine ain't never mine. Rent has to be paid; 'lectric bill has to be paid. Groceries ain't cheap."

Because I was trying to get his permission to keep Bones, I didn't bother to point out that he spent more money on booze than he did for food. "But how can I save money to get me through the year? I was hoping to be able to save some this summer to help carry me through the off-season when the work might be slower."

He seemed to laugh at me with his eyes. "That's your problem, now ain't it?"

I decided that it was as fair a deal as I was likely to get. I would pay rent, but I had my dog.

And anyway, I could find ways around giving them all my leftover money.

After my dad went inside to finish what little was left of his whiskey, I walked out to where I had left Bones. He was still there, waiting for me.

# 2

The next day I spent time with Bones, sneaking leftovers out to him from the kitchen and letting him get to know me. I ended up giving him bread and some gravy that had been in the refrigerator for a few days, along with some baloney and stale rice. It wasn't much of a meal, but he ate it the way he had everything else—in huge gulps.

I sat with him trying to figure out what breed of dog he was. I had no idea. Later, the vet told me he appeared to be a yellow lab mix. Healthy, he would weigh about seventy pounds or more, maybe eighty. The first time I took him to the vet he weighed only thirty-seven pounds.

When it was almost time for the party boats to return, I made my way to the boat docks. I walked up just as the boats were arriving so Tommy wouldn't have much time to question me. If the boats were just docking, he would be forced to start asking for work as the tourists disembarked. Also, if he told me to get lost, I could ignore him because he would be too busy getting work to do anything about it. Of course, I would have to face him later if that happened, but I would deal with it then.

I arrived with my pliers, filet knife, and fish scaler. The pliers were for gripping the skin of those few fish that needed to be skinned. Skinning was an extra thirty cents per fish, which was only necessary for certain ones, so I was hoping that I could get a few of them. As I expected, Tommy saw me coming and walked over to me, a look of doubt on his face. I could tell he was prepared to send me packing, regardless of my saying I'd turned thirteen.

"What you think your doin', kid?" he asked, sneering at me.

"I just turned thirteen and was going to clean fish."

"When's your birthday?" It felt like a job interview and I guess in a way, it was.

"I turned thirteen on Wednesday."

"What year you born?"

"1955."

It took him a moment to do the simple math in

his head. He was still suspicious. "Ain't you Cookie's kid?" Cookie was my dad's nickname. He had been a cook in the navy, but he rarely did any cooking anymore.

"Yeah." I stood there in a posture that I hoped was a mixture of defiance and respect for his self-proclaimed authority.

"I didn't think your birthday was in summer. I always thought it was later."

"You're probably thinking of my brother. He went in the marines." I silently prayed my lie would work. My brother's birthday was in April.

He eyed me. Deciding he couldn't prove I was lying, I suppose, he nodded.

"Take the end of the line," he said, unhappy about the added competition but forced to stick to his own rule.

The end of the line meant I wasn't allowed to be the first to greet the tourists. I had to be last in the line of kids asking to clean fish. I would end up asking the people that the other boys were too busy to take, and it was no guarantee anyone would be hiring anyway. I sighed, again figuring this would be the best deal I could get.

I took my place as the tourists began stepping carefully off the boat, carrying their day's catch and laughing from too much fun and beer. Tommy, of course, was first in line.

"Can I clean your fish for ya?" he asked this

one fat guy with a bad sunburn he'd feel later.

"How much?" asked Mr. Sunburn.

"Only ten cent a pound. Beats doin' it yourself."

Sunburn considered for a moment before giving the answer many of them gave once they thought about the mess and work they could escape.

"Okay, you have a deal."

One after another, the tourists filed past, many giving their fish to a kid. Some, though, weren't hiring, thinking they would clean the catch themselves or perhaps mount the best of them. The tourists were beginning to thin out, and I still didn't have any work.

The boy in front of me, a guy named Carl Hicks I didn't know but recognized from school, was asking the last tourist off the boat if he wanted his fish cleaned, mentioning the price in his pitch. The man, carrying at least twenty-five pounds of fish, was about to answer when I blurted out, "I'll clean it for nine."

The man looked at me and back at Carl, who was already glaring at me for starting a price war. Carl glanced at Tommy. Tommy had begun cleaning his customer's fish and didn't notice, but something told me that didn't make any difference. He would hear about this and beat me senseless.

"Can you go under that?" the tourist asked Carl, obviously pleased that he might benefit from a price war. It was too late to back out of it now.

Carl cut a look at me while he gave his answer. "No," he said, sounding as sullen as he looked.

"You're hired," the tourist said to me, and I took his catch to the scale for weighing. Twenty-seven pounds. I did the math in my head.

"It'll be $2.43. If you want, I can skin the triggerfish. It's better that way, and it would only be another thirty cents. That would bring it to $2.73.

"Sure," said the man.

I saw Carl step up to Tommy and speak to him. Tommy looked over at me then spoke to Carl.

I pretended not to notice, but my heart was doing back flips. I was in for it and nobody would take my side. I had been desperate and blurted out the lower price, and now I wondered how much of the money I would be allowed to keep.

Being unused to cleaning this many fish, I was the last one done, and the guy paid me $2.75 since he didn't have the exact change.

I thanked the man and started toward the dirt road that led to the highway, hoping I could get away without being stopped by the other boys. No such luck. They circled around and headed me off, surrounding me like a pack of wild dogs practiced at cornering prey.

I looked around at the circle of faces, none of them friendly. I was trapped.

Tommy did the talking. "Carl says that you

undercut the price for cleaning fish."

"What about it?" I said as if what I'd done was normal. "There isn't any sign that says there's a set price."

"Well, there is," said Tommy, menace in his tone. "No sign, but it's agreed. The price for cleanin' fish is ten cent a pound. No more." His voice hardened. "And no less."

I could hear my heart beating. "I didn't know that. I need the money kind of bad."

"Carl?" Tommy said, speaking to Carl but still looking at me with a dangerous smirk. "Did you need the money, or was it just for skippin' coins across the water?"

Carl said, "Yeah, I needed it."

Tommy continued staring at me. "We all need the money, kid. That's the idea here. This is my cigarette money."

"Same here," said Carl, and my head spun around to him again. "What should I do for my cigarettes, kid?"

"Maybe we could light him up and smoke him," suggested one of the other boys. Cruel laughter rippled through the pack.

"I'm sorry, I spoke without thinking. It won't happen again, I promise."

"You're right about that, at least," said Tommy. He looked at the other boys, and I knew it was the signal to attack me. I wondered what I would look like when they finished with me.

With a rush, they were on top of me, pummeling and kicking. Fortunately, we rarely wore shoes in the summer. Still, I felt a sharp pain in my side as a boy kicked me in the ribs. I tasted blood when Carl punched me in the mouth. I could feel the teeth loosen as my cut lip ballooned. My nose felt broken, and one eye was already swelling shut.

Finally, the boys parted from their handiwork, moving once again into a circle to consider me the way any animal pack looks at fallen prey. Carl was reaching into my pockets and taking the money, including the dime I had found beside the road on my way to the docks that afternoon. I had thought I was lucky when I found it.

I lay there crying as defeat settled on me, but it was more than that. I wondered where I would get money to feed Bones. I couldn't keep taking groceries out of my house. If my parents caught me, they would beat me too, even though that rarely happened, but stealing from my family would surely lead to a severe whipping.

The thought of not being able to feed Bones was worse than the beating I had received at the hands of this senseless mob who were more interested in where they found their next pack of smokes than in saving a good dog's life. I probably couldn't keep Bones. My dad would make me put him down instead, explaining if I couldn't make the money to feed and care for him, he would be better off dead. I even began to worry about the money my dad would expect for my rent.

Tommy leaned over me and growled, "You're banned from the docks, kid. You show up again and the beatin' will be worse. You got me?"

I did. He had just sentenced my dog to death. I wondered where I could find more work but couldn't think through the pain and the threat of loss. The idea anyone would hire a kid with a broken nose, a fat lip, a black eye, and probably a few cracked ribs seemed ridiculous.

Bones was as good as dead.

The sun was nearly setting when the boys began their walk toward the highway, leaving me in the sand. Carl called out his final insult. "Thanks for cleaning those fish for me." They went away, their harsh laughter sounding through the approaching dusk.

I managed to sit up and take inventory of my injuries. Maybe my nose wasn't broken, and perhaps my ribs were only bruised. Still, I ached all over. Against the onslaught, I could do no better than wrap my arms around my head and hope for the best. Fighting back would have been useless. The tears were drying, and the flow of blood from my nose and mouth had nearly stopped. I was wondering what I looked like when a man's voice rang out from the dimness nearby.

"They sure got the best of you."

I looked up but the last flashes of the setting sun gleamed behind him, preventing me from seeing him clearly. I squinted, trying to soften the glare, my vision also hindered by the swelling around my right eye.

"What?" I'd heard him, but I couldn't think of anything else to say.

"I said that they sure got the best of you."

"There were seven of them."

"I know. I saw."

It took a moment to understand that a grown man had witnessed my beating without even saying anything to my attackers. It had not been a fair fight.

"Why didn't you stop them?" I asked.

"Well, first it wasn't any of my business, but mostly it occurred to me that seven strong, young boys who would attack a kid smaller than they were would think nothing of taking revenge on an old man like me."

*Great, another coward*, I thought. "Who are you?" I finally asked.

"Mr. Pittman. Henry Pittman. I live in the broken-down bus."

That made things a bit clearer. I knew who he was. Down by the docks, near where the ground rose sharply uphill to the highway, a dilapidated school bus had sat for as long as I could remember. All the tires were flat, and the engine was gone. Curtains hung in the windows, which were always closed, even in the summer heat. Its owner was a man who looked to me like the actor Burl Ives. I guessed he was in his mid-to-late fifties, maybe older, though it turned out he was only fifty-three. He had a salt-and-pepper goatee and mustache to match his thinning hair, and he was a man who carried nearly half his weight around his middle. I sometimes saw him drinking beer in Kirby's Oyster Bar, where my father worked.

As I considered his explanation for not stopping the attack, I realized, coward or not, he was right. If he had tried to break up the fight, Tommy and the other boys would have paid him no attention until they had nothing better to do than harass an old man. Then, they would remember his attempts and act as if it had been a tremendous problem for them at the time.

"Who are you?" he asked.

"I'm Jack."

"Do you have a last name, Jack?"

"Turner."

He looked at me with dawning recognition. "You're Cookie's boy, aren't you?"

"Yeah. He works at Kirby's," I added without needing to because I could think of nothing else to say.

"I know. I go there sometimes for a beer."

"Yeah. I've seen you in there."

"Come to think of it, I've seen you there, too. You want to come in and sit for a minute and get bandaged up?" he asked, gesturing toward the bus as if it were an award-winning hospital.

"That's alright," I said. I didn't relish the thought of spending the evening keeping the old guy company. "I'm not hurt that bad."

"Well, at least you could wash the blood off your face. You look like something out of a horror movie." Then he chuckled. "They could call it *I Was a Teenage Punching Bag*."

Ignoring his attempt at humor, I realized he was probably right. I didn't want to go home looking like this. I stood and brushed the dirt and sand off as best I could and began to trudge up to where he was standing. As I approached, his large body blocked the sun, allowing me to see him more clearly. He was smiling at me as if he'd been expecting me for some time. It was a friendly smile that warmed the ice blue of his eyes. He had no pity in his gaze, just understanding. I'd always ignored him before, figuring he was just the crazy old guy living in the broken-down bus.

We walked to the bus and I followed him inside, never thinking he could be dangerous. I guess it was a different time back then. I wonder now how often unfounded fears prevent us from getting to know good people.

"Sit over there at the table," he said as we entered, pointing at the small, cloth-covered table and two lone chairs perched along one side of the bus. As I sat, he shuffled toward the rear.

While he was back there, I took time to look around the bus I had wondered about so often. Just how did an old man live in a bus? Where was the bed? Leaning out from my seat, I noticed the answer to my question. About half way back, squeezed between a small dresser and something that looked like a free-standing closet, sat a bed, or at least what passed for one. A thin mattress covered a small frame, which I recognized as an old, folding army cot. A threadbare blanket was spread neatly over the foot of the bed. A yellowed pillowcase that matched the dingy sheets covered the shapeless pillow. Toward the front of the bus, maybe three feet in front of the dresser that sat perpendicular to the wall, was the small table where I now sat. It was one of those chrome-legged tables so often found in cheap diners. The chair I sat in was chrome as well, with thin, red plastic that served as its upholstery. The plastic covering was torn in spots, allowing the thin padding beneath to poke out in small tufts. It reminded me of soft, white hair. Another ragged chair like it stood opposite me between the table and dresser like a boxing referee. A curtain was spread the width of the bus beyond the closet. I assumed it was where the bathroom was because once when I was walking by, I had seen pipes that connected the bottom of the bus to something below the ground, probably a septic system.

He returned and removed some bandages and peroxide from the small first-aid kit he had brought from the back.

"Mr. Pittman, I…"

"Call me Hank," he said, inspecting his supplies. "All my friends call me Hank."

"Well, Hank," I said, trying out the idea of calling an adult by his first name, "you don't need to do this. I'm fine."

"It's the least I can do, seeing as how I couldn't stop it."

Without further conversation, he arranged his materials like a doctor before beginning to work on my injuries. I decided I liked him. He was friendly and easy-going, and he didn't treat me like a little kid, which I appreciated. Many adults talked to kids my age as if we were barely smart enough to walk and breathe at the same time.

While he fixed me up, he talked about fishing, the tourists, his bus, and the fishing boats, asking for my thoughts on each topic, talking to me as if I had legitimate opinions. No other adults treated me as if I mattered.

"Alright. Go look at yourself," he said when

he'd finished, sitting back proudly.

I looked around for a mirror. "Where?"

He chuckled. "Oh, sorry. Go through the curtain and you'll see the bathroom. You'll find a shaving mirror on the little table where the washbowl is."

I went through the curtain where a small battery-operated camping lantern lit an area that I was sure nobody besides Hank had ever been. A space that took up the rear five or six feet of the bus housed a toilet and small shower, both badly in need of cleaning. A tiny table sat nearby with a filthy porcelain bowl that he used for a bathroom sink, its faucet standing on one of the pipes that led down into the ground below. Anchored to the table where the bowl sat was a small, round mirror connected to an arm that would expand and collapse like an accordion, allowing the mirror to be raised to the height of the person using it. I stretched out the mirror and took stock of my injuries and Hank's doctoring.

Hank had mostly just cleaned off the blood and put band-aids on the cuts. I had a black eye and a swollen lip that I knew was cut on the inside. My nose reminded me of a tiny rose in full bloom. A cut on my left cheek stood out near the black eye. A small butterfly bandage held the cut on my cheek closed. I thought it looked as if it needed a couple of stitches, but I would never see a real doctor because my parents didn't believe in medical help unless it would save someone's life. The lip that seemed to weigh six pounds wasn't as bad as I'd thought. It was swollen, but not nearly as big as it felt. I liked Hank's handiwork and I liked Hank. He hadn't gone overboard with the bandages, and I thought they made me look tough.

I turned to leave and noticed a wall with some black and white photographs. I could tell that some were of Hank when he was a lot younger, but I didn't know who the other people were. One of Hank and a woman caught my attention, and I figured she must have been his girlfriend or wife or something. They were smiling and looked as if they liked each other. Another was of Hank and a small boy, with a younger girl looking on from behind them. I wondered if they were his children, and it was strange to think that this man who lived in a bus by the beach had kids somewhere. Then, I saw one of Hank in a military uniform. He was young, probably in his twenties or early thirties, and he had a bunch of medals and ribbons on his chest. One medal looked special. The only medal I recognized, a purple heart, was also pinned on him. I wondered how he was injured since they only gave it to people hurt in battle.

I had been in the bathroom long enough and went back out to where Hank sat putting away the first aid supplies. I considered asking him about the pictures, but I did not want to get in a long conversation with him about them.

I thanked him and started to say goodbye when he asked me to sit for a while.

"I don't get many visitors. And you haven't told me why you were so desperate to earn money that you would risk crossing the likes of those dock boys by starting a price war," he said. Apparently, he'd heard more than I thought. "That boy Tommy is headed for no good, and it took a lot of nerve to do something you must have known would make him mad."

I wondered if Hank would understand my problem, so I gave him the chance to prove he did. I told him how I found Bones and how my dad said I could keep him as long as I could pay for his needs. When I'd finished, Hank squinted at me. "You mean you're doing this for a starving dog?"

"Yes."

He looked at me so long it made me uncomfortable before he said, "So what are you going to do now? You can't go back to cleaning fish after what happened."

I shrugged, as much at a loss as he was. "I guess I'll go door-to-door asking for work. Maybe I could mow lawns with people's mowers. I don't have one to use. Or I could run errands or do other chores. I know I'll do something though. I'm not sure how long I can get away with feeding Bones our leftovers without getting caught." A thought occurred to me. "Or maybe I could get a paper route."

"You have a bike?" he asked, his tone telling me he knew the answer.

"I could walk my route," I answered confidently.

Hank shook his head. "Take too long. People would be calling the paper complaining."

"Oh," I mumbled. "I guess you're right."

He reached into his pocket and withdrew his wallet, fishing out two dollars. "Here, take this and get your dog some food. What you do with the rest is your business."

"I don't take charity," I said. I wasn't insulted. Charity had been offered before; I just didn't accept it.

"It's not charity," he insisted. I looked at Hank. He was holding out the money and eyeing me strangely. I could tell he was thinking about something, considering something that somehow involved me, and for a moment I wondered if I hadn't been wrong about his intentions. He set the dollar bills on the table. "You really want to work, don't you?"

"Of course." Where was he going with this?

"Come by tomorrow morning and I'll have something for you to do. This is just an advance."

"What do you want me to do?"

"We can start with cleaning up around here. I'm getting too old to do some of the things that need doing, and I could use someone to help me."

"But what about after tomorrow? You can't keep paying me money. Excuse me for saying so," I said, looking around at the bus and its sparse furnishings, "but it doesn't look like you have a lot of it to spare."

A funny look spread over his face and he said, "You're right. I don't. But I have those two and three more like them for you tomorrow. We can figure out what comes after that." He must have figured out what I was thinking. "You won't have to do anything, well, odd. I'm not like that."

I considered his offer and finally reached down and picked up the money, stuffing it deep in my front pocket.

The next thing I knew I was on my way to Grayson's Market for some dog food for Bones and a Coke for me. I bought two cans of the cheapest dog food they had, figuring Bones wouldn't mind. After I paid, I had $1.41 left. When I arrived home, I fed Bones both cans and gave my mom the dollar for rent and hid the forty-one cents in a jar that I placed under a loose floorboard I knew about in my bedroom closet. This would be my savings for vet bills and maybe even running away some day.

Of course, my mom saw my face and asked what happened. I told her I'd been in a fight, but she should see the other kid. She didn't ask if she could look at it closer or who had bandaged me up, and I didn't tell her. She returned to the sofa, the TV, and her beer. A lot of kids would be bothered by that, but I was used to it. She and my dad loved me, I guess. It's just they loved their booze more.

I went outside to feed Bones and sit with him for a bit. He was still too weak to play much, but he seemed to enjoy being with me. I ended up just sitting and petting him while watching the stars turn in the sky.

When I stood to go inside, he was sleeping soundly. I had fed him both cans of dog food—a feast for him—although the can only recommended one. I figured he had some catching up to do.

I had promised Hank I would be at his place at eight o'clock the next morning, so I went to bed to try to get some sleep. Still, it took a while to fall asleep because of the soreness and the distant lightning that periodically threw bright flashes through the thin curtains of my bedroom. I wondered how Bones was handling the coming storm but decided that would be a small thing compared to what he'd already been through.

It had been a full day, and the memory of it kept rolling around in my mind, preventing me from getting to sleep for a while. In my memories, though, I held off the pack of boys single-handedly, even preventing them from jumping Hank and robbing him too.

I knew none of that had happened, of course, but that didn't matter. My imagination was like my mother's beer or my dad's whiskey. It made me feel better than reality did.

3

The following morning, I woke up later than I'd wanted, but still leaving enough time to make it to Hank's by eight. The storm had knocked out the power along with the alarm clock by my bed, so I dressed quickly and went to check on Bones before heading to Hank's and my first day of work.

It was still raining, and I had no rain gear. I wore only a pair of cutoff jeans and a t-shirt.

As I walked along the street toward the harbor, I stopped to look at the roads swollen with rainwater. My street sported a pair of temporary rivers along each side. These street-side rapids had always been a private playground for me. I loved to drop small sticks in the torrents and watch as the temporary rapids carried the twigs along to a destination only the water knew. I would follow the paths of nature's intent until the twigs either became mired in a tangle of debris, where I would leave them, or were washed down a sewer line that eventually emptied into the Gulf of Mexico down at the waterfront, where the twigs, if they made it that far, would continue their unknown journey.

Because I had stopped along the way to drop a few twigs and watch their voyage, I was late showing up at Hank's. When I arrived, I knocked on the bus's doors, which swung open immediately.

"Get in here!" Hank said. "Don't you know we're under a tornado warning?"

Looking inside the bus, I wasn't sure if I would be safer inside or out. Even a small tornado could toss Hank's makeshift home around as easily as I could throw a matchbox car. I stood there, undecided until Hank said, "Well?" I made my decision and stepped up into the bus, standing on the entry steps, dripping.

"Let me get you some towels to dry off," he said and went to the cabinet for some towels.

"I didn't expect you today, what with the weather the way it is," he said, staring at me as he handed me the towels.

"If I didn't show up, I'd owe you the two dollars you gave me, and I've already spent it on Bones and rent."

"Rent?" he asked, surprised. I hadn't told him that part of my story.

"Yeah, that was another thing. My dad said if I

was earning money, I had to pay rent."

Hank looked at me and shook his head. I didn't know what he was thinking, but he looked troubled. I offered my dad's explanation. "If I get the idea all the money I make is mine, I'll be disappointed."

"Your dad told you that?" Hank asked. I nodded. "How much you pay him of that two dollars?"

"A dollar. I gave it to my mom last night."

"And what did she do with it?"

I shrugged. "Don't know. None of my business anyway since it's their money."

"Jack," he said with a sigh, "nobody pays half their earnings in rent, especially if said rent is based on what the tenant earns."

I looked back at him, confused. "So, how much should I pay? I kept out forty-one cents," I said, proud of my planning. "My dad said that whatever didn't go for Bones went for rent, but I have to save up to take Bones to the vet." I left out the part about saving up to run away. Hank was a nice man, but that was one subject adults didn't take kindly to, no matter how good the reason for leaving might be.

"If you applied for a home loan, they would figure you could afford up to a third of your take-home pay if you didn't owe too many other bills."

I wondered how he knew this. After all, he wasn't exactly living in a nice home here. In fact, my house was probably worth more, but I ignored that argument. "You mean I should pay my parents a third of what I make?" I asked instead.

"At the most."

I stood on the bottom step inside the doorway, rubbing the towel over my scalp and clothing. My shirt would dry quickly, but the shorts were another matter. The thick denim would hold the water for a couple of hours, but I was used to that even if I hated wearing wet shorts. Like most of Denton's kids in summer, I wore no socks or shoes, so that wouldn't be a problem at least.

When I had managed to dry myself enough to stop dripping, I took the seat Hank offered me, the same one I'd sat in the evening before. I draped the towel over the seat to keep it dry.

Hank had a four-burner propane camp stove and he had put a coffee pot on. When it was finished percolating, Hank made himself a cup of black coffee and offered me some as well. I was surprised since nobody had ever offered me coffee before. I accepted and sipped the hot brew, feeling like an adult, though not one, as it turned out, who particularly liked coffee.

"It can be an acquired taste," Hank said, grinning at me.

I plunged on, forcing myself to drink so I could learn to love it as much as most of the adults I knew did. My dad had said that beer, wine, and liquor were acquired tastes, and I figured if I was going to acquire one, I would be better off drinking coffee. I'd seen what the others could do.

Once he'd finished his first cup, Hank stood, put on a large raincoat, and opened the doors of the bus, saying, "Wait here. I'll be right back."

"Where you going?" I asked, curious where he would go in this torrent. I was a kid, walking in a storm was nothing for me. He was an old man.

"I'm going to get some bacon and eggs out of the refrigerator. We can have breakfast."

"What if a tornado comes?" I asked.

"You'll hear it before it gets here. Just crawl under the bus and pray if you do." He stepped out into the wind and rain.

"Wait! What refrigerator?" I asked, but he was already gone.

I watched out the window beside me as he shuffled as quickly as he could toward the boat docks. Taking out a key, he opened the offices for the party boats that moored there and went inside. Minutes later, he was rushing back toward the bus, a carton of eggs and a package of bacon in his hands. I wondered if I had just witnessed a theft.

When he came back into the bus, he could see the questions in my face.

"I watch over the docks when nobody's here, sort of like a security guard. In return, Jerry Moreland lets me put my refrigerator in his office and use a sink to wash dishes and such. I let Jerry have one shelf of the fridge in case he wants to put a soda or two in there. I have no power in here, so I can't have a fridge. It's what's called a symbiotic relationship. Jerry helps me and I help him."

"Oh," I said.

The various branches of the Moreland family, a widespread hodgepodge of David, the family patriarch, and his two sons, both of whom had grown children, owned most of the large party boats in Denton along with much of the property in the town. Jerry Moreland owned the docks where Hank had his bus parked—or his home, depending on how you looked at it.

There had also been two Moreland daughters, but they had married. One moved to Tallahassee and the other to Atlanta. The rumor was they rarely came back to Denton because they hated their father. As much as my dad wasn't perfect, I still loved him, so I wondered why Mr. Moreland's daughters hated him so. There had also been another son, but I heard he'd died.

Mr. David Moreland's wife had died of cancer years ago, but young women were often seen at the family homestead though the faces changed on a nearly monthly basis. When I was about seven, I heard my dad say the faces changed, but not the figures. He had laughed at his joke, but I hadn't understood it at the time.

Hank started the bacon cooking over the camp

stove while we continued getting to know each other.

"Why aren't you afraid of a tornado?" I asked. He'd looked worried enough when I had arrived that morning, but since I'd set foot inside, the worry had dropped to non-existent.

"Because, you shouldn't be afraid of something you can't control. If Ol' Mother Nature decides to sweep my bus away, there's not much I can do about it. I know I'd hear it before it hit, so I'd have time to crawl under the bus."

"Couldn't it still sweep you out with the bus?"

"Same answer. No use wasting time being afraid of something you can't do anything about."

"So the idea of a tornado or hurricane doesn't bother you?" I asked.

"I didn't say things like that don't bother me. I respect them and the unbelievable power they have, but I'm not afraid of them. Fear makes people freeze up. When it comes time to act, you can't. That's more dangerous than storms."

After breakfast, the rain let up, and I figured the tornadoes wouldn't be coming for Hank's bus that day. I rose from my seat, looked around and said, "So what do you want me to work on today?"

"Well, I was going to have you scrubbing the outside of the bus, but there's no use in doing that now. We'll need a dry spell for that since I want to paint it." He looked around. "I'm not sure what you can do, actually."

"How about if I clean your bathroom? No offense, but I noticed last night it could use it."

Hank looked at me, surprised at my offer. "You'd clean my bathroom?"

"Of course. I owe you." I didn't really want to clean it, but it was true I owed him and I didn't like feeling that hanging over my head. Without waiting for a response, I went to the back of the bus. "Where's the sponges and cleaner?" I called.

"Bottom of the closet," he said, and I went to work. When I'd finished a short time later, the entire area was spotless. I was proud of my work and hoped Hank would appreciate it.

"All done," I announced.

He came to look and whistled at the results. "You've done well."

Pointing at the picture of him and the lady that I'd seen the evening before, I asked, "Who's that with you?"

He was silent and looked down at me. Finally, he said, "Maybe I'll tell you one day." I could tell my question brought up memories best left alone and was sorry I'd reminded him of them.

I continued working on the bus, cleaning the inside from front to back. By the time I left, the rain had stopped completely and the sun had started to peek out from behind the remaining clouds. He paid me the three dollars he said he would, telling me to give my parents no more than one of them, and I walked home, detouring to Grayson's Market for more dog food. This time I bought six cans and another fifteen-cent soda, which came to $1.47. This left me a dollar for rent and fifty-three cents for my savings, bringing my savings to ninety-four cents. I was starting to feel prosperous for someone not even thirteen yet.

The next day I reported to Hank's and he had me start scraping the bus down to ready it for painting, though I wasn't sure why he would spend the money and time to do that. At the end of the day, he gave me another five dollars. I tried to give him a dollar back since he was also feeding me breakfast and lunch, but he wouldn't take it. I told him he was paying me too much. Five dollars a day for a kid my age in 1968 was a mint. He assured me there would be days I would not get that much, as well as days he would have no work for me, so I should accept what he gave me and plan for the future.

I stopped at Grayson's and just bought a soda since I didn't need more dog food yet. I gave my parents $1.70 for rent, rounding up to the nearest dime, and I was left with a whopping $3.15 for my savings jar beneath my closet. In just a couple of days, I had saved $4.09.

I also stopped by the local vet's office on my way home and talked to them. The lady there said

Doctor Kelly, the vet, would look at Bones for ten dollars, but that any medicine Bones needed would be extra. She said the local humane society would pay for his shots since I was unable to afford them, and the doctor would neuter him for free as well. It was charity, but I figured it was for Bones, not me, so that was okay. I was also unsure whether or not I wanted him neutered, but the lady said if I didn't do that, the humane society wouldn't pay for the shots. I went home and apologized to Bones even though he had no more idea what was in store for him than those twigs floating down the road-wash.

Over the next few days, I managed to sock away the ten dollars needed to take Bones to the vet. I had to leave him overnight because of the surgery, which the vet almost didn't do because of Bones's condition. The lady at the welcome desk said I could pay for the medicine the next day since I had forgotten about that charge. I worked for Hank again and was able to make just enough to pay the vet off, and Bones had to wear this plastic cone around his neck for a few days to keep him from licking his stitches. I apologized to him again.

The doctor told me to feed Bones twice a day until he managed to get his weight and strength up. The next day at Hank's we started painting the bus, and I knew that soon the money train would cease stopping at my door, which made me worry about having enough to pay for all that dog food.

By the time we had finished the bus, I had managed to save over twenty dollars. I'd thought I was rich before, but now I knew better. That money would be gone before I knew it. As everyone kept telling me, dogs were expensive, especially ones that had nearly starved.

I was surprised the loss of income wasn't what bothered me the most when we finished working on the bus. It was the loss of Hank's company and friendship.

When we stepped back to admire our work, I said, "You don't have any work for me tomorrow, do you?" The words nearly caught in my throat.

"Not right now," he said, as if I hadn't asked about something vital. "You saved some money, didn't you?"

"Yeah, but—" I looked at the ground.

"But what?" Hank asked when I didn't continue. The truth was I was afraid to say more. I feared I might start crying, which would embarrass me all the way to my stomach.

I continued anyway, praying I would be able to keep my composure.

"The money isn't what's bothering me," I said.

"It isn't?" Hank asked, his tone indicating he wasn't sure what I meant.

"I—well, I like being with you. You're nicer to me than my folks are."

I felt his gaze on my shoulders as if it

magnified the sun's heat. He was silent as well for a moment before he said, "What? You thought I wouldn't want you to keep coming by for coffee in the morning?"

I looked up at him and grinned, thankful he understood something I was too young to fully grasp myself, yet those same morning coffees were what led to the problems.

4

The next morning, I left home early to have coffee with Hank, hoping he had found something else for me to do. I was worried that maybe he had been teasing me about stopping for coffee with him, and he would answer my knock with a "You again?" I knew that probably wasn't the way it was, but that's how my mind worked. I always thought I was more in the way than anything.

However, when I knocked, he smiled down at me. "C'mon in, Jack. Coffee's waiting."

Relief washed over me as I sat in my chair and began sipping the coffee he poured for me. It was hot, so I blew on the surface to cool it. The faint bitterness was familiar and welcome to me now.

"I have some good news for you," he said.

"You found more work for me to do around

here?" I asked.

"Well, I found you some work, but not here."

I was a little disappointed. Working at the bus meant I could hang around with Hank, but work was work, and money was money. "Where?"

"You know Mrs. Mary Jane Dawson?"

I furrowed my brow, thinking. "No," I said. Denton was a small town, and I at least knew most of the kids by sight, if not by name. The adults, however, were a different story.

"She's a widow, lives over on Pompano Drive. She wants someone to plant some things in her yard, work on her flower garden and maybe even plant a few summer vegetables. You up to it?"

"Yessir!" I said. This sounded like more than one day's work.

"She'll pay you what I've been paying you. Five dollars a day. If you're willing to do that, she's expecting you today around two. She'll let you know when to show up after that."

"How did you do that?" I asked.

"Do what?"

"You know, set up another job for me?"

"Oh, that." Hank stopped to think a moment before continuing. "I was out having a beer last night, and Mary Jane stopped in to slake her thirst. We're old friends, so we started talking. She asked what I'd been up to lately, and I told her that I'd hired someone to do some work for me. She wanted to know who my employee was. I told her about you and your dog, and she got right misty hearing your story."

I wondered for a moment if he'd told her about how I had the snot beaten out of me by a pack of wild animals dressed to look like boys and asked if she knew about it.

"No, I just told her you needed to make money to feed your dog and such. She asked me if you might be willing to do some gardening and yard work for her. I said I thought you might, and now she wants you to stop by today to discuss it."

I wanted to hug him, but instead I just smiled and thanked him.

"So how's your dog coming? Bones, isn't it?" he asked, changing the subject.

"He's doing well enough. He seems to be gaining weight at least. His ribs aren't as easy to see, but he still has a long way to go."

Hank smiled and said, "I'm sure he'll be fine. He has you to take care of him. Your dad say anything more about him?"

"He's not said a word since he told me I could keep him. It's almost like he's forgotten it. You don't suppose he has, do you? Bones almost never barks, so it would be easy to do."

"No, I know he knows about it. He actually mentioned it just a few nights ago when I stopped in at Kirby's while he was working."

"What'd he say?"

"He just told me his boy had found this stray dog and was working to take care of him." Hank's expression changed. "He has no idea you're working for me, does he?"

"No. We don't talk much." Even I realized how bad that sounded.

I felt him looking at me and thinking about my life again. It was almost like a smell he gave off or something. I thought about reminding him of his own words to me about not getting worked up over what can't be helped, but I didn't.

"Well," he said, breaking the uncomfortable silence. "I suppose talking a lot to me sort of makes up for it, huh?" He laughed as if he'd made a big joke, but both of us knew he hadn't.

I stood to leave, and Hank gave me the house number on Pompano where Mrs. Mary Jane Dawson lived. "Can't miss it," he said. "Lots of azalea bushes in the front yard." As I started to leave, he added, "And Jack—she's rather eccentric, but she's a nice lady when you get to know her. Keep that in mind." I wasn't sure what he meant, but I tucked the advice away for later. It turned out eccentric didn't even begin to describe her.

I walked the half mile or so to where she lived and found the house easily. Hank hadn't been kidding. She must have had a dozen or more azalea bushes inside the chain-link fenced front yard.

Ringing the doorbell, I could hear the yapping of a small dog inside. As she shuffled to the front door, she was talking to the dog.

"Hush, Yogi! He's expected."

I found it funny she named her dog after a cartoon character, but it turned out I was wrong about that. She opened the door and smiled at me. She was an older woman though I couldn't tell her exact age. Her hair was dyed black with gray roots showing beneath the cap of colored hair. A pair of bifocals with ornate frames dangled from a decorative eyeglass retainer. She put her glasses in place to size me up. "Come in!" she said as if she were greeting a relative she'd not seen in years.

As I entered, I could hear a baseball game blaring from her television, and she introduced herself and the dog. "I'm Mrs. Mary Jane Castor Dawson, but I guess you know that since I'm sure Hank sent you over. That's a mouthful, so you can call me Mrs. Dawson or just ma'am." She looked at the small poodle she carried under one arm. "And this is Yogi, named for the best catcher to ever play baseball, Yogi Berra." I didn't know if she introduced the dog that way to make sure I didn't think she named him after the cartoon character, Yogi Bear, or if she just did it that way out of habit. Next, she added, "I'm still trying to forgive him for playing that final year for the Mets." She laughed as if she'd just told the best joke in the world. "Yogi

Berra! Not my dog, Yogi! She never played baseball."

It wasn't until later that the idea I might think she meant the dog played for the Mets struck me as odd. What I had noticed was her reference to her dog as "she."

"Yogi's a boy's name," I said.

"Yeah, it is, but she doesn't know that," she said with a laugh.

Before I could respond other than wondering what I'd gotten myself into, she turned back toward the room where the TV lived. I could hear Phil Rizzuto say, "Swing and a miss for strike two!" This was followed by Joe Garagiola commenting on how the batter was a sucker for the high fast ball, thinking it was going to drop as it raced toward the plate. I followed her into the room.

"Have a seat. I'm missing my game," Mrs. Dawson said, pointing to a chair near hers. A small table between us was loaded down with crossword puzzle magazines, pens and pencils, books of matches, a pack of Kent cigarettes, a half-full ashtray, a small jar of Mentholatum ointment, Q-tips, a box of safety pins, and an open can of Budweiser on a permanent cloth coaster. The moisture on the outside of the can told me the beer was still cold. A small lamp completed the jumble on the table that seemed too small to hold all that.

She noticed me looking at the pile of her

various belongings. "Sorry, I'm a nester."

"A what?" I asked.

"A nester. I'm like a bird with a nest. I like to keep things I frequently use at hand. Makes 'em easy to get to when I want 'em." She indicated the table and her chair with a wave of her hand to show me her "nest." I just smiled, not knowing what to think of this rather odd woman who named her female dog after her favorite baseball player and kept a pile of things handy in case she needed them. The rest of the house looked spotless. Only her table was a mess.

As she reached blindly for the can of beer and brought it to her lips, her attention turned back to the ballgame, Yankees against the Orioles.

"I'll be with you at the commercial. It's two outs, and Al Downing will have this guy sitting down in no time." Sure enough, two pitches later the batter grounded to second to end the inning.

"Okay," she announced, rising from her chair with a flourish. "Let's go look at what needs to be done. Based on the last inning, the O's will be bringing in someone from the bullpen, prob'ly a leftie, so the announcers will be bumping their gums for a while to fill time." She looked at me. "I can't stand announcers, even if they played for the Yankees. All the time just 'blah, blah, blah' filling time to hear themselves talk. Sometimes I get so fed up with it I turn the sound all the way down. It's not like I can't tell what's going on from watching."

I wondered why someone who hated to listen to announcers had the TV volume turned almost all the way up, but I later realized sometimes Mrs. Dawson was just like that. Hank might call it eccentric, but I thought it was just weird.

I had never met anyone quite like Mrs. Dawson. She loved to talk—unless a ballgame was on—and she loved baseball more than any other person I've ever met. After getting to know her, I discovered she could quote the stats of nearly every player that year for the Yankees, even some of the obscure ones who rarely played, and she revered the most famous players in that team's history as if they were gods to be worshipped. Babe Ruth, whom she'd met once on a train ("A great player but a filthy mouth"), Joe DiMaggio, Lou Gehrig, Mickey Mantle, Roger Maris, Whitey Ford, and of course Yogi Berra, were the names of national heroes to her. Two years after I met her, she actually punched a man who claimed that Mantle was an alcoholic, though that statement turned out to be true.

We stepped out to her back yard, where ten plastic trays sat loaded with various plants waiting to be planted. Each tray had a dozen small compartments that held rich, black soil and a sprouting plant. Small tags identified the plants in each tray. Her back yard was enormous, at least a half acre, and an area had already been tilled, waiting for the new plants to take up residence.

"All you need to do is place each small cube of soil with its plant in the dirt over there," she said, indicating the tilled area. "Put the plants about two feet apart and in straight rows." She looked at me and made sure she had my complete attention, wagging a finger at me as she repeated, "Straight rows. Not squiggly ones. Understand?" I nodded, wondering what awaited me if they weren't straight enough for her.

She continued her instructions. "Don't bury the plants deeper in the dirt than they are already in their little plot there. Do that and you'll kill 'em." I nodded.

Peering at me over her bifocals. "Hank said you were polite and a hard worker. I trust Hank." She dusted off her hands as if she'd been working the soil. "And because I do, I'll trust you to do what I want." She went on in an effort to explain. "I had one boy working for me until two days ago. He didn't know straight from an 'S' curve."

That answered my question about what would happen if I didn't make the rows of plants straight enough.

Mrs. Dawson was anxious to get back to her game, but before she went she said, "If you work out, I'll need you here for at least the next week, maybe more. You'll be paid five dollars a day, and no, I won't haggle on that, payment to be made at the end of each day—*if* I like what you've done. If I don't, you'll be sent packing, with only a portion of the payment, depending on how close you came to pleasing me. I'll pay you two dollars for today because of the late start. Now, next commercial I'll bring out a pitcher of ice water and a glass."

Leaving me standing there blinking after her, she scurried to her back door and her ball game. She seemed friendly, but she had high demands when it came to work. She expected to be pleased with the work or the job would end immediately. I felt as though a sword were poised over my neck the entire afternoon.

She brought the water about fifteen minutes later, glanced my way, seemed satisfied, and went back to her game. When it ended, she came out to inspect my work. I'd expected this and my heart pounded while my mouth dried up. I kept working and tried to ignore her. Holding Yogi, she marched around the tilled dirt like a general inspecting the troops. She would nod, squat to look down a row, then stand and continue her inspection. Finally, she came over to where I was still working and announced, "Good work, young man! I knew Hank wouldn't steer me wrong."

I had been holding my breath without realizing it, and her pronouncement caused me to exhale audibly.

"I had you nervous, didn't I?" she asked, and I

looked up at her. She was grinning as if I were in on a wonderful joke.

I said, "Yes, ma'am. You did." I couldn't very well deny it, and besides I could see it amused her that she'd had that effect on me. Who was I to deny her a gentle laugh at my expense? She was my boss for the next week, after all, maybe more. And five dollars a day was a lot of money to me.

"Well, I'm sorry about that, but that's something you'll learn as you get older. If you're the boss, you gotta make sure everyone understands you have high expectations for them. Low expectations get even lower results. High expectations get good results."

She was smiling down at me with what can only be described as genuine affection. She liked me, apparently, and I had met her high expectations. I still wasn't sure about her, but I liked her smile.

"C'mon, Yogi," she said to the dog in her arms, "let's let our young man get back to work." She started toward the house, but turned back.

"I'm going up to the market in a few minutes. Would you like for me to get you something different to drink? A coke maybe?" she asked.

"No, thank you," I said and continued working.

"So polite, isn't he, Yogi?" she mumbled to the dog as she went back into the house. Several minutes later, she returned to the back yard.

"Where's my car?" she asked, her brow

furrowed in worry.

Her car? How would I know? "Your car?" I asked, at a loss as to why she would ask me.

"Yes. It's not in the driveway."

I looked toward the house as if I could see through it to the driveway beyond. "It's not?" I asked, realizing how dumb that sounded.

"No, it's not. I left it there. Now it's gone."

"What kind of car was it?" I asked, trying to be helpful.

"A Chevrolet Impala. 1960. Hardtop. Blue. With a dent in the passenger side rear bumper where some nut ran into it in a parking lot and drove off without so much as a howdy-do."

"I didn't see a car in the driveway when I came in," I said.

"Are you sure?" she said. "I thought I saw it out there."

"I don't believe so," I answered.

"Well, what happened to it?" she asked, as if I might know.

I shrugged. "You might want to call the police and report it – missing." I'd almost said "stolen" but stopped myself at the last second.

She seemed confused. "Yes, I suppose I should." She looked around the back yard as if the car might be playing a game of hide-and-seek and she'd spot it back there.

I returned to my work, hoping to get the row I

was working on finished before the end of the day. The sun was already moving toward the horizon, and I would need to get home to take care of Bones and fix myself something to eat. I also hoped to stop by Hank's on the way home to talk to him about my day, not to mention the strange occurrence of the disappearing car.

I finally stood and dusted off my legs and denim shorts before wiping my hands on my t-shirt. I carried the remaining trays up near the house and left them there before knocking on Mrs. Dawson's back door. Yogi was barking from a distant room.

"Jack, yes!" she said. "Come in." I opened the door as she spoke to someone standing where I couldn't see him. "This is Jack, my gardener," she said as I stepped into the room. A policeman was there, taking Mrs. Dawson's statement.

He eyed me suspiciously, as if I might have been the thief. I reached out a hand to shake, but he didn't, choosing to ignore my hand the way some people in authority will do with kids.

"How long have you been working here?" he asked me.

"Since two o'clock," I said.

"No," he said, a look of exasperation that he had to deal with such stupidity crossing his face. "I mean, how long have you been employed as Mrs. Dawson's gardener?"

I glanced at Mrs. Dawson before turning back

to him. "Since two o'clock."

A look of understanding dawned on him. "Oh, so this is your first day?" he asked. His look of suspicion deepened, his tone suggesting he thought he'd found his man. Or boy.

"Yes, I started today at two." Next, I added, in an effort to move him off me as a suspect. "The car was gone when I arrived."

"So you noticed it missing when you got here? That didn't seem strange to you?"

I suddenly felt as if I were in some sort of Abbott and Costello routine. "Why would that seem strange if I'd never been here before?" I asked, showing my own exasperation at the questions.

"So, this was your first time here?" he asked, as if this had not been stated already.

"Of course. I've never been here before today."

"Then how did you know where to go? Did you just walk down the street and say, 'I think I'll see if this lady needs a gardener?'"

Mrs. Dawson finally intervened.

"I found Jack through a mutual friend," she said. "He gave Jack my address. Believe me, officer, Jack did not steal my car."

The officer, who apparently considered himself a cross between Sherlock Holmes and Sgt. Joe Friday, glared at me. His features suggested a strong reluctance to abandon his original theory regarding the car thief.

I noticed the officer's name on his uniform: Hicks. This name rang a bell. I had found out that Carl, the guy whose price I had undercut to clean the fish that day, was named Carl Hicks. I wondered if the policeman might be Carl's older brother since he was too young to be his father, and Hicks was not a common name in Denton. I also wondered if he already knew who I was and my connection to Carl.

"Who is this mutual friend?" asked Officer Hicks.

Mrs. Dawson and I spoke at the same time. I said, "Why do you need to know?" as she said, "Hank Pittman—" but stopped suddenly in mid-reply, probably because I had said what I did. I've no idea what else she was going to say, but I was glad that whatever it was remained unsaid.

"Jack, he's just trying to do his job," Mrs. Dawson said.

"He's just trying to pin it on someone to make himself look good," I answered.

With an angry glance at me, Officer Hicks closed his notebook and said, "Well, Mrs. Dawson, Denton's a small town. I'm sure we'll find out who took your car for a joy ride." He looked at me with a sneer. "And who may have helped out."

After he left I exploded. "Why do they always want to pin it on a kid?!" I asked. "And Hank certainly had nothing to do with it!"

"Calm down, Jack. I know the police seem to be that way, but in all honesty, many crimes these days are committed by teenagers."

"I didn't see him around when I was having the snot beaten out of me down at the docks," I said, but she ignored it, thankfully. I hadn't meant to tell her that, but my anger caused me to blurt it out.

"They'll find my car and realize it had nothing to do with you."

"I won't hold my breath waiting for an apology," I answered.

"What time will you be here tomorrow?" she asked, getting her purse.

"When would you like me here?"

"Does nine sound too early?" I wondered where the bossy lady from earlier went.

"No, that sounds fine," I said as she handed me three one-dollar bills.

"Mrs. Dawson, we agreed on two," I said, surprised.

"I know, but you did such a good job, and you had to put up with the rudeness of the officer."

"I didn't think you thought he was rude," I said.

"Just because I defended his right to ask the questions doesn't mean I agree with his tone," she said as she let Yogi out of the closed room where she'd put her while Officer Hicks was there.

I put the money in my pocket and started toward the front door. Yogi was now sitting next to it, and she yapped at me as I approached. I reached down and pet her as I left.

"Oh, my," Mrs. Dawson said. "She usually doesn't like strangers at all." She looked at me. "You are rather special, Jack."

I left thinking about what had gone on that day. I decided if every day with Mrs. Dawson would be this full of drama, I might have to insist on the extra dollar.

I stopped at Grayson's and bought myself a Coke and a rawhide chew for Bones before heading for Hank's bus. When I knocked, he wasn't home. I wondered if he might be at Kirby's, so I went up the hill to see if he was there.

I stuck my head inside the door and saw my dad behind the bar shucking oysters. He didn't see me, and I saw Hank wasn't there. As I started to step back from the door, though, I saw him coming out of the men's room near the back of the bar, behind the two pool tables where a couple of guys in their early twenties were playing a game of eight-ball.

Hank saw me, and his expression seemed to be asking me what I wanted. I motioned for him to step outside, and he did.

"So how did you like Mrs. Dawson?" he asked once he was outside.

"She's definitely odd," I said. "But that's not why I stopped by." I paused for a second.

"Someone stole her car."

He looked down at me, frowning. "Really?"

"Yeah. A cop came out and asked questions and everything." Hank nodded, thinking. "The cop thought I'd done it," I added.

"You?"

"Yeah, he seemed pretty stuck on it in fact. He might come by and talk to you, too."

"Why's that?"

"Because you're the one who recommended me to Mrs. Dawson."

Hank nodded again.

"It's okay," I said. "I'm used to adults thinking I'm guilty of something or other."

Hank stared at me for a second before saying I shouldn't worry about it, that if I'd done nothing wrong, I couldn't get in any trouble. It's funny, though. I wasn't even thirteen yet, but I knew that wasn't so. People get falsely accused of things all the time. For some people, suspicion and dislike were all that was needed.

5

The next day found me back at Mrs. Dawson's. I knocked on the door and she invited me in. When I entered, I was met by Yogi, who danced around my feet.

"My goodness, she does like you," Mrs. Dawson said. "You have a way with animals."

I ignored her comment and just shrugged. "Do you want me to keep planting in the back?" I asked.

"Yes," she led the way.

When we walked out back, I saw she had been out there working already, using several tools to continue tilling the soil. "Mrs. Dawson, you don't have to do that. That's my job."

"Don't be ridiculous. I can do what I want. The last time someone tried to tell me I couldn't do something, I divorced him."

I didn't want to get into stories of her past, so I asked if she'd heard anything about her car.

"Not yet. I doubt I'll ever see it again. My car's probably half way to Miami by now. I'll just have to wait until the insurance pays off and I buy another car to be able to get anywhere on my own. I'm not sure what I'm going to do about food. I'm already out of milk, and soon I won't even have food for Yogi."

"I can go to Grayson's for you," I said.

"Oh, no," she said, shaking her head. "You have enough to do without doing my shopping, too."

"I don't mind," I said.

"Well, I don't know," she said, debating whether or not to accept my offer.

"I work for you already, don't I?"

"Yes," she said, "but as my gardener, not my errand boy."

"I really don't mind," I said again. "Besides, you can't let Yogi starve."

She looked at me, frowning, her eyebrows pinched together. I could see her resolve weakening.

"I can go this afternoon," I said, "right after lunch."

"Well okay," she said, "but you have to let me buy you a candy bar or something."

I smiled. "It's a deal."

"Well, as my mama used to say, good deeds can come from unexpected quarters." She smiled back, and again I noticed how nice it was.

I began work in the garden, moving faster than I had the day before because I no longer felt the axe over my neck, and familiarity with the job helped speed things up. Soon, I had finished the first task she'd assigned me.

I had brought some cold boiled potatoes for lunch. My mom had cooked something for dinner the night before, a rarity but not unheard of, and there had been some potatoes left over. By the time noon arrived, the cold food had warmed considerably in the sun and summer heat. I poured a glass of water from the pitcher and began to eat.

Mrs. Dawson came outside again, walking to where I sat in the dirt.

"So what's that you're eating?" she asked as she approached.

"Potatoes," I said.

She frowned. "Potatoes? What else?"

"Nothing," I said.

"A growing boy can't eat just potatoes for lunch. You need protein."

"I'm fine," I insisted.

I was hoping she wouldn't offer to make me lunch. I was happy with the potatoes.

"Nonsense." She was still frowning. "Does your mother know that's all you're having?"

I wondered for a moment if she knew who my parents were.

"Don't know. Doesn't matter anyway," I said, returning to my potatoes.

"Of course, it matters. I'll bet she wouldn't be happy with this."

I shook my head gently at her, at a complete loss as to why my lunch would bother her. "She doesn't care."

"Doesn't care?" She was incredulous, as if I had told her the Gulf had dried up. "Of course, she cares. She's your mother!"

"She doesn't care as long as I don't bother her," I said.

"You're wrong," she said. "She loves you."

"Mrs. Dawson, do you know who my parents are?"

"Of course, I do. Harold Turner and his wife— Barbara's her name, isn't it?" She used my dad's given name, making me wonder just how well she knew them. Everyone called him Cookie. Besides, my mom's name was Belinda.

"You don't know 'em much," I said. "My mom's name is Belinda." I was getting irritated, but I was trying my best to be polite.

"Okay, Barbara—Belinda. I had the first letter right."

"You were wrong, though. That's what's important. You don't really know her. If you did, you'd know she doesn't care what I eat."

She sat beside me in the dirt. "So suppose you tell me about her," she said, and I realized it wasn't a suggestion.

Swallowing the last bite of potato, I took a deep breath to calm myself and said, "You're right. She loves me I suppose. She just doesn't have time for me."

"Why not?"

I fell back on my old standby. "She just likes her beer better." Mrs. Dawson's mouth gaped as she stared at me. "It's okay," I said. "I'm used to it."

"Jack, I drink too. I like my beer, but that doesn't mean I don't care about people."

"She cares about people, too. She just likes her beer more than you like yours."

"I don't know. I like my beer a lot. It may surprise you, but I've been snockered a few times in my life. Quite a few times. But I still—well I still made sure my children ate and had what they needed."

I shrugged. "Some people aren't like you."

It was simple enough to me. Adults always became upset when they discovered I mostly took care of myself. My mother would hug me sometimes and even kiss me on top of my head until I grew too tall for her to do that. But her beer had swallowed her. It owned her. I only rented her.

"Well, I—" Mrs. Dawson began but stopped.

Standing abruptly, she strode into her house without another word.

I sat there drinking my water and wondering about adults. If I was fine with my life, why wasn't everyone else?

Finishing my water, I looked around, wondering what I should do next. Then, I remembered. I had promised I would go to the store for the few groceries she needed. After our conversation, I thought it might be a good idea to get away for a little while anyway.

Rising, I went to the pitcher of water and filled my glass again, downing it before stepping up to the back door and knocking. Yogi came to the door and barked before scampering back to Mrs. Dawson to announce my presence. A couple of minutes later, Mrs. Dawson was at the door. I could see she had freshened her makeup. She didn't wear much, and I wondered why she decided to apply more now. I thought maybe someone was dropping by.

Like me, she acted as though the conversation in the back yard had not happened.

"I promised you I would go to the store," I said. "Do you need anything more than milk and dog food?"

"Oh, yes, well, I made you a small list. It's not much since you'll have to carry the bags back here." She paused, looking back into the house. "Now, where did I put that list?" She considered this for a moment. Yogi barked. "Oh, yes. Now I remember. Thanks, Yogi," she said, and I thought again how strange she was. Hank had called her eccentric. I was starting to think she was crazy.

Stepping back into the house, she left me there, and I wondered if I had ruined our budding friendship. Crazy or not, she was my boss and I still liked her. She returned with the list and stepped outside. She did not hand it to me, though.

"Jack, I'm sorry I became upset. I've added some sandwich items on the list. You don't need to bring your lunch anymore. I'll let you make yourself a sandwich here. If you don't like ham, you can get whatever you like instead. Turkey, bologna, whatever you like."

I started to protest, but she silenced me, holding out her hand in a 'stop' gesture and saying, "You've no choice. Either you accept the lunch I offer, or you don't come back. I insist." I figured she was right about having no choice, so I took the list and the five-dollar bill, promising to bring the change and receipt.

"I trust you, Jack, but if it makes you feel better, you can bring back the receipt."

I left the house and started walking to Grayson's. When I entered, the air conditioning slammed into me, instantly chilling me from head to toe. I wasn't used to the cool of air conditioning. I'd never had it at my home, and goose bumps covered my skin as I hurried through the aisles in an attempt to get back outside to the heat.

Cathleen Grayson, one of the daughters of the owner, worked there as a cashier. She was in high school and would sometimes speak to me as I entered. I was not even thirteen yet, but when she noticed me, my heart fluttered. She was the most beautiful girl I had ever seen. She was returning to the front of the store from the back as I entered and she saw me.

"Hey, Jack. Whatcha doin' in here today? Gettin' more food for your dog?"

"No, I'm working," I said, feeling important for having a job. "I'm working for Mrs. Mary Jane Dawson, doing chores and such. She needed me to come to the store for some things."

"Oh, that's nice," she said. "I bet you're the best worker she's ever met." I grew dizzy.

"Her car was stolen, you know," I said. "That's why I told her I'd come to the store for her. She'd starve if it wasn't for me." I considered a moment. "And so would her dog, Yogi."

She smiled at me, and my toes curled. "That's real nice of you, Jack," she said and began to ring up a customer. I was disappointed someone had come along to turn her attention from me. I was surprised the air conditioning was no longer making me cold. In fact, I was rather warm.

I continued through the store, putting the items

Mrs. Dawson asked for in the small basket. When I returned to the front, Cathleen was waiting for me.

"You say her car was stolen?" she asked, picking up our conversation from where it had left off.

"Yeah. She noticed it yesterday. I was even interviewed by the cops."

"They don't think you had anything to do with it, do they?" she asked, her voice suggesting how absurd she thought that would be. I smiled.

"Nah," I lied. "They wanted to know what I saw. That kind of thing."

"Well, I hope they find it. Not having a car in Denton's no fun. Take my word for it."

She finished ringing me up while I stared at her. I wondered if she knew how I had a crush on her, and at the same time I knew being in love with a high school girl was a dead end. She surely had a dozen football players after her for dates all the time. Still, I couldn't ignore my heart.

As I walked out, she said, "Stay sweet now!" and I walked on a cloud all the way to Mrs. Dawson's.

When I approached her house, though, that changed.

A police car waited in the driveway. I wondered if it was Officer Hicks back to accuse me again. I thought about not going inside, but I had milk and it might spoil in the ninety-degree heat.

When I entered, I saw it was a different policeman. This man was wearing a suit, and he glanced my way before returning his attention to Mrs. Dawson. Next, I saw Officer Hicks was there, too, standing near the back door. He looked at me as if I were a tick he'd found crawling up his pants leg.

I took the groceries into the kitchen and set the bags down. I began placing the cold items in the refrigerator and left the rest on the counter for Mrs. Dawson to put away since I wasn't sure where she kept everything.

Standing near the doorway that led out to where Mrs. Dawson and the two policemen were, I listened in on the conversation, waiting to hear my name mentioned.

"So, tell me about the last time you drove your car," the older officer said.

"Well, let's see. I know I had it day before yesterday."

"How do you know that?" asked the older officer.

"I drove into town to meet a friend for lunch."

"Who's this friend?" he asked, and I wondered if maybe she shouldn't tell him. Her friend might be the next suspect.

"Sarah Moreland," she said. "We've been friends for years. Since high school."

Sarah Moreland was the wife of Ted Moreland, one of David Moreland's rich sons. Only an officer who wanted to lose his job would ever suspect her of stealing a car.

"What happened after that?"

"We had lunch."

I could sense the awkwardness all the way in the kitchen. He had obviously meant what had happened regarding the use of the car. I heard Officer Hicks heave an impatient sigh.

The older officer didn't miss a beat, though. "And where did you go after lunch?"

"Well, we had eaten at the Seaside Restaurant, so we decided to have a drink or two after lunch and just sit and look out at the boats. It was a late lunch, so some of the boats were coming back into harbor. Some had good catches, and we sat there talking to each other and some of the people there, including some of the boat captains that stopped by to pay respects," she said. Suddenly, irritation edged into her voice. "Why are you asking about lunch. It wasn't stolen then."

The officer ignored her question. "Did you notice anyone suspicious? Anyone watching you?"

"I'm not answering your question until you answer mine."

This time it was the older officer's turn to sigh. "I'm trying to determine if someone was watching you having lunch and followed you. Maybe he decided to steal your car later that night."

"Oh," she said.

"So will you answer my question? Did you see anyone suspicious?"

"No, not at all. In fact, I knew everyone I saw that day at lunch."

The conversation paused for a second. Suddenly, a rough hand grasped my shoulder.

"What do we have here?" Officer Hicks asked. He had come into the kitchen from the entrance behind me. "Hey, we have us an eavesdropper." He hauled me into the room.

The older cop turned to me. His nameplate read *Tyndall*. "I was going to get around to him," he said before asking, "I'm Detective Tyndall. Who are you?"

"I'm Jack. I work for Mrs. Dawson."

"Since yesterday," Officer Hicks said, his meaning clear in his tone.

"You have a last name?" Detective Tyndall asked.

"Turner."

"How about brothers? You have any older brothers?"

I knew what he was thinking. "Yeah, but he's at Parris Island."

Detective Tyndall nodded, considering my answer.

"What about older friends? You know, like high school age."

"He's friends with that old guy who lives in

that broken-down bus by the Moreland docks," Officer Hicks said.

Looking at Officer Hicks, Detective Tyndall said, "Nah. Ol' Hank wouldn't have anything to do with this." He turned back to face me. "Why were you eavesdropping?"

"Curious."

"About what?"

"Whether you'd be able to find Mrs. Dawson's car. I don't want to keep having to walk to Grayson's every day for her groceries."

Detective Tyndall smiled for the first time. "Don't blame you there." He indicated a chair beside Mrs. Dawson and I sat. Turning back to Mrs. Dawson, he said, "So what about when you left Seaside? Notice anyone then?"

"No. Sarah and I started walking back up the hill from the restaurant and I—" She stopped short, her mouth open in surprise.

Detective Tyndall's brow furrowed. "You what?"

"Oh, dear," was all she said before repeating herself. "Oh, dear."

Understanding dawned on Detective Tyndall. "What did you do with the car, Mrs. Dawson?"

I looked at Mrs. Dawson, puzzled. She was blushing about ten shades of red.

Detective Tyndall went on. "No need to be embarrassed," he said. "It happens to the best of us.

We're busy doing things and forget."

Mrs. Dawson started to whoop. She laughed so hard she was having difficulty catching her breath to talk.

"Oh, dear! Oh, my!" she said, laughing around the words. Looking first at Detective Tyndall then Officer Hicks, she said, "I shouldn't be the only one blushing, Detective!" Tears from laughing so hard were rolling down her cheeks, leaving small streaks in her fresh makeup. "I stopped to have a few beers at Kirby's, and after that I accepted a ride home because I didn't think I should be driving." She pointed a finger in Detective Tyndall's face. "I left it parked on the street in front of the police station!" Next, pointing a finger at Officer Hicks, she said, "And he's had the license plate number and a complete description for a full twenty-four hours!"

Mrs. Dawson continued to laugh at the officers' expense, whooping and chuckling as she slapped her knee. Officer Hicks turned an angry shade of red, but Detective Tyndall just smiled and shook his head before turning to Officer Hicks and saying, "I guess we'd better give Mrs. Dawson a ride to the car we've been guarding for the past two days."

I joined Mrs. Dawson in her laughter.

"I wouldn't be laughing, Mrs. Dawson," Officer Hicks said. "Filing a false police report's a serious matter!"

The detective looked at Officer Hicks. "Don't

be stupid, Dagwood. That only applies if she did it on purpose."

*Dagwood*? I laughed even harder after hearing Officer Hicks's name. I had thought Yogi was named for a cartoon character, but he was a dog. Officer Hicks had been named for a hen-pecked, comic strip buffoon. Between Dagwood and Yogi, I figured the dog ended up with the better name.

While getting control of her laughter, Mrs. Dawson said, "Jack, the azaleas out front need some pruning. Would you do that while I go with these gentlemen to retrieve my car?"

"Yes, ma'am," I said, still laughing as I went out back to get the pruning shears from the tool shed.

I continued chuckling at what had happened while I worked.

Later, when Mrs. Dawson returned and I finished my work, she called me inside. We were both still amused at what had happened.

"I was right, you know," she said.

"About what?" I asked.

"About how they wouldn't find my car. Turns out, I found it."

"And it was right under their noses," I said, grinning.

Mrs. Dawson gained control of herself and said, "On a more serious note, you'd better watch out for that Officer Hicks."

"You mean Dagwood?" I asked, chuckling.

"Yes," she said. "He seems not to like you very much."

She was right about that, but I didn't let it bother me. As it turned out, though, I should have taken her warning more seriously.

6

I woke up one morning and didn't feel like working. I'd been going hard and needed a day off mid-week. I couldn't call Mrs. Dawson because I had no phone and didn't know her number anyway, so I decided to tell her the next day that I hadn't felt well. It was dishonest, but I figured people lied to me all the time, so it was okay.

After getting dressed and taking care of Bones, I walked up to Denton Bridge and crossed it to Bayfront Island, which stretched between Denton and Wharton, a much larger town that lay about six miles west of Denton. A beach stretched behind the Ramada Inn just across the bridge where tourists would swim and sunbathe.

When I arrived, I saw Mark Hales, a guy I knew from school. Mark was in my grade, but he was two years older than everyone else because he'd been held back twice. He wasn't a good student, but he was a lot of fun to hang around with, mostly because he was willing to do, as he put it, "damn near anything." He was also the only guy I knew who grew his hair out like the Beatles. He was always getting in trouble at school for keeping his hair longer than was allowed. He once told us the principal had threatened to hold him down and shave his head. Schools were like that back then. The adults could get away with whatever they wanted, including making stupid rules about how long boys could wear their hair. Anyway, Mark was always in trouble, both in school and out, so of course he drew us younger boys to him the way a porch light draws moths. He was like Tommy in that he would commit petty crimes, but he was more fun because he wasn't a bully.

When I saw Mark at the beach, he noticed me and motioned me over. He was chatting with two girls. I didn't know the girls, so I figured they were either tourists or lived in Wharton.

"Hey, Wacky Jack!" he said. He was always calling me Wacky Jack. He got a kick out of it, and I was pleased he liked me enough to give me a nickname. "This here's Hanna and her sister, Emily."

"Hi," I said, smiling at the girls as they said hello. Hanna was about Mark's age, and her sister, Emily, was mine. They each had dark hair that fell down their backs, and their pale skin had the sheen of lotion. Hanna looked much more interested in being with Mark than Emily did. In fact, Emily didn't seem very enthusiastic that I had joined the group either. Mostly she looked bored.

"They're from the big city of Montgomery."

A lot of people from Alabama would come to the area around Denton for summer vacations. After a few minutes of talk, I learned the girls were here with their parents and were having fun at the beach but, as Hanna put it, "This is the third straight day we've been here, and so far, just hanging out here is the only thing we've done. Our parents think it's paradise, but I'm ready to do more than swim and sunbathe and go to the same damn restaurant every night."

Mark laughed. "Two pretty girls lookin' for fun. Who'd-a-thunk?"

"So where are your folks?" I asked.

The sisters exchanged a look and Hanna answered, "They kicked us out to go to the beach while they—rested—for a while."

Emily blushed, obviously embarrassed. "That's disgusting," she said.

Mark grinned at her. "Hey, we all gotta have our fun, right?"

The way Hanna looked at Mark, it was obvious she agreed. Emily, on the other hand, looked like she wanted to go somewhere and read a book or something—anything besides hang out with us.

"So, what d'ya say we go for a ride in my car?" Mark asked. This surprised me. He didn't own a car. Not only that, he was fifteen and still too young to drive on his own.

"Cool!" Hannah said.

I cut my eyes at Mark, wondering what his plan was. The four of us walked to the parking lot, Hannah walking beside Mark, who reached out and took her hand. She grinned up at him as if she'd just met Paul McCartney. Emily and I followed them as I tried to come up with something to talk about, but I couldn't think beyond wondering about the car. Finally, I said, "You like dogs?" Emily looked back at me as if surprised I could speak.

She turned her gaze back to Mark and her sister and said, "Yeah."

"I found one on the beach a while back. He was starving and only has three legs."

She looked back at me. "What d'ya want? A medal?"

I blinked at her. Her anger at her sister was one thing, but her rudeness was unexpected. "Just making conversation," I said, shrugging.

"Well, don't bother," she said, keeping her eyes forward. "You're not even going to make it to first base." First base? I wasn't even planning to step up to the plate. I just wasn't relishing the thought of several hours of cold-shouldered silence.

We approached an older model Buick I didn't recognize, and Mark opened the door for Hannah, letting her slide in to the middle of the bench-style seat, and he sat behind the wheel. "Hop in!" he said to Emily and me, grinning. Emily climbed in the back on the passenger side and slammed the door. I sat behind Mark.

I couldn't contain my curiosity any longer. "Uh, Mark?"

He glanced at me in the rearview. "Yeah?"

"Um, when did you get a car?"

"Just this morning! Cool one, ain't it?"

"Yeah," I said, not calling him on his lie. Looking back, it would have been better if I had. I could have saved us all a lot of trouble.

Mark had learned how to drive when he was maybe ten, and he expertly backed the car out of its spot, using the clutch and column shift like an old pro and peeling out. I glanced over at Emily to see if she'd thawed any and to gauge her reaction to Mark's driving. She could have been an ice sculpture. She didn't even blink as the car sped off.

Since nothing interesting would be found in Denton, Mark turned the car west toward Wharton.

"What d'ya say we head for The Side Pocket?" Mark said.

"What's that?" Hannah asked.

The Side Pocket was a local pool hall. No alcohol was served there, so minors were allowed.

However, just because no alcohol was served didn't mean kids didn't manage to find some to drink there. It was known as a place kids could find something to get drunk or high on. Knowing their business depended on local teens, the owners—an old guy named Don who walked with a limp and his chain-smoking wife, Esther—turned a blind eye to the illegal activities there, which were plentiful. A "lounge" was nestled through a door in the back, complete with sofas, chairs, and tables, where kids could do almost anything they wanted. All someone had to do was give Don or Esther a few bucks, and the lounge became "closed" to anyone else. Hannah was all for going there once Mark filled her in on the place, leaving out the uglier details about the lounge and drugs, so that's where we went.

Mark had a way with girls, and he knew it. He could talk a girl into believing almost anything. He once told me all a guy needs to get a girl was to convince her she was pretty because, as he put it, a lot of girls, even the prettiest ones, thought they were ugly as road kill. "Man, you think they find fault with guys, you should hear how they talk about themselves."

I had asked him how he knew this, and he said, "My sister." He laughed. "Even my dad tells her she's so ugly she has to tie a bone around her neck to get the dog to play with her."

I winced. Mr. Hales owned a local tourist trap,

what we called stores that sold beach-themed junk for five times what they were worth. As far as I knew, he wasn't a drunk, but it bothered me he would say that to his own daughter. Mr. Hales probably thought it was a joke, but I knew kids didn't when people said stuff like that to them. Mark's sister, Cheryl, wasn't ugly at all. She wasn't gorgeous or anything, but she wasn't bad. She also had a reputation with the boys. Like Mark, word was she would do "damn near anything." One thing I learned from Mark, though, was that you didn't need alcoholic parents to have a lousy home life. Bad parents come in all shapes and sizes.

Despite Mark's reckless driving, we arrived at the Side Pocket in one piece and parked facing the building. I was still wondering where Mark got the wheels as we walked into the pool hall. We were met inside by the Trogs blasting out "Wild Thing" on the juke box. Don and Esther might be old, but they liked our music. Esther would feed quarters into the coin-operated juke box they owned rather than leased and empty the machine's coin box each night.

Mark greeted Esther, who sat in her seat behind the counter. Don was nowhere in sight. In fact, other than Esther the place was empty. "Any new tattoos today, Esther?" Mark shouted over the music as we entered. Esther, who was covered with tattoos, just said, "None today."

Mark gave her a deposit and brought a rack of balls. Emily, who had about as much interest in playing pool as she had for anything other than looking bored, went over and sat on one of the cheap chairs along one wall. The chairs were mostly for spectators at the weekly eight ball tournaments, which carried a $25.00 prize for the winner. I knew Mark was good, and he won money playing pool. He was so good at it he told people he played pool for a living. Not only would he win the weekly tournament a lot, but he also hustled people for money on the tables. He would play well, but not as well as he could, losing a few small bets before making a big bet to try to, as he put it, "recoup my losses." It almost always worked. The guy he was hustling would make a ridiculous bet, only to see his money disappear in about five minutes. I'd been with Mark once when he did this, and it was almost comical to watch the guy realize he'd been had. I knew of only one guy who welched on the bet. Most of them would consider it a lesson learned and pay up, which Mark had told me was the number one rule of the bettor's game. "Nobody wants to be seen as a sore loser, especially when he put himself in the situation in the first place," he'd told me.

I knew better than to play against Mark, so I joined Emily in the seat next to hers. She ignored me while Mark racked the balls and broke. The fact he scratched on the break told me he was purposely messing up. Usually, he would sink two or three just on the break, and he was capable of running the table when his concentration was good enough. I had no idea why he was pretending with Hannah. It wasn't as if he was going to bet any money on the games.

Hannah wasn't good at all, and Mark did his best to teach her how to shoot. Once it was established that he was, indeed, skilled at the game, he began showing off, something he was also very good at doing.

"Watch this," he said to her. He placed the eight ball next to one corner and put the cue ball in a precise spot at the same end of the table. Holding his cue at a steep angle with his cigarette hanging loosely from his mouth, he chopped down on the cue ball, aiming for the opposite end of the table from the eight ball. His angle of attack on the cue ball caused it to jump forward before the back spin took over, and the ball reversed course, moving toward the eight ball. He missed the first time, causing the eight ball to bank off the edge of the pocket. The second time, he nailed the shot.

I had to admit it was an impressive trick shot. Hannah began bouncing up and down, clapping, and Mark smiled at her, took a drag from his smoke, and said, "You wanna visit the lounge?"

"What lounge?" Hannah asked, still chuckling.

Mark pointed at the open door at the back of

the room. "That lounge."

She looked at him and smiled as he took her hand and walked her back. The door closed behind them. I looked over at Emily, and she was shaking her head and mumbling something.

"What?" I asked.

She looked at me as if I had broken some unwritten law by speaking to her.

"I said 'whore.' My sister. She's a whore."

I looked at Emily, and she looked like she wanted to throw a pool table or something.

"Look," I said, "I'm sorry about all this. I can see you didn't want to do any of this." She squinted at me, making me uncomfortable. I remembered her line about first base. Of course. She had figured Mark out right away and thought I was aiming for the same thing. It suddenly became important that I convince her I wasn't.

"You know, I wasn't trying to get to first base or anything like that," I said. "I was just wanting to talk."

She looked at me as if deciding whether or not I was telling the truth. Her features softened a bit, and I realized what she might look like if she smiled.

"Sorry," she said, looking away. "It's just it's like this a lot with my sister. She meets some guy and if I'm with her, they both try to fix me up with someone so I'm not so much like a fifth wheel. The guy usually figures I'm like Hannah, but I'm not."

"Oh."

"Got a smoke?"

"What do you smoke?"

"Nothing but cigarettes," she said. It took me a moment to realize what she meant, and it made me laugh.

"No, I mean, what brand?"

Her lips curled up as if she might smile, but she didn't. "Kools."

I walked over to the cigarette vending machine. They don't exist anymore, but back then they were everywhere. I dropped thirty-five cents in and pulled a lever. A pack of Kools tumbled down to the tray. Taking them back to her, I indulged myself in a smoke. I didn't do it often, but I would when I was with people who smoked. Packs of matches advertising the Side Pocket were scattered everywhere, and I picked one up and lit her cigarette for her, feeling a little like Humphrey Bogart in one of the tough guy movies he made. Without thinking about it, I imitated him. "So, what brings you to a joint like this, shweetheart?"

She just looked at me and said, "That's a pretty bad Bogey imitation."

I blew out a lungful of smoke and said, "Yeah, I know."

"Tell me about your dog," Emily said, and soon we were chatting like real friends. She even smiled a few times. We had just lit up another cigarette when the door to the "lounge" opened, and Mark and Hannah strolled out. They were both sweaty, and Hannah's hair was in need of a brush. It was obvious what they'd been doing.

After Mark returned the billiard balls and paid, we started for the door. That was when things turned crazy.

We climbed into the Buick, rolled down some windows for air, and were about to back out when a Wharton police car screeched to a stop behind us, preventing us from moving. Another police car skidded to a stop next to that one, and cops were surrounding the car, guns drawn and pointed at us as if we'd just robbed a bank.

Hannah and Emily screamed. I looked at Mark and could tell he knew what was going on, and suddenly, I knew as well. I'd known all along, really. I knew Mark didn't own a car, and I knew his father drove a Ford. The car was stolen, and we were going to jail. The irony of being angry that Officer Hicks had suspected me of stealing Mrs. Dawson's car hit me, and I wanted to melt through the seat.

Both girls were crying, and I realized that as wild as Hannah was, she'd never been arrested, at least not for something as big as stealing a car.

"Hands where we can see them!" one officer, who was poised next to Mark's door, shouted.

"With your hands kept in clear sight, step out of the car!"

"I can't without reaching for the door handle," Mark said calmly, as if he was arrested every day.

The officer stepped toward the door, grabbed the handle, and flung it open while keeping his gun aimed at Mark's head. I just hoped his gun wouldn't go off accidentally.

Another officer had his sights on me and had me step out of the car as well. Both Mark and I were thrust against the car and searched. I kept looking at Mark, wondering if I could somehow keep this whole thing quiet. I had planned on telling Mrs. Dawson I was not feeling well to explain why I hadn't shown up for work. That plan was likely ruined now.

The girls, wearing snug bikinis, were obviously no danger to the cops, and soon we were all herded into police cars and shuttled to the station. We were interviewed separately, despite laws that said they couldn't talk to us without at least a parent there. After I'd told my story, it must have matched Mark's because I was told I was free to go, but they had to call my parents to come get me. I had hoped to thumb a ride, but that wouldn't do. They wanted to make sure my parents knew I'd been caught with a felon.

I told the officer the number to Kirby's, and he called and spoke to my dad. I knew how the conversation would go, but it surprised the officer that my dad told him how I made it back to Denton was up to me because he couldn't leave work without losing his job and didn't have a car or a driver's license anyway.

The officer hung up the phone and turned to me. "Is there anyone else we can call?" I thought about Mrs. Dawson. She would probably come get me, but I was still hoping she wouldn't find out what had happened. Her number was probably in the phone book. I could've called Hank, but he didn't have a phone or a car.

"No," I lied.

"Hold on a minute. I'll be right back." The officer stepped out and left me in the small room.

After a few minutes, he returned and said, "Come with me."

As we stepped out of the room, someone started yelling in the main room of the police station. As I followed the officer down the hallway, I realized the shouting was Hannah and Emily's dad. He was screaming at them, accusing them of embarrassing him and their mother as well as other accusations, while an officer tried to calm him down. I felt sorry for the girls. They weren't to blame, and Emily didn't even want to go with us.

When I entered the room, I saw both girls crying and they looked over at me as if I was the cause of all their problems. I barely had time to think that I was as much along for the ride as they were when the dad turned on me. Before I knew it, he had jumped on me and was hitting me and screaming obscenities. I avoided most of his blows by wrapping my arms around my head, but a few landed, and I knew I would have at least a black eye by that night. The inside of my lip was bleeding, too. So much for keeping my screw-up quiet.

The cops pulled the guy off me without telling him I wasn't the one who stole a car and took his daughters to a pool hall. They held the guy while he kept screaming at me as I walked out with the officer I'd been following. I felt sorry for the girls. I could tell their dad was a hothead and a bully. My dad was a drunk, but at least he left me alone.

The officer pointed to a patrol car and said, "Hop in. I'm taking you home." We drove in silence until we had left Wharton. Finally, he said, "You seem like a good enough kid. What are you doing hanging out with Mark Hales? He has a list of crimes as long as your arm, mostly petty things until now. You'd do well to stay away from him, assuming he ever comes back home. My guess is he'll end up in a reform school after this."

"Mark's not bad. He just doesn't always think things through," I said.

"You realize he could have pinned at least some of the blame on you? You'd be spending the night in jail if he had."

"But he didn't. That's what I mean by he's not bad. He told you the truth."

He was quiet for a moment before he said, "Your dad works in a bar?"

"Yeah, what about it?" I didn't see how that had anything to do with anything.

"It surprised me he didn't drop everything to come get you. Most bosses are understanding about that sort of thing. They'll let a guy leave work to take care of an emergency for their kid."

I stared out the window, wishing I was home already. "It didn't surprise me," I said. "I coulda saved you the call. Even if he could get off from work, he can't drive."

"Doesn't he know someone who could've come get you?"

I just shrugged, but he was looking at the road and didn't see. When I didn't answer, he said, "Well?"

"Maybe," I said, wishing he'd drop it.

"Well, you're not even thirteen yet. You should start making better decisions. Going joy riding with a guy in a stolen car was a bad one."

"I told you already, I didn't know it was stolen."

"You also told me you knew he was only fifteen and didn't have a car. Couldn't have one, in fact. Either way, you screwed up. You seem bright enough to me to have figured out where he got it."

The truth was I still didn't know where he got it though I had suspected it was stolen. I figured someone was stupid enough to leave the keys in the car because Mark didn't have to hotwire it to get it to start. Beyond that, I had no idea. I said nothing about this, though. I only watched out the window praying we would get to Denton so I could get out of that car.

He must have realized my silence was a plea to be left alone. When we drove up to my house, he took in the surroundings with a glance. Next, he pulled out a card and gave it to me, saying, "This is my card. If you ever feel like you need someone to talk to about stuff, give me a call."

When enough time had passed that I could look back on the day with some insight, I realized the cop was just a guy who wanted to do his best to keep me from going down the wrong path. I should have thanked him, but I didn't. I never even saw him again. The strange part is I kept his card in a small box where I store important keepsakes. To this day I don't know why I kept it, but I still can't throw it away.

The next day when I arrived at Mrs. Dawson's, she had heard all about my day off. Apparently, my dad had mentioned at work I'd been arrested for stealing a car, which of course was all wrong, but that's how he told it, probably with a hint of pride that his boy was growing up or something. Hank was in Kirby's when my dad talked about it, and he had walked all the way up to see Mrs. Dawson to tell her.

I apologized for not coming to work, explaining how Mark was the one who stole the car, and she accepted my apology, but she'd ended with a warning that if it happened again, she'd have to fire me. That scared me because I needed the money for Bones, but all I had to do to avoid that was come to work every day or at least get word to her somehow if I was truly sick.

# 7

I worked for the next few days and saved up enough to take Bones back to the vet for a checkup. When the vet saw him, he said that Bones was getting healthier by the day. Because he still didn't get much exercise, he was putting on weight since I was feeding him two cans of food twice a day, four times what he normally would get, and he'd reached fifty-two pounds. He was even beginning to stop gulping his food. The best part was the vet said I could start taking Bones out with me as long as I kept an eye on him.

I ran into Lee and Roger one day while walking home from my job. I told them the story of Mrs. Dawson's missing car, and they got a kick out of hearing about the car that couldn't be found parked in front of the police station.

"Hey, man," Lee said. "We're thinking about

going camping tomorrow night in Panther Dunes. You wanna come?"

"Sure," I said. Tomorrow was Friday, and Mrs. Dawson had already told me I could have the weekends off.

"Think we'll run into Diablo?" I asked. Diablo was the name the people of Denton called the one remaining Florida panther believed to live somewhere in the dunes that rose about a half mile inland from shore. Panther Dunes was the unofficial name for the sand hills of small scrub oaks and longleaf pines that grew there. Diablo was elusive and some didn't believe he existed, though we had heard countless stories about people seeing him. The dunes themselves covered several square miles, and enough wildlife lived there to support the large cats that were indigenous to Florida but almost never seen there anymore.

"Who knows?" Lee said. He pushed his sandy hair out of his eyes. "Roger's gonna bring his pellet gun just in case."

"You can't kill a panther with a pellet gun," I said.

"Don't wanna kill him," Roger said. "Just keep him from killin' us."

"All a pellet gun'll do is make him mad," I said.

"Well, I'm bringing my pellet gun anyway. If Diablo shows up and wants to eat you, I *might* protect you, or maybe I won't."

"Would it be okay if I brought Bones?"

Lee laughed again, commenting on the name I'd chosen for my dog before saying, "Sure. Maybe *he* could protect you from Diablo."

The next day I asked Mrs. Dawson if she believed Diablo was still living in the dunes.

"Don't know," she said. "I suppose if he'd died, someone would have found his body somewhere, but it's not likely he ever was there since if he had been, there would have surely been a female."

"Maybe he's like Hank and prefers to be alone," I said.

"Hank doesn't prefer to be alone, exactly."

"What d'ya mean?"

"How much do you know about Hank's life?"

Thinking about it, I realized I didn't know much and admitted this to Mrs. Dawson.

"The fact is he was married once. Even had two children."

I was reminded of the pictures I'd seen numerous times in the back of Hank's bus. "I've seen their pictures, I think," I said.

"Where'd you see them?"

"They're on a wall in his bus," I said. "In the back where the bathroom is."

She nodded. "I'm sure that's them."

"I asked about them once, but Hank didn't want

to talk about it."

"I don't doubt it. It was a real tragedy."

Mrs. Dawson grew quiet after that, and I figured she was thinking of Hank's wife and children. Finally, my curiosity became too much, so I asked, "What happened to them?"

"If I tell you, you can't go blabbing it all over town. More folks than Hank want to forget," she said, making me wonder why he would have their pictures up if he didn't want to remember. "And the folks that don't know don't need to know."

"I won't tell anyone," I said.

"Okay," she said. "Only reason I'm telling you is you've gotten close to him and knowing might help explain a few things."

I sat forward in my seat, anxious to hear about a tragedy so bad nobody wanted to think about it.

"Well, you see," she began, but stopped because her phone rang. She held up a finger to indicate she would continue after the call.

"Hello?" She listened for a moment, and her eyes widened in surprise and joy. "Dorothy?" I didn't know who Dorothy was, but Mrs. Dawson told me. "It's Dorothy, my sister!" she said, as if it were Mickey Mantle on the phone.

After they talked for a couple of minutes, I realized this call wasn't going to end any time soon, and I had work to do. I excused myself with a nod and smile to Mrs. Dawson and went out to the tool shed, pulling the mower out to mow the lawn.

By the time that job was finished, Mrs. Dawson had forgotten all about telling me about the tragedy in Hank's life. Either that or she'd thought about it and decided against telling me. It didn't matter what led to it; the result was the same.

After mowing, I weeded the garden I'd planted, ending my day by tilling another area where Mrs. Dawson wanted to plant a small vegetable garden.

While I was tilling, she came out to tell me she had some errands to run and she would be back soon. She climbed into her rescued car and drove off, leaving me there with my work. After I had tilled the area, I added fertilizer to the dirt and blended it in evenly, finishing a few minutes after she returned.

"So what are your plans for the weekend?" she asked. She had already forgotten I was going camping up in Panther Dunes with Lee and Roger.

"Going camping with my friends," I said, as if I'd not told her before.

"Oh, that's right. I forgot," she said, shaking her head. "Well, you boys be careful and have fun. I'll see you Monday."

She paid me for the day, and I thanked her before putting everything away and heading off toward Grayson's for last minute supplies. With any luck, Cathleen Grayson would be working today and I'd be able to brag about going camping.

I pictured her telling her friends it didn't matter I wasn't thirteen yet because I was plenty of man for her.

Cathleen wasn't there, which was probably a good thing. I had to get home and pack food for Bones and grab my pillow and a blanket, which I stuffed into another pillowcase. I splurged, spending $3.27 at Grayson's, but I had worked hard for the money and deserved it. I knew I'd have to give my parents $1.70 for rent, leaving me only three cents for my savings jar.

After I arrived home and gathered everything I needed, I went to get Bones. It would be the first place I'd taken him besides the vet's office. I figured he would enjoy the outing after being sick and starving, and I was happy to be able to finally take my dog somewhere with me. As it turned out, though, bringing him was both a blessing and a curse.

I met Lee and Roger on a path that led up into Panther Dunes. They were carrying their supplies in backpacks. I was embarrassed I only had a pillowcase to carry my things, but I knew they would more or less ignore that, which they did.

"Jeez! Is that the same dog that was starving a few weeks ago?" Roger asked when he saw Bones.

"Yep," I said. "He's starting to look like a normal dog. I mean, except for the three legs."

"Wow, man. It's amazing what a little bit of

food will do. He's still skinny but looking better."

"Yeah, he's looking pretty good," Lee said. "You're not gonna leash him?"

"Nah, he follows me wherever I go," I said. That was true, but I hadn't known it until that day. I had started to tie a rope to his collar when I went outside to get him but decided against it to see if he'd run off or walk with me. He'd stuck to me like maple syrup.

As we trudged up and down the hills toward where we planned to camp, we talked about past camping experiences.

"Hey, you guys ever been on a snipe hunt?" Roger asked.

"Yeah. What about you, Jack?" Lee asked.

"Nope. Never been that stupid," I answered.

Roger said, "One time on a Boy Scout camp out, we talked three guys who'd never heard of it into going on one. We told them they had to thump a paper bag real hard with their fingers and make this high-pitched screeching noise to draw the snipe out of hiding. We nearly died laughing at them."

"Man, I bet that was fun," I said.

"That's nothin'," Lee said. "Last summer we had these guys crawling on their bellies in the woods making snorting noises like a pig. One guy's mom got mad because he ended up with a couple ticks and chiggers from crawling in the dirt. She made him quit scouts over it."

"He coulda gotten ticks and chiggers without crawling in the dirt on a snipe hunt," I said.

"That's what the scout leader told her," Lee said, "but she was too mad to listen. Said he was a disgrace to scouting for lettin' us trick her son that way."

"Man, some parents have zero sense of humor," Roger said.

We finally arrived at the spot Lee and Roger had chosen for a campsite while exploring earlier that week. We all pitched in and assembled the tent. Next, we cleared an area and dug a place in the sand for a campfire. After fanning out to find some loose sticks and small branches for firewood and kindling, we huddled around the impromptu fire pit. Lee added some charcoal briquettes under the kindling and doused them with some charcoal lighter fluid. After that, he took out a pack of matches and struck one, holding it to the charcoal, which caught and spread the flames to the wood. Within minutes, we had a small fire going. We sat back, satisfied with the results of our work on the campsite.

We rested near the fire, basking in the joy of having nobody around to tell us what to do. Lee and Roger talked about the chores their parents would have them doing if they were home.

"I'd have to take the garbage out about now, and helping Sandra with the dishes would be waiting after dinner," Lee said.

Roger nodded. "Yeah, my little brother will have to take the garbage out for a change. Well, maybe he will. I swear, he gets away with murder sometimes. He'll be going, 'It's too heavy, Mom,' or 'Why can't it wait 'til Roger gets home?' What a baby," Roger said, switching his voice to a pouty whine to imitate his brother Ronnie.

"Yeah, I'm sure Sandra will figure something out to get help with the dishes and all," Lee said.

Their attention turned to me and my situation since I had no brothers or sisters at home to complain about. My brother had just arrived at Camp Pendleton across the country in California. He'd be shipping out in a few days to fight in Vietnam. I wondered if I'd ever see him again and doubted I would regardless of whether he survived the war. When he'd left home, he hadn't seemed anxious to return.

"Poor Jack," Lee said to Roger. "He has no one to complain about."

"Yeah, he'll have to do all his chores when he gets home," Roger said.

"I don't mind," I said, but that wasn't strictly true. What I minded was that my brother had left me holding the bag with our parents.

Needing a distraction, I sat up. "I'm hungry," I said, reaching for my supplies and pulling out a package of hot dogs and buns.

Lee's face lit up. "Now, you're talkin'."

Grabbing a thin branch, I used my knife to whittle one end to a sharp point. Lee and Roger did the same, and soon we were holding a hot dog over the fire. Bones stared at the cooking meat, licking his chops. I reached into the package of wieners and handed him one, which he gobbled down in two bites.

"He still acts like he's starving," Lee said.

"If you could down one in two bites, you'd do it, too," I said.

"Who said I can't?"

This challenge led to a contest to see who could eat his hot dog the fastest. It turned out Lee was right. He could eat his hot dog in two bites.

After our dinner of hot dogs, potato chips, and Cokes, we sat back to watch the sunset. Coastal towns barely have a dusk. The sun sets over the water, so no land forms cause the sunlight to slowly fade. Within ten minutes, the sky goes from light to dark, with only a faint red glow along the western horizon to show the sun was ever there in the first place, and even that disappears in a few minutes. The darkness descended on our campsite as if a window shade had been drawn to block the light. The fire glowed, and Roger added a few more of the thicker branches we'd found to keep it going for a while longer. We certainly weren't ready for sleep.

"So, tell us about the old guy who lives in the bus," Lee said.

"Not much to tell. He's an old guy who lives in a bus," I answered, not sure I wanted to talk about Hank.

"Why would he live in a bus? Can't he afford a house?" Roger asked.

"I guess he lives there because he wants to," I answered. "I never asked him."

"Really? That would be, like, the first thing I asked," Lee said.

"That's you."

"Come on, man. What's it like in there?" Roger said.

"It's just a bus with all the seats removed." My friends were now leaning forward, their eyes aglow with adventure, as if I were going to share the world's greatest ghost story. Heaving a deep sigh, I said, "He has a small table with a couple of metal chairs like you see in diners. He has an old army cot with a small dresser and an area in the back with a toilet, a shower, a faucet and a little table with a bowl on it for a bathroom sink."

Disappointment in my story stared back at me. It was obvious my description had not satisfied them.

"That's it?" Lee asked.

"That's it," I replied.

"What kind of guy is he?" Roger asked.

They obviously weren't going to leave this alone, so I said, "He's actually a real nice guy. He hired me when nobody else wanted to. He's as much a reason for Bones being alive as I am."

Roger worked to phrase a difficult question delicately. "Is he . . . I mean has he ever, you know, gotten 'funny' with you?"

Looking back, I guess it was a legitimate question. After all, I had wondered about Hank's motives myself early on, and I found it sad it was always the first thing people wondered when an older man wanted to befriend a boy my age. The truth was he was just a man who wanted to help me out, probably the best person I knew.

Still, Roger's question angered me. "What d'ya mean? Why would you think that? He's just a nice guy! He doesn't want anything from me! Nothing!" Tears of anger gathered in my eyes as the image of my friends blurred. "He's just a nice man!" I said in conclusion.

"Whoa, man. Don't get upset," Roger said. "I was just asking because—" He stopped suddenly. I could tell he had started to say more but thought better of it.

I stared at him. "Because why?" I demanded.

"Nothing," Roger said. "Just forget it."

"No, I won't forget it. You were going to say something else. What?" My anger rose, and I cautioned myself not to jump on Roger and beat him senseless.

"Okay. Okay. I'll tell you, but just don't get

mad," Roger said, glancing at Lee for support, and I realized Lee already knew what Roger was going to say.

Roger was silent, so I said, "Well?" as fear of what he would say stole over me.

"Well, I was in Grayson's the other day. My mom had me go there to get some bread and a few other things and, well, I heard Mrs. Polk talking to Mrs. Grayson." Mrs. Polk was the secretary at our school and one of Denton's biggest gossips. Nothing happened at school the community didn't know about within an hour, and most of what was passed on was exaggerated to the point it was no longer true.

"Go on," I prodded.

"Well, she was talking about you and that guy."

"Hank," I said, preferring Roger use his name.

"Yeah, Hank."

"And?"

"She was going on about the two of you always being alone every morning in his bus."

I wondered how she knew that. Had she been spying? "What did she say?" I said, seething. I hadn't needed to ask the question, but I was going to force Roger to tell me what she said. I was intent on having him repeat the lie as if saying it would make the accusation disappear like a fading echo.

"She didn't say you two were, well, actually *doing* anything. She was just sorta suggesting it was possible," Roger said.

"And you gotta admit, it's kinda weird an old guy wants to be your buddy," Lee said, the first thing he'd said in a while.

"I'll tell you what's weird," I said. "It's an old witch like Mrs. Polk going around spreading lies about people because she has nothing better to do, and it's my best friends thinking she's right."

"We don't believe it," Roger said.

"Then why'd you ask me?" I said.

He considered my question. "Because I guess I wanted you to tell me what I already knew."

I looked back and forth between him and Lee. They looked frightened, as if what I had started by talking about Hank truly had been the world's best ghost story. Children believe in ghosts, goblins, and evil monsters. It's not until we grow older that we find they are real after all, just not the way we read about them in children's story books. We're haunted by the ghosts of our pasts, and the goblins and evil monsters are standing in grocery stores, spreading lies without substance.

I spoke in a near whisper. "He's just a guy who's helping me out." Finally, I faced the truth. "He's better to me than my own dad."

I fed Bones before going inside the tent, leaving them behind to consider my words and either believe them or not. Lee and Roger joined me about a half hour later, but we didn't speak as they crawled inside their sleeping bags. I lay there as sleep crept up and took me. I thought all the drama of the night was over, but I was wrong.

8

I awoke to barking. Bones rarely barked, but the few times I had heard him, the sounds were muted, almost as if he were trying to converse with me. This racket was anything but muted or conversational. Bones was in a frenzy about something. I didn't know what time it was, but darkness blanketed the campsite because our fire had died.

I had left Bones outside the tent, trusting he would stay there until I woke up the next morning, but now the sound of his barking placed him at least ten yards from the doorway. I wondered what had upset him so much.

"What's up with your dog?" Lee asked, the irritation clear in his voice.

"I don't know," I said. "He usually doesn't

bark much at anything."

"Well, he's barking up a storm now," Roger said. "Can't you make him shut up?"

"Are you sure you want me to?" I asked, beginning to worry what it might be.

"It's probably just a rabbit," Lee said. "So, yeah, I do want you to."

"I don't know," I said. "Rabbits come through our yard all the time. He's never sounded this riled up before."

"Well, at least go see what it is," Roger said. "Otherwise, we'll never get back to sleep."

Lee turned on his battery-operated lantern. At that moment, a snarling growl tumbled from the night, the sound of a large cat. The hair on the back of my neck moved as I reached to grab the lantern.

"Oh, my God!" Lee said.

"It's Diablo!" Roger screeched, jumping to his backpack for his pellet gun and catching it on a strap before managing to pull it loose from the tangle of cords and straps inside. I could see its muzzle trembling as he aimed it toward the doorway as if Diablo would come crashing through it in the next few seconds.

The snarling grew wild and jumbled as Bones and Diablo began to fight. A nauseating rush of fear ran through me as I fast-crawled to the zippered doorway and grasped the zipper, yanking it up the seam to open the flaps. The zipper stuck in the fabric and I tugged at it. I finally freed the stuck zipper and bolted through the opening, pulling myself along with my hands as my feet scrabbled in the sandy dirt, I plunged toward the melee, screaming like a banshee.

My hands scurried along the ground, searching for a limb we'd not used for the fire. I found one with enough heft to cause the large cat pain if I hit him. The snarling stopped as I ran forward, the fight ending as quickly as it had begun. I could see the glow of Diablo's eyes, a yellow flash of light in the darkness that would disappear and reappear as he blinked.

A low growl came from Bones, followed by one from Diablo. I guess the large cat figured two against one wasn't fair. He turned and trotted away into the night. I couldn't see him, but I could hear him stumbling through some bushes as he slipped away.

I was startled by Roger as he said, "Sweet Jesus in a chariot race." He was standing behind me, and it occurred to me these were the same words he had used when he first laid eyes on Bones.

"Good Lord!" Lee said. He was standing beside Roger. I couldn't see their eyes in the darkness, but I would have bet they were bulging in shock at what had just happened.

"I guess we don't have to question anymore whether or not Diablo is real," Roger said.

"Unless this is the worst nightmare I've ever had," I said. "If it is, someone wake me."

We stood there in stunned silence as our eyes adjusted to the meager light, and the crickets came back to life around us. The full moon was near the western horizon, telling me it was nearing dawn, which was hurried like the dusk.

The warm wetness of my dog's tongue touched my hand. I squatted beside him and reached out to stroke his side. When I did, he whimpered and I felt the sticky wetness matting his short fur. Instant tears of fear and worry filled my eyes. Bones was bleeding. He'd either been severely scratched or bitten, maybe more than once. As the scenario of what had happened formed in my mind, I leaned down and held my dog in a gentle hug, blinking back tears.

Bones must have smelled the panther as it approached our camp and moved toward it, advancing to where he knew the cat would be. He'd started barking when Diablo came too close to ignore. Then he'd managed to get into a fight that could have killed him, might still kill him, to protect my friends and me.

Had I not been there, Diablo would surely have won the fight. Bones was still too weak to be a real match for the panther. Even healthy he couldn't have beaten Diablo. I wondered if he knew he was risking his life to protect me before deciding he probably didn't care. I had saved him from starvation, he had saved me from Diablo, and I had saved him from Diablo in return. Did that mean he still owed me a life? I didn't know, but I did know if I didn't get him to the vet's soon, he would die anyway.

"It's okay, Jack. Diablo's gone. We're safe now," I heard Roger say.

"Bones isn't safe. He's bleeding," I said.

"Where?" Lee asked.

"I don't know, but he's covered in blood."

"Maybe it's Diablo's."

"I doubt it," I said. "Get your lantern, Lee."

He went to the tent and returned with the lantern, holding it over Bones. I could see some places where the cat's teeth had left small punctures, and I was unsure how deep they were. The worst wound, though, was a gash along his back that was the source of most of the blood. I stared as the torn skin oozed a steady flow.

"We have to get him to town," I said. "He needs the vet."

"Can he walk?" Roger asked.

"Maybe, but I'm not gonna let him. Walking will just make him bleed more." I leaned over and wrapped my arms below his neck and rump and lifted him. He was heavy, but I could manage. I knew if Bones tried to walk the two miles to the vet's, he probably wouldn't live. Carrying him the entire way wouldn't kill me, and I was already aware Bones would risk his life for me.

Lee led the way, holding out the lantern to help me see the roots and such that could trip me. Falling on top of Bones certainly wouldn't help. Still, because I was hurrying, I stumbled twice when I tripped on something in the path and caught my balance just in time.

The sky to the east grew lighter, going from dark to dim in minutes, followed by total sunshine a few minutes after that. The temperature began to climb as if someone had started a fire beneath our feet.

As we neared the place where the pathway opened onto a back street, I suffered the weight of my dog with every step. My arms throbbed, and I wondered what I would have done if he had reached his normal weight.

We finally arrived at the main highway. The vet's office was still a quarter mile or so away. Lee and Roger offered to carry Bones, but I refused their offer. If I'd made it this far, I could make it the rest of the way. Besides, it was somehow something I needed to prove to Bones and myself.

When we finally arrived at the vet's, the doors were closed and locked. It was still early, of course, not even seven o'clock. On the door was an emergency number, which I memorized. I had to go another two blocks to a pay phone. Lee came with me and Roger stayed with Bones. Fishing a dime from my pocket, I dialed the emergency number and waited for an answer.

It must have rung seven times before anyone picked up. It was the number of the vet's assistant, Mrs. Terry, the nice lady who had helped me each time I'd brought Bones in before.

"It's Bones!" I cried into the receiver when she'd picked up with a sleepy "hello."

"What? Who?" she said. She still sounded groggy.

"Bones! He's hurt! He's bleeding real bad."

"Is this Jack?" she asked. Apparently, they didn't work with too many animals named Bones and she'd realized who this was on the line.

"Yes. Jack Turner. Bones got in a fight with Diablo!"

"Diablo?! The *panther*?"

"Yes, ma'am. We were camping in Panther Dunes and Diablo attacked him!"

"You're sure it was a panther?" She was having a hard time believing me.

"Yes! It was Diablo! I saw him!"

"And heard him," Lee prompted.

"And heard him!" I said into the receiver.

"Oh, dear," she said, clearly disturbed.

"Bones is bleeding real bad! I had to carry him out. Can you get the doctor and have him come in? I'm scared!" I said. Panic rose in me, trying to choke off my thinking.

"Where are you now?" she asked.

"At the pay phone down from your office."

"I'll have him there as quick as I can, hon. You go wait at the door."

With that, she hung up. I looked at Lee. "She's getting the doctor."

"This is gonna be expensive, Jack. Do you have enough saved for this?"

"I don't know, but I'll just set up a payment or something if I don't."

After we arrived back at the vet's, Roger looked at me. I could see something was bothering him. "Jack?"

"What?"

"I'm sorry about last night. I didn't mean to make you mad."

I'd forgotten all about it. Dealing with Diablo and the injuries had tossed it from my mind.

"It's okay," I said, but realized I needed more. "You don't believe it, though, do you?"

"If you say it didn't happen, it didn't happen," Roger said.

I looked at Lee. "I never believed it," he said, but something in his eyes told me he had. I dropped it, though. I could at least see he didn't believe it now, and that would have to be enough. Later, it occurred to me that was what friendship was about. Friends would irritate you and even drive you wild with anger sometimes, but you either had to let it go or let it eat the friendship alive. Lee and I had been through too much to let that happen.

Within a few minutes, the doctor arrived. Coming to the door, he unlocked it. Mrs. Terry, the lady I'd spoken to on the phone, drove in as he fumbled with the lock. I had lifted Bones and was covered in his blood. I took him into an examination room while the doctor washed up to examine the wounds.

As I laid Bones on the sterile table, I began to cry. I didn't want to think about what could happen. I feared the doctor might say it would be better to put him down. Lee and Roger stood silently beside me. I knew how they felt. It was never easy to think of anything to say in the face of tragedy. We were all helpless as we watched the doctor working on my dog.

"I don't know if I can pay for this," I said. "I'll need to probably make payments."

"Don't worry about that now," the doctor said. "We'll figure something out, I'm sure."

He never took his eyes off what he was doing while he spoke. He made remarks about what he found as he looked at the injuries.

"So Diablo did this?" he asked, astonishment in his tone. Whether his amazement came from the fact Bones was alive or that Diablo was really out there, I couldn't tell.

"Yeah," I said. "Their fighting woke me up."

"Woke us all up," Lee corrected.

Mrs. Terry came in and washed her hands while asking what she should do. I half expected the doctor to say she needed to prepare whatever drugs they would use to put Bones down.

"Help hold him down while I numb him. It's gonna need stitches," the doctor said. "I might have to knock him out. It's gonna take a while to sew him back up." He looked at me. I guess he could see the possible outcome I'd been imagining. "He's gonna be fine. He'll take a while to heal, but he's not gonna die today."

Relief flooded me, making my legs tremble.

"Is there somewhere I can sit down?" I asked.

"Why don't you boys go sit in the waiting area while we do this?" Mrs. Terry said, and ushered us out the door of the exam room, letting the door swing silently closed behind us.

I looked down and noticed how much blood was on me. My shirt front was covered, and I had drying blood on my hands and arms. I went to the bathroom down the hall and tried to clean up. When I looked in the mirror, I saw blood smeared on my neck and face. One ear was bloody as well.

I removed the shirt and tried rinsing it out in the sink, but too much of it had dried already, so I threw it in the wastebasket. I worked to clean the blood off me, and managed to get most of it. After that, I used wet paper towels to clean up the bathroom since I'd made a mess.

When I finally came out, Lee and Roger's parents were there. "We called our folks," Lee said.

"Yeah, we wanted to let them know where we were," Roger added.

Lee's father, Mr. Humphrey, looked down at me. "I hear your dog saved you fellas."

"I guess so," I said, feeling numb.

"That's a brave dog you have," Roger's dad, Mr. Cutshaw, said. Both mothers were silent, as if they were imagining what could have happened if Bones had not been there.

"I always thought he was a myth," Mr. Humphrey said and smiled. "Diablo, not your dog." He was attempting a joke, and it reminded me of the time Mrs. Dawson had done nearly the same thing when she said she wasn't talking about her dog playing baseball with the Mets. The memory made me smile.

Mr. Cutshaw glanced at Mr. Humphrey as if they shared information I didn't have before he looked down at me. "An act of bravery and heroism like that deserves a reward," he said. "Our boys are alive, and while it's no guarantee your dog saved them, it's fair to say that cat could have done quite a bit of damage if your dog hadn't been there."

"Yes," Mr. Humphrey said. "So we'd like to pay the vet bill if you don't mind. As a reward."

I looked at them. These men barely knew me. I was just a kid their boys played with, camped with, and sometimes even broke the law with. I began protesting the kindness I didn't deserve.

"No, really," I said. "I can handle it."

"I'm sure you can," Mr. Cutshaw said, "but we insist."

I was stunned. They didn't need to do this, but good deeds can come from unexpected quarters, as Mrs. Dawson said.

Putting my hand out toward the two men, I said, "Thank you." Each man took my hand and shook it.

Mrs. Terry came out of the room and smiled. "We'll be done in maybe another half hour," she said. "We think it will be best if we keep him here for the next few days to monitor his progress, so you can all go home. He'll be fine now, but he will need lots of medicine and rest. You can come back to pick him up on Monday," she said to me. She turned to go back into the exam room, but Mr. Humphrey stopped her.

"He'll need to be driven home, right?" he asked.

"Yes, he won't be able to walk very far at all for at least a week," she answered.

I wondered who would drive me to get him. Neither of my parents drove or even owned a car. I thought maybe I could ask Mrs. Dawson to do it.

Mr. Humphrey looked at me. "I'll meet you here to pick him up Monday evening at six," he said and looked at Mrs. Terry. "Will that be a good time?"

"Sure," she said. "We'll have him ready."

We still needed to break down our campsite and return home, so Lee, Roger, and I walked back out there. After we broke camp and gathered everything, we set off toward home.

It had been an emotional twenty-four hours, but I had learned a lot. I knew who my friends were, and that would come in handy in the coming weeks and months.

## 9

A couple of weeks went by while Bones healed and I worked. Mrs. Dawson had managed to find more things for me to do, so I kept busy. Not only was I now keeping her garden and lawn up, but I was also completing some of the more difficult tasks that needed doing around her house she was too old to do, like cleaning out and organizing her shed and washing and waxing her car.

Because I didn't have to get to work until nine o'clock, I had time to stop and have coffee with Hank each morning. My work day ended at five, which allowed me time to enjoy much of the remaining light. I would sometimes stop off at Hank's on my way home for a chat before going home to play with Bones, something he felt more like doing as the days passed and his wounds healed.

I had chosen to ignore what Mrs. Polk had said about Hank and me and decided she was just another adult with a dirty mind. I hadn't mentioned it to anyone else, not even Hank.

Thinking about Mrs. Polk had another effect on me. I was angry at her for being such an evil person, and these emotions sometimes interfered with the way I dealt with others, especially Mrs. Dawson since I spent more time with her than anyone else.

One morning I was angry because my mom had returned some of the dog food I'd bought so she could get money for beer.

The fact my mother was stealing from me led me to hide my money in more than one place in case my mother or father managed to find my jar beneath the floorboard in my closet. It was an easy hiding place to spot, and I didn't want them to know about all the money I'd saved if they did discover my hiding place. I still kept about twenty dollars in the jar there, but I had hidden the rest – over a hundred dollars now – in various places. It would have been nice if things were different, but they weren't.

More than that, I grew jealous of Lee and Roger and their normal family lives. Their parents would never steal from them, no matter what.

Mrs. Dawson attempted conversation the morning I'd found out my mom was stealing from me, but I wasn't in the mood to talk. My reactions to her attempts to cheer me up were abrupt and angry.

"It's a lovely day, Jack. Maybe you should take the day off," she suggested.

"Can't," I said. "I need the money to buy more dog food."

"Surely you have enough," she offered.

"Would have, but my mom stole some dog food and returned it to Grayson's for a refund."

She looked at me as if I were making this up. She still insisted my mom never thought of herself first, and this news didn't fit that opinion.

"Surely, you just forgot how many cans you had left," she said.

"Surely, I didn't," I said, wanting this conversation to end, but knowing that was impossible. "I keep a close count of how much I have because, well, because I wondered if something like this might happen."

Mrs. Dawson shook her head, and her face collapsed into a defeated frown. Looking into her eyes, I saw she finally understood what I'd known for years. My mother's alcoholism trumped everything.

I had been digging in the garden during the conversation, but I stopped to talk to Mrs. Dawson because the pain in her eyes was impossible to ignore. "She's not a bad person. It's just she's not a good person either. She needs her beer and will do almost anything to get it. She's like a junkie."

She shook her head. "Your own mother."

"I'm the unluckiest person in the world," I said. "It's like God hates me or something."

Her voice took on a firmness I hadn't expected. "Never say that," she said. "Many people are much worse off than you."

"Oh, yeah?" I said. "Show me one."

She stood there for a minute, her arms crossed.

"I'll do better than that," she said. "I'll be right back."

With that, she turned on her heel and walked inside, and I returned to my work. A few minutes later, she came back out, her purse dangling from the crook of her elbow.

"Let's go," she commanded.

"Where?"

"You'll see."

I rose and brushed myself off, wondering where we were going. She had her purse, so I knew it wasn't nearby. We would be taking her car. I'd never ridden in it, and part of me was excited to be going somewhere in the car for the first time, while another part of me was annoyed my work day had been interrupted by Mrs. Dawson's decision to take me somewhere I probably didn't want to go.

We climbed into the car, her jaw set firmly as she started it.

"Where are we going?" I asked again.

"Same answer as before. You'll see."

Her answers were abrupt, so I sat back as we rode in silence. We drove toward Denton Bridge, and I wondered if she might be taking me to see Hank. I couldn't see any reason for that, but it was the only place, other than my house, I thought she might be taking me. I started to panic. What if she were taking me home to confront my mom? If she took me there, I was going to jump out and run as soon as she stopped at the house. I couldn't accuse my mom of stealing with Mrs. Dawson standing there.

I was surprised when she didn't turn down my street. Instead, she drove over the bridge toward Wharton. I knew that had to be where she was going, since nothing but beach stretched between the two towns, and I knew she wasn't taking me to the beach.

Suddenly, the last words of our conversation in the yard hit me. *"Show me one,"* I'd said, referring to someone worse off than I was. She had answered, *"I'll do better than that."*

She was going to show me.

The pit of my stomach rolled and tightened into a knot. I couldn't imagine where we were going, but one thing I knew was I was not interested in seeing anyone worse off than I was. The thought of it was depressing. I considered jumping out and running the first time she stopped at a traffic light.

Apparently, that thought occurred to her as well. "Don't you dare jump out of this car when I stop," she said. "If you do, you're fired."

She glanced my way and I was shocked to see her eyes brimming with tears. At that point I wasn't sure what I would do, but I knew I wouldn't run.

As we drove, I looked out the window at the passing stores and houses. Wharton wasn't big, but it was at least five times the size of Denton.

Denton also had a health clinic where minor ailments and injuries could be treated by a nurse, but Wharton had a real hospital, which, as it turned out, was our destination. Mrs. Dawson steered her car onto Elm, and the massive building loomed before us, a monolith built for treating the sickest people in the county. My grandparents had died in this building, as would many people I knew. I didn't like hospitals, and as we approached it, panic settled into my chest. I thought of running again but I couldn't.

After Mrs. Dawson parked in the visitors' lot, we climbed out.

"What are we doing here?" I asked, even though I suspected the answer.

"You said to show you one person worse off than you. We're here so I can show you several."

"That's okay," I said, willing to do nearly anything to keep from going inside. "I understand now. You don't have to do this."

Walking into the building and holding the door for me, she turned to me and said, "No, Jack. I think I do."

I stared at her, seeing no way out of this. I hated hospitals. The animal hospital in Denton wasn't bad, but the ones for people frightened me. She noticed the fear. "It's just a building, Jack. It can't hurt you. I think you need to do this."

"Why?"

"So you'll stop feeling sorry for yourself," she said.

"I'm not feeling sorry for myself," I said.

"Tell you what," she said. "You meet these people and then decide if you are or not because it sure sounded like it to me, going on about how you're the unluckiest person in the world because your parents are alcoholics. Lots of children grow up in homes with alcoholic parents. It's not a good thing, but it's not the worst either."

She ended her lecture, saying, "Now, get in here and let's go see some people with real problems. This is what I'm paying you to do today."

I didn't find out until later Mrs. Dawson knew a lot of doctors because she had once worked in this hospital. She was an admissions clerk, and she ended up knowing nearly every doctor in Wharton. She knew a lot of the ward nurses, too. When we took the elevator to the fifth floor, I realized we were in the pediatric ward.

Colorful, hand-drawn and painted pictures by children decorated the halls. I'd never been here, and it looked different from the other wards because of the efforts to make it cheerful for the children who had to be there. When we arrived at the nurses' station, Mrs. Dawson didn't even have to speak before the nurse at the desk broke into a wide grin.

"Mary Jane! What brings you up here?"

Mrs. Dawson gestured towards me, and I was afraid for a moment she would say, *This kid thinks his life stinks, so I brought him up here to teach him a lesson,* but she didn't. All she said was, "Jack here is my gardener, and he wanted to meet some of the children on the ward. He has some great stories about his new dog."

"Well, I'm sure we can arrange that," said the nurse, whose name tag read *Anne Kennedy, R.N.* She looked at me. "What kind of dog is he?"

"The vet says he's a lab mix," I said, already wondering what I might tell a complete stranger about Bones.

"I bet he loves you," she said.

Mrs. Dawson leaned over the counter and said, "The dog nearly died saving him and some other boys from Diablo, that panther up in the sand hills."

"That was you?!" Nurse Kennedy said, surprising me. "We heard about that. We talked about how it was lucky you boys didn't end up here on the ward with us."

I was embarrassed word of what happened had made it all the way to Wharton. Denton was six miles from Wharton, and I wondered how she knew about it. Then it hit me. Roger's dad was an x-ray tech here. He must have spread the word.

"Here ya go," Nurse Kennedy said, holding out one of those cloth masks like doctors wear in surgery.

"Why do I need this?" I asked. "I'm not going into surgery, am I?" I wasn't sure I could have done that. The thought of looking into a human body made my stomach churn.

Nurse Kennedy laughed, joined by Mrs. Dawson. "No, dear. Some of the children here have diseases or even treatments that can cause them to get sick real easy if they're exposed to germs from others, so we always wear masks and gowns when we go into certain rooms."

She pointed up the hall. "You'll find a sink in the alcove there where you can scrub your hands real good with soap from the green bottle next to the sink," she said. "Scrub your hands and arms all the way to your elbows for a full minute before rinsing. Then dry them real good on a clean towel on the rack. Then come back out here." As I walked toward the alcove, she added, "And use hot water."

I did as I was told and when I arrived back at the nurse's station, I was given a gown to put on over my clothes. Mrs. Dawson was sitting behind the counter. Nurse Kennedy was already in her mask and gown.

I was already thinking I was more fortunate than some of the kids there. I had no idea such sickness even existed, especially in kids.

When we were in our masks and gowns, Mrs. Dawson said, "Anne told me about a boy about your age just down the hall. He has cancer. There's a girl just down from him. She has a disease that makes her immune system not work very well."

Cancer? I thought only adults had cancer. I had always figured it was somehow related to years of smoking cigarettes, and kids were too young to get it.

We stepped down to the room with the boy who had cancer. The moment I walked in I wanted to leave. He was the palest person I'd ever seen, and he was bald. In fact, he didn't even have eyebrows. When we entered, he was playing with a little game board with pegs.

He smiled as we came in. "Toby," Nurse Kennedy said. "This is Jack. He came by to meet you today."

"Hi," Toby said. His eyes looked sunken into his face, and dark circles hung under his eyes. He looked like he might weigh no more than fifty pounds.

"Hi," I said back and could think of nothing else to say.

"Toby's ten," Nurse Kennedy said.

I looked at Toby as if he were a science project gone wrong. I suddenly wondered if he would live as long as I had already. By the looks of him, I doubted it. I had a strong urge to cry or turn and run, but I did neither.

"You heard about those boys who were saved from that panther by a dog?" Nurse Kennedy asked, reaching out to pat Toby on the shoulder. Her touch was so gentle I thought he might not have felt it.

Toby nodded. "Yeah. I heard you talkin' about it a while back."

"Well, this is the boy who owns the dog."

Toby looked at me and smiled broadly. His dark eyes lit up and seemed to bulge from his sunken face. "Really?" he said. He acted as if he were meeting a celebrity.

I smiled back at him. "Yeah. He fought the panther and saved our lives," I said. "I had to carry him two miles to the vet to save him."

"Wow, that's cool!" he said. "My folks won't let me have a dog 'cause of the cancer."

I wasn't sure what cancer had to do with not having a dog, but I acted as if I understood, nodding. I could tell he wanted a dog, though.

"You know how to play this?" he asked, holding out the peg game. He had replaced the pegs, leaving one space empty to allow the first jump. It was kind of like checkers. When you jumped a peg, you'd remove the one you jumped. The object was to end up with only one peg.

"Sure," I said, and took the offered game. I began jumping pegs until I couldn't make another jump, ending up with three pegs. I handed it back to him after replacing the pegs for another game. "Now you try," I said.

After a few minutes of talking and playing the game, I realized we were alone. Nurse Kennedy had left. I could hear her and Mrs. Dawson outside the door talking. I talked to Toby, telling him more about Bones and Diablo. I wanted to ask him if he was going to live or not, but I knew it would be rude. Finally, I excused myself and said, "I hope you get better." He just thanked me for coming by and invited me to stop in again if I wanted to.

"Now, let's go meet Suzanne," said Nurse Kennedy, and she led us two rooms down to a closed door. A placard on the door warned that anyone entering needed to be masked and gowned. "I'll just stick my head in to make sure she's okay with having a visitor."

She stuck her head inside and said, "Suzanne? You dressed?"

I heard a sweet voice say yes. Nurse Kennedy said, "I have a visitor for you. A young boy." I blushed when Nurse Kennedy said, "He's cute, too."

"Okay," Suzanne said. She didn't sound too

excited, which made me even more uncomfortable. I wondered why every adult had to make a comment about things like that when introducing a young boy and girl to each other. It was like putting added pressure on the kids to start dating, or something.

I walked into the room. When I saw the girl propped up in bed, I was struck by how fragile she looked, like Toby, her neighbor with cancer. However, she was so small and thin it reminded me of the first time I saw Bones.

Nurse Kennedy once again mentioned Bones and how he saved us from the panther, and Suzanne seemed impressed. Still, she seemed much too tired to be meeting people she didn't know, especially a boy who had been put in the pressure situation of being called "cute."

We talked for a while, and I found out she was my age although she looked younger. I told her about the campout, and finally excused myself, saying, "You try to rest, okay?"

She smiled back at me and apologized for being so tired. I told her it was okay.

As I left the room, though, she stopped me. "Jack?" I turned back to look at her from the door. "She's right. You are cute."

I wanted to drop through the floor, but I said, "Thanks." Then I said, "You are too," even though she must have known she was too thin and sick to be cute, but I could see she would be pretty and cute if not for her disease. She smiled her thanks anyway. As I walked out of her room, I wondered how she could tell anything with all the garb I had on, including a mask. I decided she was just being polite.

It went that way all afternoon. Nurse Kennedy would introduce me to the patient, and I would stay for a short visit while Nurse Kennedy and Mrs. Dawson stood in the hallway outside the door, as if I had requested privacy.

When we were finished visiting the kids on the ward, I returned the gown and mask and we rode the elevator back down. The moment the elevator doors shut, I burst into the tears I'd been holding in since we'd arrived in Toby's room. Mrs. Dawson didn't say anything until we were in her car.

"Every life has bad things in it, Jack," she said. "It's just some lives have more bad in it than others. Keep that in mind the next time you start feeling sorry for yourself."

As I worked to stop crying, I stared at her for a moment, thinking of Hank's advice about her that first time I met her. He'd said she was eccentric. She definitely was with Yogi, the Yankees, her forgetfulness, and her tendency to talk to herself.

But I was also beginning to understand the rest of what he'd said—that I would find she was a nice lady once I grew to know her. I didn't fully realize it then, but *nice* didn't even begin to describe her. She was much more than that.

## 10

When we arrived back at Mrs. Dawson's, we went inside and I poured myself a glass of water from the pitcher in the refrigerator. When I came out of the kitchen, she called me to the living room. The TV was off, which was rare.

"Have a seat," she said. Once again, I didn't consider it a request. "This little trip reminds me I never told you about Hank's family."

I'd thought a lot about how the phone call from her sister Dorothy had interrupted us, but it would be rude to ask Mrs. Dawson to continue the story. "What about it?" I asked. I tried to be nonchalant, but I leaned forward in anticipation.

"Before I start, you have to swear to me you won't say anything to Hank about this. The only reason I was going to tell you in the first place is because you are about the closest person to him now. Not only that, but his story shows how bad things will happen to everyone. But if you tell him you know about this, he'll know where you heard it, and I don't want that. Are we clear?" I nodded.

"Hank was married once," she began, after lighting a cigarette. "She was a pretty thing, too, with dark hair and eyes so brown they looked black. Hank owned his own restaurant back then, had just opened it a month or two before they met, in fact, as well as two big deep-sea fishing boats. He'd advertise "HANK'S DAILY CATCH" on a chalk board as you walked in, and that's what it was. He'd let a couple of his deck hands fish when his boats went out after they'd cut bait and done their other duties, and that night he'd serve what they brought in. Of course, whatever it was didn't last long on the menu since a few people can catch just so many fish on a deep-sea fishing boat in one day, but it was—if you'll pardon the pun—a catchy thing for him to have on the menu because he was the only restaurant owner in the area who actually hired guys to fish for his restaurant's daily special."

"Wait a minute," I said, confused. "You mean Hank owned a restaurant and a couple of party boats?"

"Yes, he did. And that restaurant was a big success."

"Why doesn't he own them anymore?" I asked.

"That's what I'm getting to," she said. "Now, he was happily married and a successful businessman, which was no wonder, everything considered. His wife's name was Pauline. She was a Milgrove from Pensacola, and they'd met at a party in Wharton. I've never seen two people more in love.

"After they were married, she moved into his house." She stopped and looked at me. "You know that huge place that sits at the end of Souder's Point?" I nodded. "That was his house." I was stunned. That house was probably the most expensive one in Denton, other than David Moreland's mansion, and now he lived in an old, broken-down bus? What in the world had happened?

"Anyway, soon she turned up expecting their first child. It was a boy, and they named him Henry Paul, after both of them. A couple years later, their daughter, Constance Pittman was born. They doted on those children something awful, but the thing was it didn't spoil them. Hank made sure they knew what work was, and his son would work in the summer mopping the floors at the restaurant. Connie, which is what they called their girl, would clean the restrooms there, and they were no more than eight and ten."

"What happened to them?" I asked.

"Like I said, I'm getting to that." Her glare

warned me not to interrupt her again.

"Anyway, Hank never cared much for his father—I guess he had good reason—but what happened sealed the death of that relationship for good.

"You see, one night Hank's father became drunk at a party and was driving home. He shouldn't have been driving, but that's all water under the bridge now. Anyway, it so happened that Pauline and the children had gone to Pensacola to visit her mother. They were driving back from there, and both cars arrived at the intersection of Main and Orchid in Wharton at the same time. Hank's father pulled out in front of Pauline's car, and she clipped his car and swerved, running head on into another car, which was being driven by a teenager who was doing at least fifty down Main Street. That boy ended up in the hospital, but he survived. Pauline and the children were killed. Connie died at the scene, and Pauline and Henry died within a few days at the hospital."

Mrs. Dawson sat back, her story apparently finished. I was speechless for a full minute, trying to grasp the pain of something like that. No wonder he hadn't wanted to discuss the pictures that time I brought them up.

"What did Hank do?" I asked. "Just give up the restaurant and boats?"

"More or less," she answered. "He sold them

and dropped his last name entirely. He's not spoken to his father since, that I know of."

"He dropped his last name?" I asked, trying to understand.

"Yes, Jack. Hank's middle name was Pittman. His last name was Moreland, but he had it legally dropped. He's the second oldest son of David Moreland. After Ted, the oldest. Jerry, who owns the docks beside his bus, is the youngest son."

I think I went numb at this revelation. "Hank's a—Moreland?" I said, wondering if Mrs. Dawson was pulling my leg to see my reaction. It didn't seem possible that Hank was a member of the richest, most powerful family in the entire county.

"Yes," Mrs. Dawson said, "and you can't let him know that you know."

"So, he just took his middle name, Pittman, for his last name?" I asked.

"Yes," Mrs. Dawson said. "They gave their daughter their middle names. Constance was Pauline's middle name. Essentially, both their children were named after both of them."

"That must have been awful for him," I said.

"It was. He's not been the same person since, although after meeting you, he's come the closest to his old self as I've ever seen. Don't tell anyone, especially Hank, but I think he sees his son in you."

"How old was his son when he died?"

"He'd just turned eleven, I think," she said.

"About two years younger than you."

"How long ago did this happen?"

"Oh, dear. Must have been ten years or so." She thought about it for a minute. "Yes, I think it was in '58. So that would make it ten years ago this summer." I considered this. I turned three the October after the accident.

I thought of something else and wondered if Mrs. Dawson would know the answer. "Mrs. Dawson? What was his military medal for?"

"How do you know about that?" she asked, her brow furrowing slightly.

"I was in his bathroom, and I saw a picture of him in a military uniform. I think it might be army, and he's wearing a big medal with a star on it."

"He was in the army during World War II. He earned the Silver Star. That's the third highest award for valor given by the military. I don't know how he earned it. He never wanted to talk about it, which is not uncommon for war heroes. It's the cowards who want to talk about what they supposedly did in battle. But I think he earned it the same time he earned his Purple Heart after parachuting into France after D-Day."

"He was a war hero?" I asked.

"Yes. They wanted to write it up in the papers here, but Hank wouldn't let them. Said getting medals was not something to celebrate because valor never saves everyone."

I began to feel as though I'd only just now met the real Hank Pittman, or Hank Moreland, actually. He had been hiding so much from me. From everyone. He was living a lie. Not only that, but it also occurred to me that a lot of people in town knew who he really was but said nothing about it.

I felt lost, as if everything that had given order to my world had suddenly disappeared.

Mrs. Dawson rose and stretched and walked into the kitchen without a word. I had started out for the back yard when she came back and said, "I'm going to visit my sister Dorothy in Mobile next week, so I won't be needing you to come for regular work, but I do need you to stop by every day and make sure everything's okay and the plants are getting enough water. I'll pay you a dollar a day to do that. Will that be okay?"

It wasn't as if I could say no, even though the dollar just to check on things was good pay. The thing I was disappointed about was not being able to plan for the time off from work. I would have tried to set up something just for next week.

On my way home that day, I saw Hank stepping into Kirby's. I knew my dad was there, and I didn't want him to see me talking to Hank even though I wanted to after finding out about his past like that. I wouldn't have mentioned it. I just wanted to talk. I had just about walked past Kirby's when a sudden thought hit me.

I was on the other side of the highway from the bar, and I turned to stare at the door for a minute while I made up my mind. I figured I could count on Hank not to speak to me if I didn't speak to him, so I set out across the road to talk to my dad.

When I walked in, he was busy serving Hank a beer. I stood in the doorway for a moment, allowing my eyes to adjust to the pale light inside.

When my dad saw me, he was surprised. It wasn't as though I'd never stopped in at Kirby's, but it was rare. He knew if I was dropping by now, it was important. He'd been out of sorts lately because my brother Rick had shipped off for Vietnam a week before. Besides, he had to serve other people beer at work and couldn't take a drink himself, so he was always on edge when he was working.

"Jack!" he said. "What're you doing here?"

"I was wondering if you'd do me a favor," I said.

"Depends."

Out of the corner of my eye, I saw Hank look at me, holding his gaze there for a second before going back to his beer.

I continued my conversation with my dad, pretending not to notice Hank. "I was wondering if you would get me in to talk to Mr. Kirby."

My dad looked at me, suspicion clouding his face. "Why you wanna talk to him?"

"I wanted to ask him about possibly cleaning up here next week. I know he does the morning clean-up work himself before opening, and I thought maybe he'd like a week off from having to do that."

Because this would increase my rent payment, my dad was happy to speak to Mr. Kirby for me. He smiled. "Sure, son. He's in his office. Let me go see if he has time right now."

My dad hustled around from behind the bar and stepped toward the hallway in the back where Mr. Kirby kept his small office, passing the empty pool tables on the way. As he went, a customer sitting at a table with a couple of men said, "Hey, Cookie! How 'bout another round here."

"Be right on it, Bill," my dad said as he disappeared down the hall.

He was gone for a minute, and I glanced at Hank, who was ignoring me. He knew I didn't want my dad knowing I had done work for him. If he knew, he would pester Hank with questions about how much he'd paid me, how much work I did, and how much I was earning now.

A minute later my dad was rushing back into the bar, jerking his thumb over his shoulder toward the hallway. "He'll speak to you now," he said, as if I were a favorite customer.

I was on my way to the back hall when I noticed her. Mrs. Polk was sitting in a booth nursing a beer and staring at me as if I had just materialized out of the depths of Hell in a puff of smoke. I saw her cast a quick glance toward Hank, and I wondered what she was thinking. Nothing good, certainly. Just being near her like this made me queasy.

I walked past her as quickly as I could without seeming to rush, realizing at the same time she had no idea that I knew she was spreading lies about me. Her eyes crawled over me as I passed her thinking she was the one who had materialized from Hell.

I walked to Mr. Kirby's door and knocked. The walls badly needed paint, and the door was scarred with gouges. The entire building back there looked as if it would crumble soon.

"Enter!" boomed from beyond the damaged door.

I stepped in. The room was filled with cigarette smoke. An overfilled ashtray had claimed a permanent spot on his desk, which overflowed with papers. A junk-sale fluorescent desk lamp cast a soft glow over the mess. More fluorescent lighting from the ceiling filled the cramped room with pale light that made everything appear dead, Mr. Kirby included.

Mr. Kirby, who was in his fifties at least, parted his hair in a comb-over. His sparse strands of dyed hair did their best to hide what everyone but Mr.

Kirby knew couldn't be hidden. He'd been cursed with thick facial hair but mounting baldness where he wanted it most. He had a full beard and mustache that was so thick it looked as if it could hide a bird's nest. It was as though he had decided that if he couldn't grow hair on his head, he would grow it everywhere else he could.

"What is it? I'm busy," he said.

"I'm looking for some work next week," I said. "I have to earn money to pay for my dog, or my dad will have me put him down."

He looked at me as if I had just spoken an alien language or something. "Why do I care about your dog?" he asked.

"You don't, I guess, but I do. I was thinking—"

"You can't work here, kid. Gotta be at least twenty-one to serve beer." He looked almost sympathetic, as if it was sad I was so dumb that he had to explain this to me.

"No, sir. I know that. You see—"

"So what d'ya think you can do here, kid?" he asked, interrupting me before I could explain. "If you know you gotta be twenty-one, why are you wastin' my time?"

"I wasn't exactly thinking about working during business hours."

He gawked at me, bewilderment flooding his face, which was scrunched into this ball of squinty eyes and facial hair. "Huh?"

I rushed into an explanation before he threw me out. "I know you do the morning cleaning yourself trying to get the place ready to open. I have some time on my hands next week and needed to earn some money and wondered if you might like a week off from doing that."

Now, I could see the wheels turning as he thought about my suggestion. It was a tantalizing offer for him.

"If you're thinking about sneaking into the till and stealing me blind, I never put money in there until I'm about to open, so you wouldn't have the chance."

I took the insult without blinking. "That's not why I want the work. It's because I need the money for—"

"For your dog. Yeah, I heard you the first time," he said, still thinking about my offer. "How much you expect to be paid for this?" he asked. Good! We were in negotiations. The job was as good as mine.

"I figured it will take me a couple of hours, and I'd even clean your office for you," I said.

"Nah, don't need you snooping in my office," he said, still suspicious of my motives. "How does two bucks a day sound?" he asked.

"Make it four?" I countered, knowing what he would offer after that if he went up at all. If he didn't, I'd take the two dollars. That would be an extra ten for the week. Twelve if he wanted me for Saturday too.

He took the bait I'd dangled. "Three," he said, "and not a penny more."

I smiled, stood, and stuck out my hand. He looked at it for a moment as if he didn't know what it was. He stuck out his hand, and we shook on the deal. His grip, if it could be called that, was like holding a dead fish.

"Be here Monday at nine," he said. "I open at eleven, so that should give you time to clean the place up."

"Thank you, sir. You won't regret it."

"I better not, because if I do, your dad might join you on the street for puttin' you up to this."

"My dad had nothing to do with it," I protested, wondering if it was worth the effort.

"Yeah, yeah. Close the door on your way out."

As I left he said, "Don't be late, kid. You're late, you're fired. No questions asked, no explanations accepted."

I walked back out to the bar. My dad was shucking oysters for the guys in the booth who had asked for another round of beer. Hank was still there. His glass was full now, so I knew he was working on his second beer of the evening, and I wondered if he had stayed to find out how my talk with Mr. Kirby went. I nodded at him as I took a seat at the bar.

"Well?" my dad asked.

"I got the job," I said. "I have to be here at nine on Monday."

"Don't screw it up, boy." He shoved the oyster knife expertly into the back of the oyster's shell to pry it open. "My job's gone if you do." He knew his boss well. I didn't think that had occurred to him when he went back to knock on Mr. Kirby's door, but it must have come to mind while I was back there.

Hank shot me a look and said, "Congratulations, son. This calls for a Coke."

"That's okay," I said.

"I insist," Hank turned to my dad, who was finished shucking the dozen oysters. "Cookie," he said, "a cold Coke for this fine young man. Put it on my tab."

At that moment, Mrs. Polk stepped up to the bar to pay her own tab. She weaved her way to sidle up beside Hank and seemed to anchor herself to the bar between us. "You act as if you don't know him," she said to Hank.

"Well, barely," Hank said, continuing the charade for my sake. "He's Cookie's son, I believe."

I couldn't see Mrs. Polk's face, but I saw Hank's puzzled reaction to whatever expression he saw there. He told me the next morning over coffee that her eyes had a distinct "yeah, sure" quality. Of course, I knew why she would do that. He didn't because I'd not told him what Roger told me she was saying about us. It was when he told me about her look that I realized we may have made a mistake by pretending not to know each other. Doing that would only make her suspicions worse, and I was still too embarrassed about what she was saying to tell Hank, so her glare remained a mystery to him.

"At least I understand a few things now," she said as she weaved her way out the door after paying, but I had no idea what she meant.

I accepted the Coke and drank it the same way a drunk nurses a beer, drinking slowly and thinking about problems. I wasn't sure what to make of Mrs. Polk, but between Tommy and his pack, Officer Dagwood Hicks, and her, I was gathering quite a few enemies in Denton.

# 11

The next day was Friday, and I stopped at Hank's on my way to Mrs. Dawson's to have coffee with him, as usual. He was still puzzled at Mrs. Polk's reaction to him the evening before, and once again, I didn't tell him what I knew. It made me angry that she would talk about us that way, but mostly I considered it gossip that nobody in his right mind would listen to. I figured everyone would realize she was just trying to get attention for herself.

"Are you sure you don't know why she would think I know you well?" he asked.

"She was drunk, wasn't she?" I said. "Maybe that explains it." The truth wanted to spew from me like vomit, but I held it down.

"That she was," he said, though he didn't sound convinced.

This brought up another question that allowed me to change the subject. "Hank?"

He finished a sip of his coffee. "Hmm?"

"Why do people consider my parents the town drunks when people like Mrs. Polk get just as drunk?"

"That's a good question." He blew on his mug of coffee to cool it.

"What's the answer?" I wasn't going to let him off the hook that easily.

"To be honest, I don't have one though I'm not sure everyone sees your parents as the 'town drunks,' as you say. You're right about one thing, though. Mrs. Polk does indeed get drunk most days. I'd say people don't think of her as a 'town drunk' because she has a respectable job, but I'm not sure your father doesn't have one as well. I mean, he works in a bar and not the local school like she does, but that's no reason to hold him to a higher standard. In fact, it should be the opposite. You'd think working in a bar would lower people's expectations."

"That could be it," I said. "Maybe he's looked down on more because he works in a bar and she's a secretary at the school."

Hank shrugged. "Who knows? I don't think we have an actual 'town drunk,' though. Too many candidates."

That was the point I was trying to make, so I

figured it was time to change the subject again. "Mrs. Dawson took me to Wharton yesterday," I said, knowing he would ask why. He did, and I answered, "She took me to the kids' wing of the hospital."

"Oh?"

"Yeah, she said she wanted to show me people who weren't as lucky as me."

He looked at me over the rim of his mug as he sipped and asked, "And did she?"

"Yeah." I told him about Toby and Suzanne and some of the other kids I saw there.

"Why did she do that?" Hank asked.

I shrugged, but he could probably tell I knew the answer.

"Well, she's right. They say there's always someone worse off than you, no matter how bad things are."

"Even if you're dying?" I said. "I can't see any way someone's worse off than you if he's living and you're dying."

He looked at me for a moment and said, "Sometimes the ones who die are the lucky ones."

We sat there drinking our coffee in the silent bus. I knew he was talking about his family. I watched him and thought about them, both the one he lost and the one he threw away. He was a member of the wealthiest family in the area, but now people considered him to be a bum because he lived in an abandoned school bus. His silver star for heroism didn't even count anymore.

Watching him, I wondered if I could get him to tell me about his family and his past. If I could coax everything from him, I wouldn't need to avoid mentioning my conversation with Mrs. Dawson. I was afraid I might blurt something without thinking that would let him know I knew everything.

"Hank?"

"Hmm?" He was sipping his coffee again.

"Who's the lady in the pictures?"

He looked annoyed and said nothing.

I pressed on, undaunted. "And the two kids. The little boy and girl. Who are they?"

He cleared his throat and took another sip of coffee. "Just some people I once knew," was all he said.

"Are they your wife and kids?"

He stared at me, wondering how I landed on that, I'm sure. "Who've you been talking to?" he asked.

"Nobody," I lied. "I can just tell they're old pictures so they must be people who mean something to you. I mean, otherwise, why keep them up there?"

After a short pause he said, "Like I said. They're people I once knew." He returned to his coffee.

I had to give him credit for not exactly lying to

me, though. Technically, he was telling me the truth. Of course, what he was leaving out was the most important part, like what I'd left out about Mrs. Polk.

He suddenly stood and set his coffee mug down. "Don't you have to get to your job?"

"Yeah," I said and stood, too. My coffee wasn't finished, but I didn't want it anymore.

I walked to Mrs. Dawson's and thought about the past twenty-four hours. Life had gotten much more complicated in the past few weeks. I wondered if that meant I was becoming an adult, as Mrs. Dawson wished. If so, I found it to be much less fun than I thought it would be.

I didn't talk much to Mrs. Dawson that day. I was out of sorts, and she was being obsessive about packing for her trip. I'd never gone on a trip before, so I wondered what the big deal was. I always thought if you managed to pack clothes and a toothbrush, you should be set. Each time I entered her house, though, I could hear her asking Yogi's advice.

"Do I take the blue dress or the yellow one?" she asked the dog.

I once talked to Hank about how she always spoke to Yogi as if she were another person and asking for the dog's opinions. It was different from the way most people talked to and treated their dogs like people. Hank said as long as I never heard Yogi talking back, I had no problem. He laughed and told me she had always been a little bit different from everyone else.

Finally, around three o'clock that afternoon, she came outside to where I was weeding in the vegetable garden.

"I'm leaving now. It should take me a about five hours to get there, depending on the traffic."

"Okay," I said. "Have fun at your sister's."

"I will," she said. "And, Jack?"

"Yes ma'am?"

"If any vegetables ripen this week, go ahead and take them home. No sense in letting them spoil on the vine."

"Thanks," I said, wondering if my parents would ask me where I was getting fresh garden vegetables before deciding they probably wouldn't care.

"Thank you for checking on things for me." She paused for a moment, as if she wanted to say something more.

Finally, she asked, "Did you talk to Hank today?"

"Yes, ma'am," I said.

"Did you mention anything about what we talked about?"

I thought about my questions to Hank about the pictures and decided that asking what I had was not the same as letting on that she had told me about his past, so I said, "No, ma'am."

"Make sure you keep it that way. Even if you say someone else told you, he won't believe it. Nobody talks about that in Denton. Nobody."

"Why not?"

"Because David Moreland wanted it shut up, so it was shut up. After all, he was technically guilty of vehicular manslaughter and drunk driving, and he made sure it went away. He could have gone to prison, and perhaps he should have. I don't know how much it cost him to make it go away, but I'm sure it cost plenty. Now, nobody mentions it."

At least that explained why I hadn't heard it from anyone else.

"So, take care of things while I'm gone, and I'll see you a week from Monday," she said.

Putting Yogi in the front seat, she drove away and I finished my weeding. I made sure everything looked good before leaving for the weekend. I noticed a few tomatoes and cucumbers would be ready to pick next week at the latest. If my parents wanted to know where I got them, I'd say they were from Lee's mom, though I wasn't sure why I thought I needed to lie about it.

The next day was Saturday. Lee was gone with his family on a vacation, and Roger had mentioned he would be busy helping his dad with something or other. I decided to walk into town to find something to do. When I arrived, I ran into Hank coming out of Grayson's. He was carrying a small bag that held milk, coffee and cigarettes.

"Just the young man I was thinking of," he said. "Would you carry this for me?" I didn't mind doing it and had nothing else to do anyway, so I took the bag from him and we started walking to his bus.

"You up to going back to visit those kids in the hospital?" he asked.

I frowned. I had hoped he would forget about that. "Not really."

"Why not?"

"It made me uncomfortable."

"Course it did. That's why you should do it again."

That made zero sense to me, but I could tell he wouldn't take no for an answer. I heaved a sigh. "When you want to go?"

"No time like the present, as the man says."

"What man?"

He looked down at me and smiled. "Just the man," he said and chuckled. I didn't understand why he was so chipper, but he was. When we'd spoken about when I visited the hospital before, he had sounded about as anxious to go there as I did.

"How're we gonna get there?" Hank didn't have a car.

"I'm sure I can get Jerry Moreland to lend me his car. It just sits there at the docks all day, and he sometimes complains that he thinks it's going to rot from disuse."

"How does a car rot from disuse? Looks to me like it would stay new longer."

"Don't know, but it does. You park a car and leave it, things start breaking down. Battery goes dead, tires go flat, rust starts to eat it. Doesn't take long either. It's almost like it was made to do something and isn't content unless it's doing what it was made to do. Houses are the same way. A house sits empty for a year, and it starts to fall apart. Can't explain why that happens, but it does."

We walked along in silence, Hank deep in thought and me wishing we would get to his bus. The milk was getting heavy. Hank spoke up again, continuing his conversation about cars and houses because I guess he'd been thinking about it as we walked along.

"People are the same way, I guess. When people are doing what they're supposed to be doing, they're a lot happier." He paused. "And one thing people are supposed to do is make others feel good. That's why we're going to the hospital today." I began to wonder if he hadn't gotten a head start drinking his beer. He wasn't acting like himself. He was far too cheerful.

Twenty minutes later we were heading west toward Wharton in Jerry Moreland's car. I wasn't as upset as I had been when Mrs. Dawson had forced me to go, but I still wasn't happy. I would much rather have been fishing or just hanging out with Bones. Anything besides this.

We pulled into the lot and parked. When we climbed out, I looked at Hank and was surprised to see he had stopped still and was looking up at the hospital. It took me a moment to realize he was staring at a particular window, or at least that was what it looked like to me. He was staring up at a spot on an upper floor and not moving. The cheerful mood had disappeared. He was pale, and I realized he was afraid. His enthusiasm for coming here was gone, and I realized he was at least as afraid as I had been. Suddenly, it hit me. His wife and children had been brought here after his father had caused the fatal accident. It wasn't until years later that I realized how difficult this trip had been for him. His show of joy was masking a deep fear. My fear had been a childish one. His was real like a fire that had consumed him without killing him. This was his attempt to face that fear. At the time I just thought he was only remembering. Now, I know he was in agony because remembering isn't the same as reliving.

We went into the hospital and rode the elevator up to the pediatric floor. Once we were there, he excused himself, saying he had something else to do and would meet me back there later. To this day I don't know where he went, but I suspect it was to the floor where his family had been taken.

When I walked into the pediatric ward, Nurse Kennedy wasn't on duty. I stopped at the nurse's station and spoke to the person there. I looked at her name tag, which read *Dawn Burton, R.N.*, and I spoke to her.

"Nurse Burton?"

She looked up at me from her work and smiled. "Yes?"

"Hi. My name's Jack Turner. I was in here the other day. Nurse Kennedy showed me around, and I met—"

"You're Jack?" she said, as if she'd heard of me, interrupting what was probably going to be a long, confusing explanation about why a kid my age would be stupid enough to come back to the hospital to visit some kids he barely knew.

"Yes, ma'am."

"Anne told us about you!" she said and turned to another lady there who had just hung up the phone. "Frieda? This is Jack! The boy Anne told us about!"

Frieda, who was near sixty and must have weighed over two-hundred pounds, stepped to the counter and held out her hand to shake mine. "Hello, Jack. We're so happy to have you stop by." She wore her long, salt and pepper hair in a ponytail that swayed with her movements as she walked. Her nametag said her last name was Webster.

"So what brings you up here?" Nurse Burton said. "Anne said you lived in Denton. Did Mary Jane bring you again?"

I decided I didn't want to go into it all, so I lied. "My grandfather dropped me off. He's making me come here, and he'll pick me up later."

Nurse Burton spoke up and what she said made me blush. "Well, let's get you masked and gowned because I know for certain that Suzanne will be happy to see you."

I'd almost forgotten about the girl's last comment to me about how she thought I was cute, and I wished again that I was anywhere but here.

Nurse Webster must have noticed my cheeks turning red because she said, "Hush, Dawn. You're embarrassing the boy." She turned to me and said, "Go ahead and wash up over at the sink. You probably know the routine."

When I was washed, masked, and gowned, I stepped down to Toby's room first, stopping to pick up a game of checkers I had seen in a room marked LOUNGE when I'd been there before.

When Toby saw me, he smiled as if one of the Beatles had entered his room.

"Hey!" he said.

"Hey, yourself," I said. I held out the checkerboard. "You like to play checkers?"

He nodded, still grinning, and I sat on the edge of his bed to play, placing the game on the special table they have in hospital rooms for the patients to eat from. After two games, we had each won one apiece, so of course we had to play a third to break the tie.

In the middle of that game, though, Toby became too tired to play and he had to quit. He said I would have probably won anyway.

"Why are you so tired like this?" I asked. "Seems to me being in a hospital would give you plenty of rest." It was not even lunchtime yet, and he looked worn out.

"It's the stuff they give me for the cancer," he said. "They make me awful tired sometimes."

"Oh," I said. "Sorry."

"It's okay," he said. "You get used to it."

"Yeah, I know all about getting used to stuff," I said.

"Yeah?" he said. "What do you get used to?"

I figured maybe hearing about my life would cheer him up, so I said, "My parents are the town drunks. Sometimes life with them isn't that great."

"How so?" he asked. He was tired, but he seemed truly interested.

I went on to explain how my mom likes her beer more than me and how my dad makes me pay rent so he'll have more money for booze.

"I guess life's not perfect for anyone," he said, looking sad.

I realized maybe my plan to cheer him up

hadn't worked, so I finished up by telling him how much fun it was to have Bones. I told him about Bones seeing himself in a mirror and how he'd thought another dog was there, and Toby started laughing. Finally, I started telling him about my job with Mrs. Dawson and talked about how she would ask her dog's opinion on things. He thought that was funny, so I felt better.

Finally, Nurse Burton stuck her head in and said I had to give Toby some time for rest. Toby and I said good-bye and he asked when I'd be coming again. I told him I wasn't sure, but I'd try to stop in again soon.

When I left the room and the door closed, Nurse Burton said, "Suzanne knows you're here, and she's anxious to see you."

That made me nervous. I tried to get out of seeing her, but Nurse Burton said it would hurt Suzanne's feelings if I didn't at least stop in for a short visit. "Just five minutes," she said. "She was happy to hear you came back."

I looked at Nurse Burton and confessed, "She said I was cute."

She laughed and said, "Well, you are."

"Nobody can be cute in this get-up," I said, holding out my hands to indicate the gown and mask. "She was just trying to make me feel better about Nurse Kennedy saying I was cute, but it only embarrassed me more."

Nurse Burton looked down at me and smiled. "She wasn't trying to make you feel better. She was being honest. She always says what's on her mind. Ask her yourself, she'll tell you."

She put the mask over her face and said, "Let me make sure she's decent." She opened the door to Suzanne's room and said, "He's here to see you. You ready?"

I heard Suzanne say she was, and the next thing I knew I was being more or less pushed into the room as Nurse Burton came out.

"Hi," I said, hoping the mask would cover my blushing.

"Hi," she said. "Won't you come have a seat?" Though the words were formal, her tone was friendly.

I did as she asked and sat there at a complete loss for words.

"I'm sorry if I embarrassed you the other day. I didn't mean to."

"It's okay, you didn't embarrass me."

She giggled and it sounded like a wind chime.

"Did you mean it?" I asked, suddenly wanting to know.

"I always say what I mean and mean what I say," she said. "I think they *are* the same, no matter what the March Hare and the others said."

I realized she was referring to *Alice in Wonderland*, but I'd never read it and didn't want to sound stupid, so I just laughed as if I understood completely.

"Can I ask you something?" I said.

"Sure."

"Nurse Burton said you always say what's on your mind and I should ask you about it."

"What about it?" she asked, curiosity in her eyes.

"Why do you? I mean, most people never say what they're really thinking."

"A few months ago, I realized I wasn't going to live that long, and that if I wanted to say something to someone, I should because I didn't know if I'd ever have the chance again."

"Oh."

"It's not like they hadn't been telling me I was going to die younger than most girls. It's just that I sort of, well, finally understood what that meant."

"I see," I said, even though I didn't.

"So now if I want to say something to someone, I do. I mean, not mean things or stuff like that. Just, you know, the good stuff. I wouldn't want the last thing someone remembered me saying to them to be mean. But the good stuff, that's different."

"Uh-huh," I said. It was all I could think to say.

She pointed to my gloved hands and said, "Take those off and put on some fresh ones. They're over there." She pointed to a table near a window where a box of surgical gloves sat. I did as she asked. After my new gloves were on, she asked me to give her a pair.

She put her gloves on and held one hand out to me. I realized she wanted me to hold her hand. Nervously, I took her offered hand and was surprised at its warmth.

She smiled. "I'll never actually have a boyfriend, but if I could, I'd want you to be him."

I certainly wasn't used to such open honesty, but her words made me smile. Looking at her now, I realized I'd only been lying to myself when I thought she would know she wasn't cute because she was so pale and sick.

For the next ten minutes, we just sat there, holding hands and talking about things I no longer remember. I fell in love in those ten minutes, and maybe she did too. I'll never know. Perhaps she was too embarrassed herself to follow her own rule and say she had fallen in love with someone she really didn't know. Or maybe she knew it wasn't love, just a first crush. In either case, she became my first girlfriend and I became her first boyfriend, and our entire relationship lasted only ten minutes. I like to think I made her happy that day. I like to think I gave her something she thought she would never have and that I received something that I thought I would never deserve.

When I left Suzanne's room, Hank was waiting

for me at the nurse's station. He was chatting with the two nurses and a man who was there to draw blood from a patient. When he saw me, he said, "Well, it's time to go."

We left after saying good-bye to everyone else there. When we arrived back at the car, he said, "Your grandfather?"

"I didn't want to go into details, and I figured it would be easier that way."

"Okay, just don't make lying a habit."

"You didn't tell them you weren't my grandfather, did you?"

"I was too shocked to speak when they said, 'You must be Jack's grandfather. He mentioned you had brought him.' I played along to save you the embarrassment."

"Okay, thanks," I said.

We drove back to Denton in silence, each of us in our own private thoughts about this trip. Part of me wanted to go back and visit them again, and part of me didn't. I decided I would if the opportunity came up.

The truth is I never saw either Toby or Suzanne again. Events that were about to take control of my life got in the way, and by the time I was able to get back to the hospital to visit, they weren't there anymore. I asked Nurse Burton if they'd died, but she said she couldn't tell me due to privacy issues. To this day, I hope they remembered me before they went away. I know I will always remember them. And I hope Suzanne knew how I felt even though I never developed the ability to say what I mean and mean what I say. She was the only person I ever met who had the courage to try.

# 12

The next day when I went by Hank's for coffee, I brought Bones, who was well enough to tag along with me. He had regained some of his strength, and his weight was almost within the average range for a dog his size and age.

"Bones!" Hank said, as we entered his bus for coffee and whatever Hank had that might please my dog. Bones greeted him with a sniff and wag of the tail, allowing Hank to scratch him behind his ears before he curled up at my feet. Hank tossed him some leftover sausage, which he gulped down.

After a few minutes, Hank asked me if I wanted to go hunting for Diablo. I told him that would be fine, and we left to go looking for the panther with Hank carrying his sixteen-gauge shotgun. It turned out he didn't want to hunt the cat so much as spend some time with me outside to talk about things, as well as allow Bones to get some exercise.

As we walked, he finally said, "You were wanting to know about those pictures." It was a statement, not a question.

"Yeah," I said.

"I guess you can tell I don't want to talk about it, but I'm going to because—well, because you deserve to know who they were."

"Were they your wife and kids?" I asked to prompt him.

He looked down at the shotgun in his hands and began inspecting it, as if it might hold the answers he looked for. "Yeah, they were, but I guess you probably figured that out already."

"What happened to them?"

"Died." It was all he said, and I wondered if he would say anything else.

When he didn't, I asked, "How'd they die?"

"Car wreck. I lost all of them in a matter of seconds."

"I'm sorry," I said.

"Me, too. And I'm sorry I made you leave Friday morning. Like I said, you deserve better."

"It's okay," I said.

I thought of something and decided I would make him admit one thing to me. "My friend said you're really a Moreland."

He stared at me, his brow pinched. "Who told you that?"

"A friend." That was the truth, but I added a lie to it to remove any suspicion from Mrs. Dawson. "He says his dad told him."

Hank looked at the ground for several seconds before looking back at me. "Yes. I dropped my last name for personal reasons."

"You're the middle son people say died?"

"Yes, and that part of me did die, so they're not lying to you." He looked around at the underbrush as if it held comfort or a better answer. "That's all I'll tell you."

We were passing Helmer's Creek. It wasn't really a creek. It was a man-made canal cut through a low area of Panther Dunes years before I was born. I still don't know why it was there, but I suppose they had their reasons when it was created. A plank footbridge crossed it near where we stood.

I wiped the sweat that was gathering on my brow and realized the day was already much too hot. I'd heard the weather report, and the high was expected to top a hundred. It seemed close to that already. The water, the sun shimmering on it, invited me in. It had apparently invited Bones as well. He plunged in, swam across to the other side, huffing through his mouth, then reversed and swam back to where we were. He looked as if he had a big smile on his face, and I marveled that a three-legged dog could swim and not go in circles.

"You mind if I go swimming?" I asked.

"Suit yourself," Hank answered.

I removed my shoes and shirt and began to wade into the canal, but then I thought better of it. I didn't want my denim shorts to chafe at me all day, which they would if I walked around in them in the hot sun until they dried, and that would take an hour or two. The added heat of the day would make me miserable.

I turned to Hank. "You mind if I go skinny-dipping?"

He considered my question, shrugged, and said, "Suit yourself."

Stepping up onto the shore, I shucked my shorts and underwear. I'd never been naked in front of Hank before, but he was paying me no attention anyway, and I figured he'd seen his share of naked boys in his life. Besides, I trusted him completely. He deserved my trust more than I deserved to know his history.

I waded back into the water and splashed around, cooling off from the heat of the sun that had gripped me moments before. Bones swam around me, seeming to want to play some canine version of tag.

After refreshing myself in the canal, I crawled back onto the shore and quickly dressed. I wasn't exactly used to going naked outside, and the feeling was an odd one.

I noticed Hank still ignoring me as I dressed.

"Sorry if I embarrassed you," I said.

"No, mostly I'm jealous. I'd like to take a dip in this heat myself."

"Why don't you?" I asked.

"You're still young," he said. "I'm old. There's a difference."

I could see his point. As I mentioned, he was probably used to seeing naked boys in his lifetime, but I'd never seen a naked man. I was thankful he didn't take me up on my suggestion.

Once I was dressed and we were again on our way in our half-hearted search for Diablo, I pressed Hank for details about the car accident. He refused to give them, though, saying only that the details didn't matter. The fact they were gone was all that did.

I decided he probably would never tell me his father was the one responsible, so I left it at that. His father, David Moreland, was in his eighties. Maybe once the man died, Hank would volunteer the information. At least he had told me some of it.

We finally gave up on our hunt, as we had known we would, and returned to Hank's bus. He invited me to stay for lunch, and I accepted. He gave Bones some leftovers he retrieved from the refrigerator in Jerry Moreland's office when he went to get the lunchmeat for the sandwiches we made. He also had a couple of Cokes, and we drank them, washing the ham and cheese sandwiches down and enjoying the fizz of carbonation that tickled our throats.

After lunch, I said good-bye and said I would drop by Monday morning on my way to work at Kirby's.

On Monday I rose early to get to Kirby's for work. Mr. Kirby's warning to arrive on time stayed with me, and I didn't want to lose my job the first day. I fed Bones and rushed off, anxious to get started.

When I walked in, Mr. Kirby was standing behind the bar, counting inventory. He looked at me and barked, "Start with the bathrooms. They both gotta be cleaned."

"Where are the cleaning supplies?" I asked.

"In a closet between the men's and women's."

I walked to the back and found the closet and went to work. The bathrooms were filthy, as if they'd not been properly cleaned in months. I scrubbed and polished, working quickly since I knew plenty more had to be done by eleven.

After I mopped both bathrooms, I was putting away some of the supplies when Mr. Kirby entered the men's restroom to use it. As he closed the door and turned on the light, I heard him exclaim, "Holy cow!" When he came out, he said, "You did a pretty good job there."

"Thank you," I said. "What's next?"

"I like that, kid. Eager to get the job done. If you were old enough, I'd hire you full time."

I ignored that because, first I wasn't old enough to serve beer, and second I wouldn't want to work for him full time if I were. I just stared at him, shifting my weight from one foot to the other as I tried to be patient.

"Go out front and sweep and mop the floors, including behind the bar. And be sure to do as good a job as you did on the bathrooms."

I took the broom from the closet and set to work. The bar had booths where many of the customers sat. More dirt and grime lay underneath them than one day could account for. The last time this work had been done was Saturday because Kirby's is closed on Sunday, but I could see Mr. Kirby wasn't nearly as thorough in his cleaning as he wanted me to be.

I swept dirt and bits of paper from beneath the booths. Suddenly, my eyes fell on something that had come scooting out from under one of the benches of a booth as I swept. I stared in disbelief at what I saw.

Sitting amid the dust and filth swept from under the booth was a folded twenty-dollar bill. I glanced around to make sure Mr. Kirby wasn't watching and picked it up as if it were Charlie's golden ticket. I'd been reading Roald Dahl's book

*Charlie and the Chocolate Factory* at night in bed that summer, and I suddenly knew how Charlie felt upon finding the ticket. I wondered who had dropped the money there, and for a second, I considered asking Mr. Kirby if anyone had asked about a lost twenty-dollar-bill, but I immediately thought better of it. First, I doubted my boss would allow me to keep it, saying that yes, someone had asked about it, and he would be sure to get it to that person, but he would just pocket it. Second, I doubted anyone would have asked about it. This was a bar, after all. I understood that if money was found here, it would be kept. If any place existed where "Finders keepers, losers weepers" stood true, it was in a place like this. If I knew that, certainly whoever lost the money knew it too. Twenty dollars was a lot of money in 1968, even to adults. And just by doing a thorough job, I was now twenty dollars richer. Pocketing the bill, I grinned and went back to work, hoping to find more money, but I didn't.

I asked Mr. Kirby what was next, and he told me to take out the garbage, including the four large aluminum cans behind the back door that were filled with the oyster shells from Saturday's business. It was my job to dump the cans in a special dumpster out back, which would be picked up by a company that coarse-ground them, bleached them in the sun, and sold them for fill and unpaved street coverings.

I struggled with this job because the cans were so heavy, but I managed to heave them up high enough to empty them into the dumpster.

When I was done, Mr. Kirby told me to rub down the bar and all the table tops with a soft cloth and make sure plenty of clean beer mugs were available. These were kept in another closet behind the bar, which I already knew about since I'd seen my dad retrieve some before. I opened the closet and gradually pulled out a dozen racks of mugs and set them on a low pallet behind the bar before wiping down the bar and tables.

I finished that easily and went to Mr. Kirby.

"That's it," he said. "You're a good worker."

"Thanks."

"You wanna earn a little more?"

I asked how I could do that, and what would I earn.

"Good focus, kid," he said. "Always make sure about the money."

I stood there, silently waiting.

"Anyway, I looked into it and as long as you don't actually serve anyone any alcohol, you can work here. In fact, in the summer like this, you can work full time."

Uh-oh. Here it was. The full time offer.

"I don't want to work full time," I said. "I have other things to do."

"Yeah, I figured as much," he said. "But would

you be okay with comin' back around three o'clock and do some touch-up cleaning after the lunch customers leave? You work so well, I'm willin' to give you another three bucks for it."

"What kind of touch-up cleaning would I do?"

He smiled at me as if proud of a protégé. "Mostly what you just done, just while customers are here. I think they'd appreciate a cleaner bathroom in the evening, when most of my customers come in. And when they're not quite full, those oyster shell cans would be easier to lift, which would make lifting them tomorrow that much easier as well." As I stood there considering his offer, he added, "If you'll do it, I'll give you a raise for the morning work, too. Four instead of three, starting today. You did a good job, kid. A lot better than I expected."

I looked at him and saw he was being sincere, which surprised me. Adding the twenty that I'd found meant I would pocket twenty-seven dollars for the day, cash. I knew of adults who worked full time that didn't make close to that much in a day. Plenty of them, in fact, my own father included.

"You have a deal," I said.

He smiled and I left after collecting my four dollars for the morning's work. I insisted on collecting my payment after the work was done instead of being paid the full amount after my afternoon shift. Again, he smiled at me, this time shaking his head and chuckling.

Before walking out the door, another thought occurred to me. "Mr. Kirby?"

"Yeah?"

"Would you mind not telling my dad how much I make?"

He squinted at me, puzzled, but said, "Sure, kid. What you make is between us."

I left, went home, and hid the money. I put the twenty in a paper bag I kept under my mattress and put the four dollars in my hiding place beneath the loose floorboard in the closet.

I returned that afternoon just before three o'clock. My dad had started his shift at noon, and I said hello to him. I had told him already about the extra work in the afternoon, and of course he had smiled. When he asked how much I made, I said, "Just three bucks." I wished I could be honest with him about making seven dollars for the day, but I couldn't. If he found out I made more, I could claim I thought he had asked about how much I made for the afternoon work. I would owe him $1.70 for rent. He would assume I used the rest on Bones.

I did my job, the only difference being that I had to work around the customers while trying not to interfere with them although at three o'clock the place was mostly deserted. Still, I tried to be invisible as much as possible.

When I left, I saw Mr. Kirby in his office and

he paid me the three dollars.

The next day was about the same, except that I no longer had to ask what to do. The fact that I had cleaned the place so thoroughly the day before, as well as emptied the cans of shells to make the morning work easier, it took me a full thirty-five minutes less to finish in the morning.

I returned at three, and the second I entered the bar, I knew there would be trouble.

Mr. Kirby sometimes had a man working behind the bar named Mitch. He was as rough a character as I'd ever known. What hair he had was thin and graying. He had a round face that always looked in need of a shave. His nose bore a spider's web of tiny veins and was slightly crooked, the result of breaking his nose more than once in fights, and his eyes were an icy blue-gray.

I only knew a few things about him, but they were enough. First, it was clear to see that his daughter, who was seventeen, despised him. The second thing was he had done time in prison for killing a man in a fight. He'd been found guilty of manslaughter and had served six years of a ten-year sentence. I knew all about his time in prison, but I had no idea why his daughter hated him so much. She did, though. Mitch brought his family to our house several times, and Mitch would brag about how pretty she was while she did her best to be anywhere but next to him. He would drape his arm around her shoulders, and she would cringe. He was the only adult I feared in Denton.

Mitch was behind the bar that day, along with my dad. When I entered, my father motioned for me to come behind the bar. Mitch was arguing with a man, a customer I'd seen before whose name I didn't know. The customer was already drunk, and they were going back and forth about something or other that I couldn't follow.

As I walked around behind the bar, I noticed my dad putting the .32 caliber revolver that Mr. Kirby kept under the bar for protection in his pocket. My dad had told me it was always loaded, but with the safety on. I didn't know why he would do that, but it meant danger to me. He saw that I had noticed what he'd done and said nothing, but the look in his eyes said for me to keep my mouth shut.

"Mr. Kirby's out right now," my dad said. "Just take a seat over there." He pointed to a barstool that stood next to the end wall behind the bar, where Mr. Kirby would sit sometimes and chat with some of his customers.

As I climbed up onto the tall stool, Mitch said something I didn't hear. The other man said, "You saying that's so?"

Mitch cursed and said, "Yep."

The man stared into Mitch's face and said, "Then you're a damn liar."

I thought Mitch was going to explode. His face

was red with fury, and he did his best to climb over the bar to get to the man. Mitch was not very tall, and his feet couldn't reach high enough to find anything to step up on to help him jump over the bar and onto the man. Not only that, but Mitch was also in his fifties and wasn't that agile anymore.

His gaze darted around the area beneath the lip of the bar, and I realized with horror that he was looking for the revolver. When he couldn't find it, he grabbed a truncheon Mr. Kirby kept back there for what I supposed were the customers who didn't deserve to be shot. He then began to trot around the bar as fast as he could.

My father just looked at the drunk man whose life he had saved without the man's knowledge. The man calmly sipped his beer as if a devil from Hell weren't rushing at him with a weighted club in his hand. The thought that Mitch had killed a man in a fight ran through my mind, and I wondered if my father's actions would end up being for nothing after all.

Mitch leapt upon the guy, swinging the stick in a high arc that landed on the man's head with a *clop* that I heard from my seat, causing me to flinch.

The customer collapsed in a heap on the hard floor. Mitch, after calling the unconscious man a host of foul names, asked my dad for a glass of water, which he poured on the man's face. I found it ironic that Mitch held his hand over the man's nose and mouth to prevent him from inhaling some of the water. After all, if he'd been able to locate the pistol, the man would be lying on the floor either dead or dying.

The customer came to and struggled to a sitting position and managed to hoist himself back up onto his barstool. At that moment Mr. Kirby walked through the front door, totally unaware of what had just happened.

Oddly, I was the first thing he noticed as I sat behind the bar on what was his stool. He stopped short and stared at me.

"Taking a break?" he asked, bewildered that I was not hard at work.

My dad nodded at Mitch and the customer. "There was a little disagreement, and I thought it best for him to be back here."

Mr. Kirby looked around, the reality of what had gone on dawning on him. "Oh, okay."

Without another word, he went back to his office with the bag of office supplies he had purchased, but not before telling me my break was over. I noticed my dad return the revolver to its place under the bar, and I took that to mean it was safe for me to get up and do my job.

The man had started to bleed from a cut on his head and my dad tossed him some rags, which the guy pressed against his wound. He apologized to Mitch and started crying, becoming nothing more than another drunk who had lost control of himself. Mitch just cussed the man and came back behind the bar, possibly thinking how close he had come to killing a man whose only mistake had been getting drunk and calling Mitch a liar.

I had no idea what might have gone through Mitch's head. I was busy doing my job and thinking that some men act like boys while some boys have to become men before they should.

Three days later Mitch was stabbed to death by his daughter while he slept. It caused a brief sensation. The scandal died along with the daughter when she committed suicide by hanging herself in her jail cell a few days after that. It wasn't until later that I realized everything that had been going on. It made me sad for the daughter, who was very pretty but also very fragile. But it made me angry at Mitch, who had ended up causing three deaths in his lifetime, including his own, plus another near-miss with the drunk customer.

## 13

Wednesday, I came to work after having coffee with Hank and finished faster than I had the day before. It was getting easier to clean up because everything wasn't so filthy to begin with. I spent the rest of the day until I had to be back at work fishing with Lee and Roger. We didn't catch much, certainly not as many as we caught the day Bones showed up. After cleaning my fish, I stored them in our refrigerator for later, needing to shoo Bones away as I carried the fillets to keep him from eating them himself, though he did enjoy the scraps.

I went to work that afternoon. Hank was there when I went in, drinking a beer, and I went to work without a word to him. My dad was behind the bar and paid as much attention to me when I came in as Hank did.

As I was in the back cleaning the bathrooms, I heard my dad shout, "What?!" I wondered if another fight was about to break out, so I went out to the main area of the bar. What I saw made my heart drop.

Officer Hicks was there, bending Hank over the bar and putting handcuffs on him. I heard Hank's head thud against the hard wood. I saw him wince as Hicks put the cuffs on.

I thought I might faint when another officer, this one in a brown suit and tie, said, "Henry Pittman, you are under arrest for taking indecent liberties with a minor."

My dad stared at me as I entered the room. "What is this about?!" he shouted. "These cops say he's been messing with you!"

"I—I don't know," I stammered. "Hank?"

Hank looked at me and said, "Someone lied about us." His tone was not what I would expect in those circumstances. He sounded as if he were telling me a baseball score.

My face burned with hot embarrassment—not because we had done anything, but because I knew where this came from and I'd done nothing to stop it. I had thought nobody would believe such trash. Not only that, but I was also embarrassed because my dad thought it was true. He looked at me as if I were a particularly disgusting piece of the filth I'd cleaned from the floor.

"She's crazy!" I shouted. "She doesn't know what she's talking about!"

"Who?!" my dad demanded.

"How is it you know it was a woman who said anything?" the detective said, his voice echoing menace.

It wasn't until I spoke to Hank's attorney later that I realized I was just making it worse. I was having a hard time understanding what I considered sheer stupidity by the police. Of course, I hadn't been aware of how quickly people accept someone's guilt, especially when sex was involved. I didn't know it at the time, but I was about to get a crash course in how ugly people could be.

I had thought people would ignore Mrs. Polk's accusations since everyone knew she was a gossip who told more lies than anyone else in town. I figured they would view her the way they viewed my parents—a drunk whose word couldn't be trusted. Until that moment, I had viewed her as dirty-minded but mostly harmless, yet this changed things. This turned my world upside down. The fact that she had gone to the police and leveled charges without an ounce of proof, and that she had been believed to the point that they were arresting the one man in the world who did things for me because he cared, not because he wanted something from me in return, all made my head spin. It was as if God had walked through the door and announced that from now on, all water would flow uphill.

I stared as Officer Hicks shoved Hank toward the door and pushed him into a police cruiser.

"You better come with me," the detective said to me. "We'll need to get your statement."

"Wait a minute," my dad said. "Shouldn't his mother or me be there when you talk to him?"

"He's not under arrest; he's the victim here. Besides, you can allow us to talk to him without a parent, and I think he'd be more forthcoming in his statement without one of you there."

"I don't have a statement!" I said, seething.

The detective walked up and put his hand on my shoulder as if he cared about me and said, "It's all over now. He won't hurt you anymore. You don't have to protect him."

His hand felt like a large spider and I shrugged it off, glaring at him. "He doesn't need me to protect him because he didn't do anything! He never touched me! There's your statement!"

The detective looked at my father and said, "He's just upset. He'll get over it and once he realizes it's over, he'll talk to us."

I suppose he was just doing his job as he saw it, but I didn't understand that. He had arrested my best friend. Hank had told me the first time I talked to him after Tommy and his mob had beaten me nearly senseless that he didn't want anything like that from me. I'd sat alone with him in his bus nearly every day since then, and he'd never made the first move that caused me suspicion. Not only that, but he'd completely ignored me when I went skinny-dipping that time.

Now, they were saying he had done awful things to me, and it didn't matter that I said he hadn't.

I glared at the detective and was about to say something else, but my dad spoke first.

"Jack!"

I turned to him, my eyes brimming with tears of rage and sadness. They began to flow down my cheeks as I said, "Dad, they have it all wrong!"

"Go down there and tell the truth!" he said. His tone accused me of lying—and more. I stared at him, wondering how I could make him believe me. "Go on!" he said, "and don't come home until you do."

I was stunned. I could think of nothing else to do but go with the detective. As I shuffled out of the bar, I heard Mr. Kirby from near the hallway that went to his office. "And you don't have to come back here at all," he said to me. Great! On top of everything else, I was fired.

I climbed into the passenger seat of the detective's car, wondering how things could have gone this wrong so quickly. My best friend was in jail for something he didn't do, and I was the only person who could set people straight, but nobody would believe me. I rode in the front seat of the detective's car to the police station hating Mrs. Polk with a passion.

When we arrived at the station, I climbed out of the car, slamming the door as I did. We entered the building and the detective escorted me into a small room with a table and two uncomfortable chairs. He indicated for me to sit in one and I did. He took the other and said, "Do you want something to drink? A Coke maybe?"

I realized I was thirsty and asked if they had any root beer. He said he would check. He walked out of the room and the door closed behind him. I checked the knob, hoping to get out of this disgusting room and walk out of the police station. Although he said I wasn't under arrest, the door to the room was locked from the outside, and I couldn't get out. I looked around the room. The dingy gray walls hovered over me. Even the metal table and chairs were gray, just a slightly darker shade. A large reel-to-reel tape recorder perched on the table. The room had no windows, only what I figured must be one of those large two-way mirrors on one wall. I knew I was being watched, and I held up a middle finger at whoever might be out there.

Sitting back down, I waited for the detective to return with my root beer. It hit me that Hank was also somewhere in this place, probably in his own gray room. The word *interrogation* hit me and I wanted to cry again. I stopped myself, though. I didn't want to give them the satisfaction of knowing I was scared.

When the detective returned, he said, "We don't have any root beer, but I have Officer Hicks going out to buy you one."

I was pleased that he had to run an errand for me. That was the only pleasure I had, though. I stared at the table and said, "I won't drink it if he opens it."

He laughed and said, "We're not going to poison you."

I shrugged and said, "You must not know him very well."

The detective ignored my remark and reached over to the tape recorder. Pressing some buttons, he spoke clearly into the microphone on the table. "This is Detective Lieutenant Daryl Hodges. I am interviewing Jack Turner, the alleged victim of Mr. Henry Pittman, who has been accused of sexual assault on a minor and related charges. The date is August 4, 1968; the time is 3:47 P.M." Looking at me, he said, "Please state your name and date of birth for the record, Jack."

He spoke to me as if I had called him on the phone, begging him to allow me to come make a statement accusing Hank of despicable behavior. I heard my dad ordering me to tell the truth, and that was exactly what I intended to do. I leaned forward toward the small microphone and said, "I'm Jack Turner. I was born October 16, 1955. I have nothing more to say because Hank didn't do anything to me, no matter what that lying bitch Mrs. Polk said. Everyone in town knows she lies more often than she blinks. This is just another lie from her filthy mind."

Detective Hodges looked at me for a moment, seemed to make a decision, and said, "How do you know it was Mrs. Polk who filed the complaint?"

"A friend of mine heard her telling someone, but it's a lie."

"He told you about it?"

"Well, he asked me about it."

"Because he believed it to be true?"

"No, he—" I said, then bit my words off. Roger *had* believed it. I had seen it in his eyes. I looked at the detective who just stared back as if he had all day and night to wait for me to tell what he thought was the truth.

"He did believe it until I told him it wasn't true. *He* believed me," I said.

"So why didn't you come tell us that she was spreading these lies? Didn't you know she would eventually come talk to us?"

"No, I didn't know that," I said. "I figured nobody sane would believe such hogwash."

"Your friend believed it," Detective Hodges said, smiling at me as if he'd caught me in a lie.

"He's different. He's a kid. Not only that, but I know him, and he'll believe anything. I thought grown-ups would see it for what it was—a woman with a dirty mind with nothing better to do than to go around telling lies."

I saw his expression change for a second before he seemed to change his mind about something. "When an upstanding citizen comes in and tells us a man is molesting a young boy, we always take that seriously." He paused when a knock sounded at the door, followed by Officer Hicks sticking his head in and handing a root beer to the lieutenant. Detective Hodges took it and set the open cold drink down on the table in front of me. Officer Hicks gave me a smirk of superiority and left, closing the door. I was reminded how much I hated him. I didn't touch the drink the entire time I was there. I knew he hadn't tried to poison me, but I wouldn't be surprised if he'd done something disgusting like spit in it.

"As I was saying, we always take such complaints seriously. Now, you have your root beer, why not tell us what happened. That way you can go home and I can go home and the man who molested you can go to jail."

"He didn't molest me!" I shouted. "How many times do I have to say that?"

"You don't have to protect him," he said. "No matter what he told you he would do if you told."

"He didn't say he would do anything if I told."

"So, you're saying there *is* something to tell?"

"No! Your twisting my words!" At that moment I had my first true understanding of the word *rage*.

He came at me from a different angle. "You said a moment ago that your friend was a kid and would believe anything."

"Yeah, so?"

"That means it would be easy to convince him you were right and the woman he heard was wrong, correct?"

I considered his question. "Maybe, yeah, but what I told him was the truth."

"What if I told you someone else had spoken to us about you and Mr. Pittman?"

"Who?"

He ignored my question. "What if I told you someone saw you get naked for Henry just the other day?"

"Get naked for him?! What are you talking about?"

"Someone saw you take off all your clothes while the two of you were hiking in Panther Dunes. This person says you thought you were alone, but you were seen getting naked for him—and more."

"I—I just got—I was just skinny-dipping in Helmer's Creek! That's all!"

"That's not the story I heard."

"In that case, someone else is lying!" I said. "I

didn't do anything with him! I was just swimming!"

"So, someone else is lying? Someone totally different from the lady you claim is a gossip? And we're supposed to believe you?"

"Who said that?" I demanded. "Who?!"

"I'm not at liberty to divulge that right now. Mr. Pittman's attorney will get that information from the district attorney."

I sat back, remembering that day when it was so hot I needed to take a dip but didn't want to walk around in wet shorts all day. I scolded myself for taking off my shorts, but later I realized it wouldn't have made a difference. Whoever had told the detective about it had implied that something other than swimming had taken place, but nothing else had. Was this person saying something terrible just to get Hank in trouble? I couldn't imagine anyone that evil. Who would lie just to watch a good man go to jail? It was the meanest thing I could imagine anyone doing. I wondered if some unseen force had decided to make our lives miserable. At least now I understood why the police insisted I was lying to protect Hank. Two people were spreading lies when I'd thought only one had.

I leaned toward Detective Hodges and the recorder and said, "I've made my statement. I don't care who is saying what, nothing happened between Hank and me. He never touched me. He never even suggested anything like that. It was never a part of our talks other than once he told me he wasn't like that. He's a nice man. He has helped me many times, and what these people are doing to him is *wrong*. I don't care if I have to be here all night, all day tomorrow, and all night again without anything to eat or drink. I'm not changing my story because I'm the one telling the truth, so to say anything happened would be a lie just like the ones these other people are telling." I looked directly into the detective's eyes as I spoke. If nothing else, he believed I would never say Hank did anything bad to me.

He looked at his watch, and said into the recorder, "The time is 4:36 P.M. This interview with Jack Turner concerning the actions of Henry Pittman is over." He reached over and switched the recorder off. Turning to me, he said, "If you change your mind and want to tell us what happened, just call the department. I'll leave word to put you through to me."

"I already told you what happened—nothing," I said. "You people have it all wrong. If he did those terrible things to me, why wouldn't I tell you?"

He stood and said, "You wouldn't be the first." Next, he sighed and added, "Nor the last."

He escorted me out of the room and to the front desk. Officer Hicks was there, and Detective Hodges told him to give me a ride home. I told him I would rather walk. What I didn't say was I'd rather he cut my legs off than make me ride in a car with Officer Hicks.

I glanced back at Detective Hodges and wondered why nobody believed me. I walked home, trying to figure out who had seen me skinny-dipping and lied about it. Mrs. Polk was a gossip who spread lies. I had asked Mrs. Dawson about her once, and she had told me that Mrs. Polk talked herself into believing what her imagination cooked up to fill her dull life with something she thought was exciting. This other person, the one who had lied about what he saw when I went swimming without clothes was evil. Mrs. Polk had seen that I spent a lot of time alone with Hank inside his bus and let her imagination run wild with the possibilities, convincing herself Hank was molesting me. The second person told a lie only to hurt me and Hank.

I had no idea how I would convince anyone that Hank hadn't touched me, but I was determined to find a way if I could.

## 14

The next day, I woke up early and went out to feed Bones, but for the first time since I found him, he didn't seem hungry. This surprised me. Even after he started gaining weight, he acted as though he'd never eat again. He had slowed down some, but he still ate too fast.

I checked him over, and he didn't seem to be hurt, so I figured he might be sick. I thought about taking him to the vet's, but that cost money and I had just lost a job.

I was thinking about what I should do when my dad called me from our back door.

"Yes sir?" I asked as I approached. We had not spoken since I had left Kirby's with Detective Hodges.

"So what happened yesterday?" he asked. I could tell by his tone he was in not in the best mood.

"I did what you said. I told them the truth."

He eyed me, apparently realizing this could mean more than one thing. "And what's the truth?"

I took a deep breath, thinking this could get ugly. My dad rarely disciplined me, but he'd whipped me before, usually when he was in a mood like this. I figured if I lied now, I could get worse later. That was one thing about my dad. Lying to him could send him into a rage.

"I told him that Hank didn't touch me." My father's eyes flashed. "He didn't, Dad! I can't say he did if he didn't."

"Why you been hanging around with him? Mrs. Polk came in last night, and I asked her about what she saw. She tells me you been spending lots of time inside that bus o' his. Why would you be in there with him?"

"We just drink coffee and talk."

"What about?"

"Just stuff. Life, Bones, my work. He's the one who helped me get work, Dad."

"I didn't see him helping you get work at Kirby's," he said. I wanted to tell him that I got that job myself, but crossing him would just make him madder. Besides, I didn't want to think about it because that made me remember I'd lost the job because of Mrs. Polk, but I reminded myself that hadn't been the worst thing to happen because of her.

"I swear, Dad. He never touched me."

"Nobody'll believe that, you know."

I had gotten a taste of that with Detective Hodges, but I still thought the people of Denton would think differently as long as they had not been poisoned by Mrs. Polk's lies or the ones told by whoever had seen me go skinny-dipping.

"They'll believe it when I tell them," I said. My father laughed, but his laugh held no humor.

"You'll see," he said. "He's a Moreland, you know. Got money. If he did anything to you, we could get him to pay." For the first time in my life I wanted to hit my father. I wanted to knock him out. Money? This was about money to him? I couldn't hit him, of course, so I just stared back in disgust.

"So, you think about that, boy," he said and went back inside to his breakfast of toast and coffee, which always held some *Old Crow*, his whiskey of choice because it was cheap. He didn't care that Hank was in jail for something he didn't do. He just wanted me to say something happened so he could get Hank to pay him money. Hating my father nearly as much as I hated Mrs. Polk, I went back to Bones, who looked as sad as I felt.

"It's okay, boy. We'll convince everyone," I said although I knew it was probably just wishful thinking. I also worried Bones might be sick and wondered what I would do about it.

When I stood to go find Lee and Roger for some company, I tried to get Bones to go with me, but he didn't seem interested at all. I left him there and worried about either him or Hank all the way to Lee's house. I pushed thoughts of my dad away.

It wasn't like Bones not to go with me. If he were sick, I'd have a hard time coming up with enough to pay the vet after paying for dog food and my rent. I had savings, but that was supposed to last through the school year, which was approaching much faster than the last day of school ever did.

"Hey! Nyeaah, what's up, Doc?" Lee said, imitating Bugs Bunny, when he came to the door.

"Bad news," I said.

He could probably see from my face I wasn't kidding. "Really? What happened?"

"Bones might be sick, but believe it or not, that's not the worst of it." Lee stared at me, waiting for an explanation. "They arrested Hank."

"Arrested him?! What for?" His jaw dropped in disbelief.

I took a deep breath and said, "They believe he molested me."

Lee's eyes narrowed. "Didn't you tell them he didn't?"

"Until I was blue in the face, but they think I'm protecting him or afraid he might do something to me if I say he did anything. They're crazy!"

"Damn! Did Old Lady Polk tell them?"

"Yeah. They never said it, but I could tell. And there's something else."

"What?"

"Hank and I went hunting for Diablo one day, and—."

"Why would you do a crazy thing like that?" Lee asked, interrupting me.

"We mostly wanted to take a walk and talk."

"Oh."

"Anyway, we were out there in Panther Dunes, and it grew mighty hot, so I decided to take a dip in Helmer's Creek."

"So?"

"So, I decided I didn't want to have wet denim shorts on all day, so I—"

"Holy Moly! You didn't!"

"Yeah, I did. I didn't think anything of it, and neither did Hank. He didn't even look at me, but someone was out there watching us. He told the cops we were, well, *doing* something together."

"Like what?"

I couldn't believe his question. "What d'ya think? But this person's making it up. He's making it sound like we did something awful, when all we did was talk while Bones and I swam around."

"What happened then?"

"Nothing. I got out of the water, got dressed,

and we kept hunting for Diablo."

"Man, this is bad. He could go to jail for a long time."

"I know. I have to think of some way to convince them it never happened."

"Don't know how you're gonna do that if they won't believe you."

"I have to. I can't let him go to prison for something I know he never did."

We grew quiet. I was doing my best to find something to help Hank and coming up empty. I had no idea what Lee might have been thinking. As we sat on his front steps, Roger came ambling up the street. He waved and approached us, smiling as if he hadn't a care in the world. When he saw me, though, he stopped in his tracks.

"What's wrong?"

I explained what had happened to Hank. When I told him about someone seeing me go skinny-dipping, he grew pale. I could see right away he knew about this already.

"What?" I said.

"I think I know who it was that saw you," Roger said.

I squinted at him. "Who?"

"You're not gonna like this," he said.

"I don't care. I'll find out eventually."

"It was actually two people." I stared at him, waiting. "It was Tommy and Carl."

"Tommy Gordon and Carl Hicks?" I asked, wishing it would be anyone but them.

Roger said, "You know any other Tommy and Carl?"

"How do you know?" I asked.

"I heard them talking about it, but I didn't realize they were talking about you and Hank."

This was worse than I'd thought. Of all people to be involved in this, it was just my luck that it was the two who led the attack at the docks. Like most kids, I had people who didn't like me very much, but these two were the only guys I would say were true enemies. Not only that, but Carl's older brother was the same Officer Hicks who had made it clear he liked me about as much as Carl did.

"Man, what am I gonna do?" I said. "Officer Hicks is sure to push this as far as he can." I wondered if maybe he had encouraged his brother and Tommy to come forward. He may have even helped them come up with the lie that Hank and I had done something we shouldn't. It was easy to see that this story had been created after they saw me swimming as a way to bolster Mrs. Polk's lies.

On the other hand, maybe Tommy and Carl had come up with the story by themselves. They were certainly capable. Finally, I realized it didn't matter who had made up the story. The result was the same. The only hope I had was to be able to convince people of the lie. I wondered how I'd do that when not even the police believed me. Still, these weren't the most honest, respected citizens in Denton. Maybe I could convince enough people they were lying. On the other hand, I was the son of a couple of drunks. Why would anyone believe me?

Finally, I turned to my friends to see if they had an idea. "How can I convince people nothing happened?"

"Maybe I can say I was with you and nothing happened," Roger said.

"Nah," said Lee. "They'd figure out you're lying. That would just make people believe those guys more."

I was getting more and more depressed over this, and I needed a distraction, so I suggested we go to Denton park and throw a football or something, so we did.

Later, I went home and found Bones was even sicker than he had been when I left him that morning. He acted too tired to move and his nose was bleeding. He had thrown up recently, and I could see blood in it. My heart hammered at the sight of him. I realized I would have to take him to the vet and worry about the cost later. I rushed back to Lee's house and asked if I could borrow his bicycle and the old Radio Flier wagon he had from when he was little. I figured I could put Bones in the wagon and tie the handle to the back of the bike and pull him to the vet's instead of carrying him. He was much too weak to walk that far.

"Sure," Lee said when I'd explained what was happening. "You need any help?" I told him I would handle it if he'd help me tie the wagon to the bike.

I rushed home and loaded Bones into the wagon to take him to the vet's. I hoped the doctor would be able to look at him. If he had too much to do, he might not be able to see Bones today. Mostly, I worried what might be wrong with Bones. I was too busy hurrying to cry, though. That happened later.

I pulled up at the vet's office and dashed inside. Alerted by the bell over the door, Mrs. Terry came out of a room in back and saw me. "What is it, Jack?" She could probably see the worry in my face.

"Bones is sick," I said. "Real sick."

"Where is he?"

"Outside in a wagon."

"What kind of symptoms does he have?" She hurried from behind the counter.

As she followed me outside, I told her about his nosebleed, his inactivity, and the vomit with blood in it. When she saw Bones, she said, "Bring him inside."

I leaned down and picked him up as she opened the door for us. She led me directly into an examination room as a lady who was sitting in the waiting area stared at us, her eyes wide.

"Put him on the examination table," Mrs. Terry said and left the room. She returned with the doctor a minute later and immediately took Bones's temperature while the doctor washed up.

"What do we have here today?" the vet asked. I could tell his easygoing tone was meant to stop me from worrying, but it didn't.

He looked into Bones's mouth, eyes, nose and ears. Next, he listened to his heart. His brow furrowed. I could tell he didn't like what he was seeing and hearing.

"I'm going to need to take some blood and do some tests," he said.

"What is it?" I asked.

"Not sure yet, but I have some suspicions," he said. Mrs. Terry was back in the room in less than a minute after leaving for everything needed to draw blood. The fact she was in a hurry worried me even more.

The doctor swabbed a place on Bones's foreleg while Mrs. Terry tied a rubber strap above where he'd swabbed. He stuck the needle into the skin, and I watched as he withdrew blood from the vein. When he had what he needed, he handed the syringe to Mrs. Terry and said, "I need a CBC and toxicity panel." She took it and left the room.

The doctor turned to me and said, "I'm not going to lie to you. He's sick. Lethargy is never a good thing in a dog, and he's having some trouble breathing. He's running a fever, too. Would he have access to any rat poison?"

Rat poison? "No, sir."

"What about antifreeze, bleach or paint thinner?"

"No. Do you think he's been poisoned?"

"It's a possibility. His nosebleed and vomiting, along with his other symptoms, suggest rat poison, but other possibilities exist, so we need to rule them out."

As if on cue, Bones began to wretch. The doctor reached over and lifted Bones a bit to prevent him from choking. He threw up, and once again I could see blood in it.

I was surprised to see the doctor collect a sample of it in a test tube, which he took with him as he left the room. I began to cry as the realization my dog might have been poisoned hit me. I thought that meant he was going to die. I'd rescued him from starvation only to see him poisoned. I wondered where he could have found anything like that, especially rat poison. As far as I knew my dad didn't keep any kinds of poisons around the house except ant and roach spray. He refused to have most types of poisons because he had a little brother who had swallowed some when he was young.

I wracked my brain to think of where Bones may have gotten into any poison, but I couldn't come up with anything.

The doctor came back and said, "I'm fairly certain he ate some rat poison," he said. "His gums are pale, he's bleeding internally, throwing up, and having problems breathing."

"Is he going to die?" I asked, near panic by now.

"I won't say he won't, but there is a treatment. It all depends on how much he ingested."

Mrs. Terry entered the room with an IV to begin a blood transfusion.

"What's the treatment?"

"It appears to be what's known as an ACR poison, or anticoagulant rodenticide. It attacks the body's ability to produce vitamin K dependent blood clotting factors. Treatment involves giving blood transfusions and vitamin K1, mostly."

"Can't you pump his stomach?" I asked.

"That wouldn't do any good. He ingested it a couple of days ago. It takes that long to get him sick like this."

I leaned down and gently hugged Bones, who lay there, too sick to respond. I grew angry that I hadn't brought him to the vet first thing that morning, but I wasn't sure if that made a difference at this point. I asked the doctor about that. He said it didn't matter, but I wondered if he was telling the truth.

"I think he should stay here for the next few

days," he said, and I wondered again how I would pay for this. I knew it could be hundreds of dollars, and I didn't have that much, not even near it. My friends' parents had paid the vet bill when Bones was hurt fighting Diablo, but I couldn't depend on having them do that every time Bones was sick or injured. I could do nothing right now except agree with the doctor.

"Can you think of any way he could have consumed any poison?" the doctor asked.

I shook my head and said, "No. My dad doesn't keep poisons around the house," I said.

He looked troubled and said, "Do you know anyone who might want to hurt him?"

That hadn't occurred to me, but suddenly I realized that this was the only explanation. Someone had poisoned my dog. I didn't know if it was done to hurt Bones or me, but I figured it was probably me they were actually after. I could think of two people right away who might do that: Tommy or Carl. Maybe both of them.

"I guess I know two people who might do that," I said.

"Who?" he asked me. When I told him, he said, "Tommy Gordon, maybe, but Carl Hicks comes from a good family. I can't see him doing something like this. His brother's a police officer."

He obviously didn't know Carl the way I did. Nor did he know Officer Hicks as well either.

People always judge others on appearance, though, or they base opinions on who someone's parents are. I'd never met Carl's parents, but their younger son was a bully. Their older son was not much different, and just because he wore a policeman's uniform or his parents were well liked didn't change that.

Every kid I knew would understand this completely, but adults seemed to forget it. It was confusing, and I realized that as nice as my dog's vet was, I would never be able to explain it to him.

I just said, "They're both capable of it. Believe me."

I talked to him about how much it would cost to take care of Bones. He estimated it could be as much as three-hundred-dollars, depending on how soon Bones could go home.

He could see this made me worry, so he said, "We can cross that bridge when we get to it." He smiled at me, but it wasn't as reassuring as he probably hoped it would be.

15

The next day crept by without Bones. I didn't have to feed him, and he wasn't there to spend any time with, so I walked to the vet's office to check on him. All the way there, I worried that he had died in the night. The emotion was so strong I almost started crying twice on the way there.

The day was already starting to cook, and it was barely eight o'clock. I thought about going swimming later to cool off, and this made me think about Hank and his situation. I decided if Bones was alright, I would stop by the jail to see if I could talk to him. I needed to find out who his attorney was so I could talk to him about the case. I needed to make sure his lawyer knew my side of the story.

Of course, Hank would tell him the same thing I would, but I needed to tell my side.

I arrived at the vet's and stood outside for a few minutes while I gathered the courage to go in. Finally, because nothing would change by putting it off, I went inside. It was a good sign that Mrs. Terry smiled at me. She wouldn't be smiling if she had bad news.

"Hey, Jack!" she said. "He's doing a lot better. Do you want to see him?"

My muscles relaxed, and I started breathing normally again. "Sure!"

She led me back to the kennel, and I saw the doctor on the way. He smiled too and said, "He's responding well to the treatment, so I think we were right about the diagnosis."

Bones was lying on the concrete floor of his kennel. When he saw me, he raised his head a bit and wagged his tail. He still didn't get up, but this was a lot more than he was doing the last time I saw him. He licked his chops and sneezed, and I laughed. They let me into the pen, and I sat on the floor to pet him, hug him and talk to him. I must have told him I loved him a hundred times. He licked my face, and I thanked the vet and Mrs. Terry at least ten times as I saw them walk by the kennel door.

As I left I started worrying about the cost of all this vet care again. I still had no idea how I was going to pay for it. I had only about $140 in my savings. I knew nobody that I could ask for the money. If I asked my dad, Bones would be dead an hour later, and besides, he didn't have that kind of money either. The only other adults I knew well enough to even ask—Hank and Mrs. Dawson—certainly couldn't afford that much money, not to mention Hank had enough problems of his own. I still had the job with Mrs. Dawson, but that wouldn't last forever.

I arrived at the police station and went inside. Other than a police officer at a desk, I was the only person in the room.

I didn't know the officer, and as I stepped up to the desk, he put aside his newspaper and said, "Can I help you?" He didn't sound happy that I'd interrupted his reading.

"I was wondering if I could see Hank Pittman," I said.

He frowned at me as if I had just asked to see the president.

"Who?"

"Hank Pittman."

"What's he in here for?"

I didn't want to say what Hank was charged with. It was so untrue that saying it would give the charges credit they didn't deserve. He was still looking at me, waiting for an answer. I swallowed though my mouth had gone dry. His stare forced me to speak the words. "He's charged with touching a minor." I wasn't sure what the exact charges were. The officer scowled at me.

"He put up bail yesterday," he said. "Are you the kid he touched?"

I looked directly into his eyes and said, "No, I'm the kid they say he touched, but he didn't."

He nodded with a smirk as if he expected that answer before going back to his newspaper and ignoring me.

I turned and walked out, pushing the door open so hard it slammed against the wall and bounced back. I heard him holler, "Hey!" as I walked away, but I ignored him the way he had ignored me.

I walked as fast as I could to Hank's. I needed to talk to him and find out when I could talk to his lawyer.

When I arrived, I knocked on the door. It didn't occur to me that I shouldn't be talking to him, considering the charges against him, but it had certainly occurred to Hank. I heard him shout from inside the bus, "I can't talk to you!"

I hollered back, "But I have to talk to you!"

It was silent inside the bus before he said, "Then, you have to go find a witness, an adult, to be with us when we talk."

I hated this. We couldn't even talk to each other anymore without an adult there. It was crazy. I'd have gone to get Mrs. Dawson, but she wasn't home yet from Mobile. She wouldn't be home for another three days, and I couldn't wait that long. I looked over at the docks, where I knew boat captains and others would be. I wondered if any of them would help out and thought about Hank's brother, Jerry.

When I walked into the party boat offices Jerry Moreland owned, I saw the last person in the world I wanted to see. Tommy Gordon stood at the counter. He didn't notice me at first, but when he did, I stood there staring at him. I thought about how he may have been the person who poisoned Bones. I also thought about how he and Carl had lied to the police about what they saw. Until a few days ago, I never knew I could hate someone so much. I would either have to leave quickly or I would be shouting and swearing at him in a few seconds. However, he must have decided I wouldn't leave until he had what he thought of as fun with me.

"Your boyfriend ain't here," he said. "I think he's in his luxury bus."

He could beat me up without trying, but suddenly I didn't care. Jerry Moreland was behind the counter, and I wondered why he would allow a hoodlum to talk about his brother that way. Then, I wondered if he was afraid of Tommy and his gang as well. When I'd asked Hank why he had allowed the gang to beat me up, he had said he didn't want them after him. Hank was just being wise about self-preservation. I wondered if his brother was doing the same thing, so it fell to me to start yelling at Tommy. "You know we never did anything! You lied! You said we had! That you saw it! But you know we never did! If you were there and saw me, you know he never did anything!"

Tommy's initial response was to stand there, gaping at me, wide-eyed. I'm sure he had no idea such anger could be inside me. I kept going, letting him have it. "And you probably poisoned my dog! He's at the vet's now, and I don't know how I'll pay for it! And it's your fault! Or maybe it was Carl, but I know one of you did it!"

"I don't know what the hell you're talkin' about," Tommy said. "You never did what?" He looked at Jerry Moreland and spun a finger around his ear in a "he's crazy" gesture.

"I'm talking about you telling the cops you saw Hank and me and how you saw him doing bad stuff with me, but we both know you're lying! And I'm talking about how you fed my dog rat poison that nearly killed him!"

Tommy glanced over at Mr. Moreland with a smirk. "Kid's crazy!" he said. "I don't know what he's talkin' about."

He was a terrible liar, which made me wonder how in the world the police would believe a word he said. It took me years to figure out it was because they wanted to believe it.

I noticed Mr. Moreland was looking at Tommy suspiciously, his brows knitted in an expression of doubt. At first I thought Mr. Moreland doubted what I was saying, but it slowly dawned on me he might believe me. If nothing else, he wasn't happy with Tommy.

"What about your dog?" Mr. Moreland asked me.

"Someone fed him rat poison," I said. "I don't know anyone who'd give him anything like that other than Tommy or Carl Hicks. They both hate me as much as I hate them."

"I'm tellin' you the kid's crazy." Tommy glared a warning at me.

I ignored his threat and kept ranting. "And he and Carl told the police your brother and I were doing stuff when they saw me skinny-dipping and Hank was there with me, but he knows all that happened was that I went swimming without my shorts because I didn't want to walk around all day with wet shorts."

Jerry Moreland looked at Tommy and said, "Maybe you should go for now." Tommy scowled at me as he walked out, and I was reminded how he looked the day Carl told him I had undercut the price to clean fish. I wondered if I had another beating in my future. It seemed a safe bet the answer was yes. I would just have to make sure

Bones was not fed more poison. Tommy could do what he wanted to me, but the thought he might try to kill my dog again made me think of doing something violent myself.

After Tommy left, Mr. Moreland turned to me. "Were you telling the truth? Did he make things up about you and Hank?"

"Yes. A friend of mine told me he overheard him and Carl Hicks talking about it. They told the police that Hank and I did stuff when I went skinny-dipping once and Hank was there, but I swear we didn't. All I did was go swimming without my clothes and dressed immediately when I got out." I must have sounded crazy with the need to be believed.

"Calm down," he said. "I probably know Hank better than anyone in the world, and he's not like what they're saying."

I suddenly remembered the reason I had come here in the first place.

"Mr. Moreland, I need to talk to Hank, but he said I needed an adult in the room first. Would you let us come in here and talk so we won't be alone together?"

He looked at me for a moment before replying. "Okay, but I have things I need to do. Don't take long."

I thanked him and ran to Hank's bus and banged on the door. "Come to the docks. Your brother said we can talk in there," I shouted.

"Are you sure we need to do this?" he asked, the door still closed. I could tell he wasn't too keen on the idea of meeting and talking. I couldn't blame him, I guess. If someone like Mrs. Polk saw us together, she might get ideas and spread more lies.

"Yes, I'm positive!" I said and ran off to the party boat office.

A few minutes later Hank walked in, wearing a frown. It looked permanent.

He spoke to his brother, thanking him and promising we wouldn't be long before turning to me and saying, "I'm sorry for all this. I should have seen it coming."

I didn't want to get into what I'd known before everything hit the fan, so instead I asked who his lawyer was.

"Shelton and Shelton," Hank said, naming a husband and wife I'd actually heard of. They were considered the best criminal defense attorneys in the county, if not the entire region. They were in the newspapers and on television frequently since they represented people in some important cases. Their office was in Wharton, though.

"I need to speak to them," I said. "I need to tell them this is all a lie."

"First, they know that," Hank said. "Second, they will want to talk to you, but at the proper time. They'll schedule an interview."

I'd seen Perry Mason on TV, and this brought up a question. "Will I have to give a deposition?"

"No," Hank said, "not with them, just interviewed. The Sheltons will call you as a witness if the judge allows it."

"Why wouldn't the judge allow me to testify?" I asked.

"He'll have to determine if you know what it means to testify under oath."

"What do you mean?" I asked.

Hank heaved a sigh and Jerry Moreland said, "When a young person like you is in court, the judge has to make sure you know the difference between lying and telling the truth." I looked at Mr. Moreland and considered for the first time that Hank might end up in jail for a long time.

"I know the difference," I said.

"We know that, but you'll have to convince the judge," Hank said.

"And the DA will do his best to make it look as if you don't know the difference because he'll know your testimony won't support the allegations against Hank," Jerry said.

"When will the trial be?" I asked.

"Not for months," said Hank.

"When can I talk to your lawyers?"

"They have your address. They'll probably send an investigator to your house," Hank said.

"No," I said, "that's not a good idea. My dad

thinks I'm lying."

"Your father?" Jerry asked, disbelief in his voice.

"Yeah." I could tell he thought that was weird, but at the time I considered it normal. My dad always thought the worst.

"You want to meet the investigator here?" Jerry asked, and I nodded.

"I'll contact the Sheltons and let them know," Hank said. "Stop by here tomorrow and Jerry will tell you when, but I don't think you and I should be seen talking. It might look bad."

I guess he could see the disappointment in my face. "Only until the trial's over," he said.

Suddenly, I remembered the other reason I needed to talk to Hank. "Oh, one other thing. Bones is sick," I said. "Someone poisoned him. I'm pretty sure it was Tommy or Carl."

"What makes you think that?" Hank said. "If he was poisoned, it could have been a lot of things. Lots of poisonous plants grow around here, you know. Oleander's everywhere." Oleander was a plant commonly found in Denton near the beach. Signs were placed everywhere warning people how poisonous they were.

"Oleander doesn't grow near my house, though," I said. "And anytime he's been away from my house, I was with him. I'd never let him eat oleander or any other plants."

"Does the vet know what kind of poison it was?" Jerry asked.

"He's pretty sure it was rat poison. Anyway, the treatment for that worked."

"What makes you think Tommy and Carl did it?" Jerry asked.

"They're the only ones I know who are hateful and cruel enough to do that."

"We can't do anything about it without proof," Hank said. "The good thing is Bones is going to be okay."

"Yeah, but it's gonna cost a lot of money," I said. "That's money I needed to get me through the school year."

"How much will it cost?" Jerry asked.

"About three-hundred dollars, maybe more."

I saw Hank and Jerry exchange a look.

"Do you need a job?" Jerry asked.

"Well, I have one right now," I said. "I go back to work Monday."

"Could you use another one?" Jerry said. "That's what Tommy was in here about—a permanent job."

I wondered what Tommy might say if he found out I took the job he wanted. Whatever it was, it wouldn't be good. He might want revenge. Finally, I decided he would be coming after me anyway, no matter what happened. It was just who he was.

"What kind of job?" I asked.

"Cleaning up around here. Maybe eventually working behind the counter to help customers."

"How many hours a day?"

"They have rules about that," Jerry said. "Child labor laws. I'd just need you for three hours a day. You won't be on payroll. I'll pay you under the table."

"Are you doing this because you feel sorry for me?" I asked. I didn't want pity.

"No, I'm doing this because I need someone to do a little work here, and I know Hank has a high opinion of you and your work."

I looked at Hank, and he shrugged.

"How much does it pay?" I asked.

Jerry chuckled. "Hank said he paid you five dollars a day. I'll pay that."

That was a lot for only three hours. I did the math. I'd need to work for Jerry for seventy days to make $350. And school was starting in a couple of weeks. "What about when school starts?" I asked.

"If you stop by for an hour before school and two hours after, I'll keep you on," he said. "I'll need you on weekends, especially. Are you willing to do that?"

I glanced over at Hank and he shrugged again. In ten weeks, I'd have enough to pay the vet bill, as long as he would let me set up a payment plan. That would allow me to keep some of the money I had made so far to cover dog food and my rent. I would also be able to keep my job with Mrs. Dawson until school started.

I held out my hand to Jerry. "It's a deal," I said, and he shook my hand. I walked out of there thinking that I may have my enemies, but I had some friends too. I was hopeful about the outcome of the trial and was handling my debts as well.

## 16

The next morning, I was at the Moreland docks by six o'clock, just as the boats were pulling out for a day of deep-sea fishing. I was anxious to get started on my new job, but I was also planning to go by Mrs. Dawson's afterwards to do some work for her as well since she was scheduled to be home last night. If I could make ten dollars a day, I'd be rich, as far as I was concerned.

As I walked into the store, Jerry raised his eyebrows at me. "Whoa! You are the early riser, aren't you?" he said.

"I just wanted to get started."

"Okay, you can begin by giving me a hand with the boxes in the back seat of my car," he said.

I went outside, opened the car door and grabbed one of the four boxes there, hustling it up the steps and into the store, where Jerry stood holding the door open.

"Set it on the table in my office," Jerry said. I went into his office, which was through a door behind the sales counter, and noticed an expensive mahogany table along one wall. Placing the first box there, I scampered out to the car to get the second box.

Jerry was leaning into the car to get a box, and I said, "I can get these, Mr. Moreland."

He stepped back and watched me get the second box and rush inside to put it down on the table. Returning, I saw he was still standing there. I looked at him and cocked an eyebrow. "What is it?" I asked. He was looking at me as if I'd grown another ear.

"Nothing," he said. "I just never had an employee hustle like you."

I didn't want to tell him I had to do as much as I could while I was there to make sure he wanted to keep me on during school, so I just shrugged. I was a good student and knew I could keep up, even while working, so it was important I keep the job. Besides, I liked Jerry and thought I would enjoy working for him.

He followed me inside when I had grabbed the last box, and after I set it down, he said, "Jack, I need you to stock some shelves. Are you up to it?"

"Sure."

He sold fishing tackle, such as lures, fishing line, nets, rods and reels—just about everything someone would need to go fishing. He showed me a storeroom in back where he kept his stock and said I should go around the store and note places where I could replenish the items sold there. After that, he took me around the storeroom again and explained how he had organized the supplies. It was easy because the merchandise was arranged just like it was out in the store. For instance, fishing rods were in the front left corner of the store, and in the storeroom, they were located in the same corner. Three islands of boxes of merchandise corresponded to the three long shelves of items for sale in the middle of the store. The only difference was that things were much farther apart in the store to allow the customers room to stroll around and shop.

I spent the next half hour stocking shelves, working as fast as I could. Then trouble struck.

I heard the ding of the bell above the door but ignored it. I was busy setting out boxes of various fishing lures on a shelf.

"Hello, Tommy," I heard Jerry say and stopped what I was doing to look over. Dread ran down my spine, making me shiver. I wondered if I looked as frightened as I felt. I now had the job Tommy had been doing his best to get. It seemed just like the time I had undercut the price for cleaning fish all the boys agreed to charge. Once again, I had undercut someone; only this time it was Tommy himself, not one of his thugs. I wondered for a second if Jerry had mentioned Tommy's name when he walked in to let me know he was there.

Tommy was looking at me, his eyes squinted in hate. "What're you doing here?" he asked me.

"He works for me," Jerry said. "Started today."

"What about me?" Tommy asked. "I was here just yesterday asking about a job. In fact, I was here first."

"I decided to hire Jack instead. Who was first doesn't mean anything." Jerry sounded unconcerned but I was scared. That Jerry didn't seem to fear what Tommy might do to him made me wonder if he was naïve to the ways of people like Tommy Gordon and his gang, but that didn't seem likely.

Tommy looked over at me again, his face an angry red. Turning back to Jerry, he said, "I'm stronger than he is. I can lift a lot more."

"That may be true," Jerry said, turning back to his work, "but Jack's strong enough to do what I need, and I decided to hire him."

"But his folks are a couple of drunks," Tommy said, as if that would be a good reason to fire me immediately and hire him instead.

"I'm aware they're alcoholics," Jerry said. "Hired him anyway. Now, if you have nothing else, we have work to do here. You're welcome to continue cleaning fish on the docks every evening, of course."

Jerry's almost rude dismissal of Tommy made me worry for the man's safety. Tommy would seek revenge. I suddenly wondered if Jerry had a dog and hoped with all my might he didn't.

Tommy said nothing more to Jerry but stepped over to me. I had gone back to work, hoping ignoring Tommy would make him pass me by without comment. No such luck. He leaned over me and whispered, "Better watch that dog o' yours. Next time I might use something stronger or maybe just shoot him instead. Or maybe I'll just lynch him." Menace dripped from the words.

The blood drained from my face and thought I might faint. He had just confessed he had poisoned Bones. Of course, he could have been bluffing, but I didn't think so. He knew he could tell me the truth, and I could do nothing about it. Jerry had gone into his office. I was alone with Tommy in the store, so nobody heard what he said to me. It was my word against his, and my word didn't stand for anything in Denton. As Tommy said, I was the son of a couple of drunks. Who would believe me? The police had already shown they would rather believe someone like Tommy.

I looked up at him and wanted to punch him in the face, but of course I never would. He smiled without humor and glanced around to make sure

Jerry wasn't watching. Reaching out, he picked up a small box that held a fishing lure, a red and white one gleaming in the light of the store. He pocketed it. Grinning at me, he turned and walked out.

I'd like to say I told Jerry what he did, but I didn't. He might have wondered why I didn't stop Tommy myself, or at least call out, ordering him to put the lure back or pay for it. I was too afraid, though. Too afraid of what Tommy might do to me, but more afraid of what he might do to my dog. All I did was mention to Jerry he might want to keep an eye on Tommy if he comes in because I wouldn't be surprised if he tried to steal something. He agreed before adding, "That's one reason you're here." It made me want to crawl into a hole.

I left work that day depressed. I decided the only thing to do would be to pay for the lure myself. It was the only way to make myself feel a little better. I could bring the money the next day to buy the same lure and put it back when Jerry wasn't looking, the opposite of shoplifting. The lure cost nearly four dollars, meaning basically I was working at the store for nearly a day to pay for Tommy's lure and my cowardice.

I walked over to Mrs. Dawson's to do my work for her. She'd heard about what happened to Hank from a neighbor, and she was full of questions since she'd been off visiting her sister in Mobile. "I leave for one week, and the whole world goes to Hell in a hand basket," she said, indicating a chair for me to sit in while she fixed herself some tea.

"That's pretty well the way it is," I said. "They're saying he did things to me that never happened. Now, Hank'll be going on trial and everything. And it's all my fault."

"How is it your fault?" she asked.

"Because," I said. "If I'd just been patient about getting work cleaning fish, the other guys wouldn't have attacked me like that, and Hank wouldn't have ever known me. Then, Mrs. Polk wouldn't have something to say about us."

"That's nonsense!" Mrs. Dawson said. "Hank is your friend, and a good one! The best one you have, in fact! It's that Mrs. Polk who's at fault! The old busy-body! Certainly not you!"

She was as angry as I'd ever seen her.

"Don't you dare think any of this is your fault!" she said, her face pinched and her eyes slits of anger.

"But Hank's going to go to jail!" I said. "And nobody believes me when I tell them nothing happened!"

"That's because people prefer to think the worst of others. Makes them believe they're better than everyone else. I've seen it a thousand times before. Human nature, I suppose. So, don't you think for one second that you're the problem. Anyway, I believe you, and I'll bet I'm not the only person who does."

"My own father doesn't even believe me! It's not fair!"

"No, Jack," she said, her voice suddenly calmer, "it's not fair. But in the meantime, we're going to do what we can to get people to believe you."

I looked at her for the first time since she'd become angry, and through the blur of my tears, I could see her eyes brimming as well.

I hugged her and she held me while I cried, touching my hair and shushing me softly. I wondered if that was how it felt to have a mother who cared for me more than anything else.

When I'd gained control of myself, I sat back, wiping my face on my sleeve. "I'm sorry," I said. "I didn't mean to ruin your first day back."

She took my chin firmly in her hand, looked in my eyes and said, "Jack, none of this is your fault. You have to see your way clear to forgive yourself, even though you have nothing to forgive. We have work to do for Hank, and it won't get done sitting on the pity pot."

I didn't want to argue about it, so I shrugged and said, "Okay, what do we have to do?"

"Figure a way to make people believe you," she said.

"How?"

"I'm not sure yet, but we'll find a way."

I had gardening and lawn work to do for Mrs. Dawson and needed to get started on it. "I need to mow your grass and do some weeding," I said.

An odd look crossed her face, as if she had more bad news. "Jack, you might want to wait on that."

"What for?"

"Well," she began, and I braced myself for more bad news. I had no idea what it would be, but I could tell she didn't want to say it, so I knew it wasn't good. I continued to stare at her as she worked up the courage to tell me whatever it was I needed to know. She sighed deeply and said, "Jack, there's something you don't know that I need to tell you."

"What is it?" My heart sank. I suddenly realized I was being fired. I didn't know why, but it hit me like a solid punch in the gut.

"I can't keep you working for me anymore," she said.

"Why not?"

She took another deep breath and let it out slowly. "Because I don't have the money."

"What happened?" I asked. I wondered if she'd been robbed or if someone had swindled her out of her money or something.

"The truth is . . . well . . . I'm not the one who's been paying you."

"Who did?" I asked, suddenly knowing the

answer just before she said it.

"Hank."

Although I had figured out the answer, that didn't mean I understood it. "Hank?" I asked. "How? Why?"

"The day before you came to work for me, I ran into Hank at Kirby's, just as we told you. But when Hank asked me if I wanted to hire you, I told him I didn't have the money to do that. He'd been paying you five dollars a day, and I wouldn't have been able to pay you more than one or two, if that. I'm on a fixed income, and it's barely enough to get by."

"Oh," I said, unable to think of anything else to say.

"You remember I told you how I'd not seen my sister in years? It's because I couldn't afford to go. She paid me back the money I needed to make the trip when I arrived. The only time I paid you anything out of my own pocket was when I paid you the extra dollar that time. The truth is I'm pretty broke."

I still didn't know what to say.

"Hank knew you wouldn't take any charity to help you raise Bones," she continued, "so he told me he'd give me the cash each week to pay you. Every Saturday night we'd meet at Kirby's and he'd give me twenty-five dollars in five-dollar bills for the following week."

I tried to grasp what she was telling me, as if

she'd just told me the moon really was made of cheese. I thought about what she was saying. I knew why he'd done it but preferred not to think about it. It was too close to the reasons I felt miserable.

She looked down, perhaps ashamed she couldn't afford to keep me on. I dealt with it by telling myself the job would be ending soon anyway, since school would be starting in a few weeks. Also, yard work wasn't needed once autumn arrived, not even in Florida. "With Hank's problems and having to pay his attorneys, I don't think it would be right to keep taking money to pay you for your work, even if it's only five dollars."

I rose from my seat and said, "Thank you, Mrs. Dawson. I appreciate what you did. I'll be starting back to school soon anyway, and I did manage to pick up another job at the Moreland docks." I was angry, but I guess I should've been happy for any job under the circumstances.

She smiled at me. "We can still do what we can to help Hank. I'm not sure what yet, but we'll come up with something." As it turned out, it was nice to think we'd figure out a way to help Hank, but we never did. The truth was our only weapon, but nobody cared to hear it.

On my way home, I dropped by to see Bones. After spending some time with him, I stopped by the docks to see if Jerry would go get Hank and bring him to the docks to talk. When I arrived, though, Jerry told me that Hank had borrowed his car to go see his attorneys. I walked home and worried the rest of the afternoon about Hank and Bones. The day that had started with such promise with a new second job hadn't gone well at all. My job with Mrs. Dawson was over, and Tommy had found another reason to make my life miserable. It occurred to me that if he wanted to ruin my life, he would need to get in line.

17

Two days later, the doctor allowed Bones to come home. He agreed to let me make payments and lowered the bill some as well. I would pay for the medicines, and he took a discount on his fee. The total came to $120. I didn't argue; the charity was for Bones. I gave him half of the money with a promise to pay the rest at ten dollars a week.

The following week I was questioned about Hank by the Sheltons' investigator, Mr. Pinnix. He stopped by the docks around nine o'clock one morning, and Jerry told me to take a break to talk to him. I had nothing much to tell other than the truth. I told him about being beaten up by the other boys and how Hank had seen it and given me a job. I talked about the day I went skinny-dipping and how Hank barely even looked at me. When I told Mr.

Pinnix how Hank had paid my wages when I was working for Mrs. Dawson, he said, "You might want to keep that under your hat."

"Why?" I asked. I thought it was something that would show how nice Hank was.

"Because the DA would twist that around to suggest Mr. Pittman was paying you off for your silence."

My jaw dropped at this news. I was surprised that Hank's best actions could be turned against him. It made me wonder why anyone ever made an effort to help other people if being nice could be twisted to make them look bad.

I asked Mr. Pinnix if it was true that Tommy and Carl would testify about the skinny-dipping, and how they would lie about what they saw. He told me they would, so I told him about Tommy's confession to poisoning Bones and how he said he would be back and use a stronger poison next time. Mr. Pinnix said while it may be true, it could not be proved. "It would just be your word against his."

When we finished, Mr. Pinnix told me he might have to talk to me again before the trial, and Mr. and Mrs. Shelton would need to see me before then to discuss my testimony. I thanked him and he left, allowing me to get back to work.

I stopped by Mrs. Dawson's several times over the last weeks of summer vacation just to talk to her and see how she was doing. I even mowed her yard for free, although she complained about it. Still, I couldn't let her do the mowing. I asked her once how she could afford the guy who couldn't plant in straight rows and she laughed. "I made that up," she said. "I hadn't had anyone planting or doing anything else. I just wanted to make sure you were careful."

I laughed with her about that. I talked about how nervous I was that first day, wondering if she was going to fire me if the rows weren't straight enough.

"Sorry about that, Jack. I had to keep up appearances, though."

Hank was correct, even if she hadn't been the one paying me. She was a stickler for good work and a little eccentric. I still liked her for a lot of reasons, but mostly because she was always on my side when I was right and told me why she wasn't if I was wrong.

Yogi spent most of my time there sitting in my lap and getting me to pet her. I enjoyed the attention she gave me and the funny way she craved the same from me. Petting her relaxed me. I wondered if she and Bones would get along, despite the difference in their size.

Finally, the first day of school arrived. I had been dreading this day, but not for the reasons most kids my age did. I knew when I went back to school, I would see Mrs. Polk, the school's secretary. She had ruined my life and Hank's with her gossip and accusations. I'd mentioned my dread to Mrs. Dawson, who told me to ignore her as much as possible and to remember that she probably thought she was saving my life. I couldn't understand that, but I did as Mrs. Dawson asked.

Because Denton was such a small community back then, the school held only enough students to fill one class for each grade level, so we all moved together up through the grades. Therefore, I was well acquainted with each of the other students, having gone to school with most of them for the past seven years. That year I started eighth grade, the highest grade at school in Denton. After that, we had to take a bus to Wharton to attend high school.

Just because I had been attending school with the same kids for years didn't mean they would all be forgiving or understanding when it came to my situation involving Hank. When I arrived at school, I was met mostly with either stares or the backs of heads. I had thought some of them were my friends. Only Lee and Roger remained loyal and ignored the reactions from the other students.

Even my teacher, Mrs. Woodruff, treated me as if she wished I had moved away. Denton used only one teacher per grade level for all subjects, so I was stuck with her all day. I always sat in one of the front seats to avoid distractions, but Mrs. Woodruff had a different idea. She made me move to the seat farthest from her desk, isolating me in the back corner, where she ignored me for the most part for the rest of the year. Most of the teachers I've known were good ones, but she was the exception.

One guy in my class was named Bob Ebert. We had never talked that much. I always thought he was kind of creepy because he liked to hug all the girls. They all thought he was sweet, calling him "Huggy Bob." I knew better, though. He was anything but sweet. He was just tall and handsome and he knew it.

That first day of school, Huggy Bob made it clear I was no longer just another guy in his class. He began looking at me with absolute hatred. His nose curled up when he walked past me, as if he smelled something awful, and he would make some comment about the room's stench.

The biggest problem, though, began when Mrs. Woodruff walked out of the room for some reason, and we were left on our own. A minute or two after she was gone, Bob came over to where I was sitting in my desk working on the word problems from math class.

When he reached my desk, he said, "You know something? You smell bad."

I knew he was just trying to pick a fight. I tried to ignore him, hoping he would lose interest, but a couple of girls turned our way. Within seconds the entire room was watching.

"What's the matter? You deaf too, you pervert?" I had Mrs. Polk to thank for this.

I looked up at him as I realized this would not end well. I said, "No, I'm not deaf. I'm just trying to do my work."

"So, what're you gonna do about that stink?" he asked. "Some of the girls have complained and I thought I'd be a nice guy and let you know."

"I took a shower this morning," I said. "Maybe you're smelling someone a little closer to where you're standing."

His bully's grin faltered a bit as he tried to figure out if I was referring to him. I was, but I wasn't sure he'd realize it. He looked at the seat in front of me as if I might be talking about someone else, but it was empty. I was in the last seat in the row. Then to make sure he had figured it out right, he said, "Are you talkin' about me?"

"Leave him alone, Bob," said a voice. I looked up and saw Roger and Lee approaching. It had been Lee who spoke.

"You two need to back off," Bob said. "This doesn't concern you."

"Maybe not—" Lee began, but I held up a hand. I didn't want them to get in trouble for defending me. I could defend myself.

"It's okay, Lee," I said. "I can handle it."

Bob turned back to me and smiled as if he had already won the fight. I rose from my seat, and he stood his ground. "You asked if I meant you," I said. "As a matter of fact, I did."

Bob's eyes narrowed, and I saw his anger flare as his jaw tightened.

The next thing I knew, someone behind me pushed me into Bob, causing him to flail at me. He pushed me back and jumped on me. My fist landed on the side of his head as we rolled to the hard floor. Excited squeals from the girls and shouts from the guys filled the room. Yells of "Fight! Fight!" echoed as we rolled and punched each other, landing few blows of any consequence.

Suddenly, we were being lifted and pulled apart. Mrs. Woodruff was there with Mr. Balzer, the principal. At the time, I couldn't figure out why he was here. He usually stayed in his office and ventured out only when it was necessary or to go home.

They marched us to the office. Bob was walking on his own. Neither Mrs. Woodruff nor Mr. Balzer so much as touched him. Mr. Balzer was steering me with a strong grip on my arm that left a bruise. It was as if both assumed I had started the fight. The double standard continued once we were in Mr. Balzer's office.

"Have a seat!" Mr. Balzer said, steering me toward a chair while pointing at a chair for Bob, who sat as if he owned the building, a smirk plastered on his face.

"You both are in a load of trouble!" he began, though his gaze was fastened on me alone. Mrs. Woodruff stood in a corner with her arms crossed. She wasn't looking at Bob either.

It dawned on me Bob would not be in any trouble.

"He started it," I said. "I was just sitting at my desk doing my math."

"Is that true?" Balzer said to Bob.

"He's been spoilin' for a fight," Bob said. "I was just tired of listenin' to him go on about how he was gonna beat me up."

"That's a lie," I said.

"That's a serious allegation," Mr. Balzer said to me.

"It's not an allegation; it's the truth," I said.

Balzer stared at me. "Well, we have no way to prove he's lying," Balzer said, as if he couldn't ask any of the students who witnessed the exchange, not that any besides Lee and Roger would defend me.

"He slammed into me," Bob said. "I had no choice but to fight back."

"Someone pushed me into him," I answered.

"Who pushed you?" Balzer asked.

"I don't know," I admitted, knowing that wasn't a good answer. "They were behind me. Bob swung at me and I had to defend myself."

"There, then," Balzer said, as if my response was the key to the entire situation. "You say one thing and he says another." He looked over at Mrs. Woodruff and said, "Do you think a warning will do this time, Mrs. Woodruff?"

"Yes," she said, "as long as Jack understands he is walking on thin ice here." Her meaning was clear. If it happened again, I would be the one found guilty of fighting. Bob, or whoever else might be involved, would suffer no consequences.

"The next time this happens, someone will get suspended from school," Balzer said, still looking only at me. "I hope you can control yourself." Again, he glanced at Mrs. Woodruff. "Allow me a few minutes to discuss this with Mrs. Woodruff. You boys can wait in the main office."

Sitting in the front office was nearly as bad as getting in trouble for fighting. Mrs. Polk was there, so I'd be forced to sit in the room with her. Bob and I walked out into the front office and took seats while I did my best not to look at Mrs. Polk. She wouldn't let me get away with that, though.

"Shame on you boys!" she said. "I heard every word of your fight on the intercom."

This surprised me. "You did?" I asked, despite my promise to ignore her. Her words surprised me that much. If she heard them, how was it that Bob was not in any trouble?

"Yes!" Mrs. Polk said. "Mrs. Woodruff came in and she and Mr. Balzer immediately turned on the intercom to Mrs. Woodruff's room. Teachers do that sometimes, you know, just to see what happens. They heard everything you both said." She wasn't aware neither of us had been punished and assumed swift justice had been dealt to us both.

I glanced at Bob, but he was not surprised at all. I wasn't sure what to think. He was smiling at me as if to say I should watch my step. Based on what Mrs. Polk had just said, I agreed with him. Bob's smirk told me he understood the situation. I'd been set up, and the warning about another time had been to justify a suspension later. Of course, there would be another fight, probably sooner than later, and I would be the only one punished.

"I don't blame you, though, Jack," she said, "after all you've been through this summer."

I wanted to scream at her to mind her own damn business and to tell her that everything wrong in my life right then was her fault, including this fight. I followed Mrs. Dawson's advice and held my tongue, though, which was not easy.

When I left school that day, I caught up with Roger and Lee as they walked home and I walked to work. I could have ridden a school bus, but I thought that would just be asking for trouble since more fights started on the bus than at school. Lee and Roger always chose to ride in the morning and walk home after school.

I explained what I'd learned about being set up, and they both suggested I do my best to lie low for a while. "If you don't get in trouble soon, they'll forget about it," Lee said.

I hoped they were right. I didn't need a suspension on top of everything else. Before we parted near the docks, they promised to do their best to try to keep guys off me. I didn't know if that would work, and I told them not to get themselves in hot water on account of me, but they said it was no problem.

When I arrived at work, Jerry had a surprise for me. He told me he would teach me about working behind the counter. He was going to train me to help customers, including doing the paperwork for tickets to go fishing on one of the deep-sea fishing boats. That was an involved process, and I was determined not to make any mistakes.

I considered this a promotion. It showed he trusted me and liked my work. Tommy hadn't come into the store since my first day, or at least he hadn't when I was there, which was all I cared about. Thinking of how he stole the lure made me feel guilty that Jerry trusted me so much, but I decided to let it go. If it happened again, I wouldn't let Tommy get away with it. He was already planning to kill my dog, not to mention his intent to commit perjury against Hank and me in court. Compared to those things, I couldn't see much else he could do to hurt me.

That was the first day I worked at the store in

the afternoon, and when the boats came in, Tommy and his gang were outside, waiting to get work cleaning fish. As the boys waited for the tourists, I saw Tommy looking through the store's front window at me. We were headed for some sort of showdown, and I was not looking forward to it, despite doing my best to convince myself I didn't care. I would rather have a tooth filled without being numbed first, in fact. His glare promised violence, and I knew it was a promise he would keep.

The next day at school I sat in my desk at the back of the room and did my work while trying to ignore everyone around me. I barely acknowledged Lee and Roger except for joining them for lunch, as usual. Lunch and other times we weren't under direct supervision provided the best opportunities for someone to start something, and I did my best to keep my two friends nearby. After lunch, we sat in the cafeteria until it was time to go back to class. Before this mess, we had always gone out to the basketball courts to shoot baskets and have fun. Now we didn't take the chance.

Later that day, I had a question in math. I raised my hand, but Mrs. Woodruff ignored me. She treated me as if I had disappeared. Finally, I gave up and did my best without knowing if what I was doing was right or not. It became the year I taught myself.

One day about a week after the fight, the trouble started again. Mrs. Woodruff looked around the room as we began working on some math and said, "Lee, would you and Roger come help me carry some boxes of books from the book room?"

I knew immediately this would be the day. I don't know if asking my only friends in the room to help was an accident or on purpose, but the result was the same. Any help I might get if attacked, as well as anyone willing to back my side of any story, disappeared as the door closed behind them.

Bob stood up within seconds and headed for my desk.

"We never finished that fight," he said.

Looking up at his smug face from where I sat, I figured I would at least make him throw the first punch just in case someone decided to tell the truth.

"You mean the one you and Mrs. Woodruff set up?"

"I don't know what you're talkin' about," he said.

"Don't you think it's convenient that the only friends I have in here were the ones called out to help move the books?" I continued staring at him, waiting for his fist to come at my face.

He smiled. "Yeah."

That's when it happened. I saw his shoulder twitch, and his right fist flew toward my face. I was barely able to deflect it while ducking to avoid the blow. The next thing I knew we were both on the floor, rolling around to the same chorus of "Fight! Fight!" from the kids jumbling for a ringside spot to watch.

When Mrs. Woodruff walked in with Lee and Roger carrying boxes of books, she shouted, "Stop that right now!"

Four boys who had been cheering the brawl stepped forward and pulled the two of us apart. I took some satisfaction that Bob's eye was swelling where I'd hit him. He had probably thought he would get out of this without a mark on him.

We were once again taken to the office, and I was suspended for three days, which back then also meant I would receive zeroes on all assignments given during that time. Bob, who claimed I started the fight by walking to his desk and hitting him in the eye, despite the fact we had obviously been fighting where I sat, received nothing but the black eye.

Nothing like that happened again, either because I was getting the better of Bob in the fight and he decided to avoid me or because Mrs. Woodruff figured more would be overkill. I had been given the message I was on my own that year in school, and Mrs. Woodruff was spared the necessity of seeing me in her classroom for three days. I could have told her I was also spared several unpleasant interactions during my suspension, but she wouldn't have believed me. Either that or she wouldn't have cared.

When I attended high school in Wharton, I met many fine teachers, but I never forgot Mrs. Woodruff. I wondered whether it would have mattered if she had gone into another profession. Would she have been as cruel? Finally, I decided that evil brings only evil, regardless of the circumstances. In her own way, she was worse than Mrs. Polk, who at least thought she was being a good citizen despite the truth, and more like Tommy, who did what he did because he was deep-down mean.

## 18

Within a few weeks I was working behind the counter for Jerry more and more, helping the few locals when they came in to buy fishing gear. Autumn was in full swing, which on Florida's northern Gulf coast was little more than a cooling of temperatures, shorter days and longer nights. Still, the tourists disappeared and Denton became a sort of ghost town.

Jerry had begun going home for an hour or so when I would show up in the afternoon for a break away from the store. I would stock shelves, clean up a little, and wait on the few customers who came in. I knew most of them by now, and they would speak to me. I found it funny that the men in town accepted me much more readily than the women did after Hank's arrest. The women acted as if I had some disease they might catch, but the men just acted the same as always.

One afternoon I was dusting shelves when the bell over the door announced a customer. I looked up and my heart skipped a beat. Tommy walked in with Carl marching behind him, their smirks forecasting their intent.

"Well, well," Tommy said, "what have we here? Jack Turner hard at work doin' the job I was supposed to have?"

"He's a chronic job thief," Carl said. "First he steals my job cleaning fish then steals your job at the Moreland Docks."

"Whatcha think we should do 'bout that?" Tommy said. I could tell this had all been rehearsed beforehand like a little drama they had written.

Carl looked around the store. "Maybe we should use some of that fishing line to hang him."

"Or we could jus' stop by his house and poison his dog again," Tommy said, laughing as if it was the world's funniest joke.

"Yeah," Carl said. "We need to use more rat poison, this time, though."

"Who knew the dog was so healthy after nearly starvin' to death?" said Tommy.

I stood there wondering what they might do. I knew they wouldn't hang me, of course, but they might decide to beat me up, which I'd prefer to anything they might do to Bones.

"Last time I was in here, I found a nice lure," Tommy said.

"Yeah," Carl said. "I could use a new lure myself." He walked over to the shelf of lures and started pawing through them, scattering boxes of them on the floor. "Sorry, I guess you're gonna have to clean this up, huh?" He laughed as he continued creating a mess.

"Actually," Tommy said, "I need a new rod and reel." He stepped over to where the rods and reels were kept and began checking them out as if he would buy one.

"Yeah," Carl said and joined Tommy. "Me too."

After looking them over for a while, they each chose one of our more expensive Zebco reels and a fiberglass Shakespeare rod. Each pair would have cost about $35 if they paid for them, a lot of money back then.

Tommy looked over at me and said, "I think I'll take these."

Carl nodded. "Good choice."

They strolled out of the store with the rods and reels. I called after them to stop or I'd call the police, but they just cussed at me and continued walking. I knew Carl believed he had nothing to fear from the police since his brother was a cop.

Instead of calling the police, I called Jerry and told him what had happened. He swore on the phone and said, "I'll be right there."

When he arrived, he called the police. My heart

sank when I saw Officer Hicks arrive less than three minutes after Jerry made the phone call, so he hadn't been far from the docks when the radio call went out. I wondered if he'd been waiting for the call up on the highway. Climbing slowly out of the cruiser, Officer Dagwood Hicks shuffled up the ramp leading to the store and entered. Reluctance made his every movement slow, as if he would rather be anywhere but there.

"Okay, what happened?" he said.

"Two boys came into the store and walked out with a rod and reel each they didn't pay for," Jerry said.

"Did you see them walk out with them?" Hicks asked.

"I didn't, but my employee did."

Officer Hicks looked at me and back at Jerry. "I've known this kid to tell a few lies," he said. My heart thumped as rage rose in my chest.

Jerry looked at Hicks in total disbelief, as if he couldn't comprehend what had been said. He frowned and said, "That's funny. I've found him to be an honest young man."

"Be that as it may, is he the one making the accusation?"

"Yes," said Jerry. "He was the one here when the boys walked out with the rods and reels."

"So, what do you have to say?" Hicks asked, looking at me, his smirk telling me he wouldn't believe me, no matter what I said, or at least he would pretend not to.

I was seething. Once again, it was as if I was in a play and knew the script. I would tell him it was his brother and Tommy, and he would say I was lying. Nothing would come of the complaint. In fact, I wondered if he already knew what had taken place, having been informed by his younger brother, complete with laughs and jokes at my expense.

"You already know what I'm going to say," I said, doing my best to control my anger.

"How could I know that? I'm not Carnac the Great, you know." I would have laughed if it hadn't been so infuriating. Carnac the Great was a fortune teller Johnny Carson sometimes played on *The Tonight Show* back then. He was funny. Officer Hicks was not.

"Because, one of the boys was your brother Carl. The other was Tommy Gordon."

Officer Hicks shook his head as if I were the biggest nuisance in the world. "Are you suggesting my brother is a thief?"

I probably should have held my temper, seeing as how this was still a cop I was talking to, but I couldn't help myself. "I'm not suggesting anything. I know he's a thief. I watched him steal the rod and reel."

"You know, kid, making a false police report is serious business, and making false allegations against someone could get you in trouble for committing slander. You sure a couple of your friends didn't come in here and take them and y'all cooked up this scheme to blame my brother and his friend?"

I glanced at Jerry, and he was figuring out what was happening now, too. He could see that Officer Hicks would be zero help.

"Are you not going to investigate this?" Jerry said, his anger causing him to raise his voice a bit.

"I will when young Jack here tells the truth. Until then, he should be happy I don't charge him with filing a false police report. The only reason I don't is that I'd have to charge you, too, and mostly I see you as just falling for his lies."

He looked down at me and I could read his face. He was letting me know that I had it right but it wouldn't do any good. He was in charge, and as long as that was the case, nothing I said or did would allow me to get justice, especially when his brother was involved. He turned and sauntered out of the store, saying to Jerry, "If Jack decides to tell the truth instead of trying to get revenge on a couple of honest citizens who intend to testify against his buddy in court, then let us know."

He plopped down in his patrol car and sped off, tires spinning on the dirt-and-shell parking lot.

Jerry looked down at me, looking as if his faith in the world had been damaged. I felt bad for him.

Here I was a month short of thirteen, and I had a clearer grasp of how things worked in Denton than he did. Of course, he'd never had to deal with the cops there, especially Officer Hicks.

"Sorry. I've sorta been dealing with that for a while now," I said. "Officer Hicks has it in for me, and his brother Carl is one of the guys that beat me up when Hank and I met."

Jerry's face hardened and he lifted the phone. Glancing at a card taped on the glass top of a display case where the phone sat, he dialed the police again. After waiting for someone to answer he said, "This is Jerry Moreland. I need to speak to the chief." He listened before saying, "Okay, then, I need to speak to another high-ranking officer." Apparently, the chief wasn't available.

He waited and fidgeted, and I could tell he was growing angrier by the second while he was on hold. A customer walked in, but Jerry held out his hand and said, "Sorry, Leo, we're closed right now." Leo's eyebrows shot up and he turned and left. When someone finally came on the line, he said, "Yes, this is Jerry Moreland, down at the docks." He didn't need to say which docks.

After a second, he said, "Yes, I was just visited by one of your so-called officers who refused to investigate a shoplifting incident because it involved his younger brother. I need a real policeman to come out here to look into it. . . .Yes, that's right. . . .Would you? I would appreciate that a lot." He hung up.

"Detective Tyndall will be here soon," he said.

"I'm sorry," I said. I was, too. If he'd had anyone else here watching his store, this wouldn't be happening and I told him so.

"I'm not so sure about that. My guess is Officer Hicks would have found a reason not to look into it since his brother is involved," Jerry said. He may have been right about that, but I knew if I hadn't been watching the store, they might not have taken anything.

Detective Tyndall was a good cop, though. I knew he wouldn't make excuses the way Carl's brother had. I remembered he had been the detective who came by to talk to Mrs. Dawson about her missing car and had also found it funny when she realized what had happened. I trusted him.

When the detective arrived, he strode into the store and listened to our story. Unlike Officer Hicks, he believed me. Jerry locked the store and we climbed into the detective's car to ride with him to Tommy Gordon's house, our first stop.

When we pulled into their sand driveway, Tommy's father was sitting outside in a lawn chair drinking a beer. Empty beer cans littered the yard near him, some of them rusting, and I wondered how often he cleaned them up. Detective Tyndall climbed out and we followed.

Approaching Mr. Gordon, he said, "Avery? I received a complaint about your boy Tommy."

Mr. Gordon looked up at the detective and said, "So?"

"So, I have to talk to him. He around?"

"Tommy!" Mr. Gordon yelled.

"Yeah?!" we heard from inside the house.

"Get out here! A cop needs to talk to you!"

Tommy sauntered out as if he didn't have a care. He smiled at Detective Tyndall in greeting. "What is it?" he said.

"You been down at the docks today?"

"Which ones?" Tommy asked.

"The Moreland docks."

Tommy appeared to be thinking that over and shook his head. "No, I don't believe I have. Been to the Hastings docks, though. Somethin' wrong?"

"Do you have a new rod and reel?" Detective Tyndall asked.

"As a matter of fact, I do. Bought it just last week with the money I make cleanin' fish."

"May I see them?" said the detective.

"Sure," said Tommy going back inside to retrieve the stolen merchandise.

"Is that true?" Detective Tyndall asked Mr. Gordon.

"What?" These people were making getting to the bottom of this as difficult as possible. It made me want to scream.

"Is it true Tommy recently bought a new rod and reel?"

Mr. Gordon took a swallow of beer, burped, and said, "Yeah, I think he did, come to think of it."

"What brand?" Detective Tyndall asked. I thought he was trying to catch them in a lie.

"Don't recall," Mr. Gordon said, not falling for the trap. It was strange that such stupid people could be so smart when it came to getting away with crimes and cheating people.

At that moment, Tommy stepped outside with the rod and reel he'd taken from Jerry's store. I took one look at them and said, "That's them! Those are the ones he stole from Mr. Moreland's store. He and Carl both walked out with identical rods and reels without paying."

"You have receipts for that?" Detective Tyndall asked.

"Threw those away last week," Tommy said.

"What store did you get them from?" the detective asked.

"Sportsman's Paradise in Wharton," Tommy said.

"Maybe we'll have to go there to see if anyone remembers selling them to you."

Before anyone else could speak, Tommy said, "What did I tell ya, Dad? This kid has it in for me! I told you he'd be comin' around one day accusin' me of somethin'!"

Mr. Gordon answered without missing a beat. "Yep, that you did!"

Detective Tyndall looked at me. He wasn't accusing me of anything. In fact, I had the feeling he knew exactly what was going on. His look said he wasn't sure how to handle this. It was unexpected, though I should have seen it coming.

What I hadn't planned on—and apparently neither had Detective Tyndall—was Tommy's father being so willing to lie for his son. My dad was a drunk who worked in a bar, but I knew he would never back me in a lie. Here was Tommy Gordon's father lying through his teeth to allow his son to keep stolen property. He may have had a fairly good job as a car mechanic, but I thought he was a worse father than my dad. My own dad pretty well ignored me most of the time. My brother had no intentions of ever coming home again my parents were so bad. Yet, here was this sorry excuse of a father who was somehow considered better than mine.

"You and Tommy and I all know the truth!" I said. "He stole those and you're backing up his story."

"Boy! You callin' me a liar?" Mr. Gordon said, his voice threatening as he squinted at me from his chair. "Tyndall, you need to get that little bastard off my property, or I'm gonna make him leave."

"Calm down, Avery. We'll leave when I'm

through with my work here."

Mr. Gordon looked at Detective Tyndall and said, "Well, you're through now." His tone suggested threat and possible violence.

Detective Tyndall stood silent for a moment, weighing his options before waving his hand for us to follow him to his car. When we climbed in, I said, "Mr. Tyndall, he's lying! He stole those and his father's lying for him!"

"I know he is, but frankly, there's not much I can do about it. I can go by Sportsman's Paradise, but my guess is they won't remember him, and the fact is I can't arrest him on that. He has a solid story that his father will back him on. Our hands are tied."

"What about Carl?" Jerry asked. "We could go there and see what he says."

"That's where I was headed," the detective said.

We drove over to Carl's house, climbed out of the car, and walked up to the door. After knocking, we waited until Carl's mother came to the door.

"Yes?" she said.

"Is your son home?" Detective Tyndall asked.

"Which one? I got three."

"Carl."

"I think so. Hold on." She walked into the house and returned with Carl.

Detective Tyndall took a different approach.

"Afternoon, Carl," he said. "Can we come in?"

"Sure," Carl said. He looked even less nervous than Tommy had, if that were possible.

He opened the door and stepped aside for us to enter. Jerry and I followed.

"Anything wrong?" Carl asked.

"Yes, there's been an accusation I'm looking into. Where have you been today?" he asked.

"Mostly right here," Carl said.

"You weren't up at the Moreland docks earlier?" the detective asked.

"No, sir. What's this about?"

"What if I told you I had a witness that says you were there and were seen leaving there with a new rod and reel?" said Detective Tyndall.

"I'd say your witness was wrong," said Carl, frowning at me. "Or lying."

"Do you have a new rod and reel?"

"No."

"Is it okay if I look around?" Detective Tyndall asked.

"Do you have a warrant?" Carl wanted to know.

"Didn't think I'd need one."

"You thought wrong," Carl said. "My brother's a cop. I know my rights."

"I was just thinking that you would want to cooperate if you'd done nothing wrong," Detective Tyndall said.

"Then you thought wrong again," Carl said.

It was frustrating how these guys were able to avoid getting in trouble. I realized this would go nowhere. Tommy and Carl seemed to have an answer for everything.

After a few more questions and no real answers, we returned to the car and talked to Detective Tyndall as he drove us back to the docks. I was beside myself.

"Can't you get a warrant?" I asked.

"It's not as easy as they make it look on television," he said. "You have to convince a judge that searching someone's home is necessary—or warranted.

"But I saw them steal the rods and reels!" I said.

"Yes, but their attorneys, if it went that far, would be able to question your story. Both boys have suggested reasonable motives for you to go after them. Juries and judges weigh such things as rather significant," Detective Tyndall said.

"But if you get a warrant, you'd find the rod and reel he says he doesn't have," I said.

"I doubt it. He'd have hidden it somewhere else by then," Detective Tyndall said, and I finally understood he was right.

"Don't worry about it," Jerry said, his first words spoken in a while. "I'll absorb the loss and ban those two from the docks."

That wasn't what I wanted. They deserved to be charged with stealing.

The next day, Jerry drove by their homes and left a written notice that if they ever came onto his property again, they would be arrested and charged with criminal trespass. He even had a camera there to take their picture if they showed up. I knew that would not make them happy, especially if they wanted to clean fish next summer, but it allowed me to call the police immediately if they showed up, and that was a relief.

## 19

I didn't see Tommy again until the trial. I didn't see Carl more than a few times, and never at the docks. He was a year ahead of me at school, so he attended the high school in Wharton. I continued to be ignored at school by nearly everyone but Lee and Roger.

One good thing happened that year, though. I actually received Christmas presents. Hank, Jerry and Mrs. Dawson gave me gifts. I knew Mrs. Dawson couldn't afford them, but she assured me she didn't go overboard. "I just couldn't afford a hundred dollars a month," she said. Hank had bought me things, but he wasn't able to come to our holiday dinner since I was there. I hated that we couldn't even be in the same room.

When I visited Mrs. Dawson in early December and saw the gifts for me under the tree, I was surprised and realized I had to buy them some as well.

"You didn't have to do that," I said. I'd never received a present at Christmas before. I hadn't even received a gift from my parents on my birthday other than some clothes from Goodwill. They said they didn't get me Christmas gifts or buy a tree because they didn't celebrate the holiday, but I had accepted the truth and thought nothing of it. When I saw the gifts under Mrs. Dawson's tree, I nearly cried.

I sat with Mrs. Dawson and admired her tree. "I've never received a Christmas gift before," I said.

"Never?" she said, incredulous.

"Nope. My parents don't celebrate it."

"Well, you have to come here for Christmas gifts and dinner. I make a mean turkey and dressing."

I hadn't had a real Christmas dinner either. I accepted her invitation with a smile.

That weekend, I went to the small five and dime in Denton and bought each of them the same gift: a Christmas decoration that could hang on a wall or outside. They weren't expensive, but I hoped they would like them. Mrs. Dawson let me wrap them at her house one day while she stayed out of the room so her gift would be a surprise.

I joined Mrs. Dawson for Christmas, and Jerry came over too. He said that Hank sent his best and hoped he could join me next time. We exchanged gifts and had dinner. Jerry took Hank a plate of turkey, dressing, giblet gravy, mashed potatoes, corn, green beans, two deviled eggs and some cranberry sauce. It was quite a feast.

I was given new clothes from Sears instead of Goodwill, a baseball glove, and a large candy cane. Hank gave me a sleeping bag and sent along a box of dog biscuits for Bones, who came with me to Mrs. Dawson's. It was a great party and I hated to see it end.

As we ate, it occurred to me that Jerry and Mrs. Dawson were both single, but they didn't act like more than friends. Still, I thought they made a nice couple and told them so. They laughed so hard it embarrassed me, but they assured me it was okay. They explained they were just friends and always would be.

"I'd never want another man sleeping in my bed every night if my life depended on it!" Mrs. Dawson said, laughing loudly.

I walked home hoping Hank would be free of this mess soon. His trial was scheduled to start in a few weeks, and I was both looking forward to it and dreading it. When Bones and I reached home, we went to bed. My parents were already passed out, so I allowed Bones to sleep with me instead of outside since it was Christmas. I had been bringing him inside once in a while for several weeks now, ever since Halloween when the kids walking around in creepy costumes made him a little crazy, and now he slept in my room nearly as often as he slept outside.

The weeks leading up to the trial were also busy for me. I was deposed by the prosecution to find out what I would say in the trial if they called me. I told them everything, leaving nothing out except how Hank had paid my salary when I worked for Mrs. Dawson. The prosecution decided it would not call me as a witness, but the Sheltons planned to, and they discussed with me how the prosecutor would attack my story as being coerced by Hank.

"I'm sure he can't wait to cross-examine you," Mr. Shelton said. "He thinks he can make it look as though you're being intimidated by Hank, even if you don't admit it. In fact, he's thinking if you continue to deny it, that will help his case."

"If my testimony doesn't help Hank, why am I testifying?" I asked.

"Because I intend to make sure the jury sees through his ploy, and besides I didn't say your testimony won't help Hank. It will, but the cross-examination will help him even more if we handle it right. I'm going to allow the prosecutor to browbeat you to a point. That will make him look like a bully to the jury. I know Joshua Metz, the assistant district attorney who's prosecuting the case. He has a history of going after defense witnesses with both barrels. He'll work so hard trying to get you to admit Hank is intimidating you that the jury won't like him, and juries often allow such feelings to influence their deliberations. Not only that, but you also have an honest look about you. When you tell the truth, it sounds like the truth and looks like the truth. Fact is, I wish I had as strong a witness as you for all my cases.

"Also, Josh knows he has a weak case, but word is he was forced to take it to trial anyway because politics are involved here. Unfortunately, he has to proceed because the district attorney insists on it."

"How is the case weak?" I asked.

"Easy," said Mrs. Shelton. "First, you're the victim in the case, yet you're testifying for the defense. Not only that, but they have no solid evidence that Hank ever did anything to you in the first place. Josh has two boys who claim they saw things happening, but we think we'll be able to create doubt regarding their testimony."

"Then, why are they going ahead with the trial? That doesn't make sense," I said.

Mr. Shelton said, "The truth is they have to for political reasons. If the DA didn't prosecute this, the people would think Hank or his family had pulled some strings to make the charges go away. And people are starting to view this type of crime much more harshly than in the past. It used to be people would say, 'Well, that's just the way he is' and leave it at that. Now, though, they realize the damage it does to children, so they go after the people who do those things."

"And they should," Mrs. Shelton said. I looked at her because she sounded angry. She took a breath and let it out slowly. "Unfortunately, though, when charges like this are made against someone who did nothing, the DA has no choice but to take it to trial unless they find clear evidence the suspect couldn't have done it."

"Don't worry," Mr. Shelton said. "We've found out a few things that will make the jury question whether or not it happened, in addition to your testimony."

I asked what they knew, but they wouldn't share it with me. They seemed confident, but I wasn't so sure. Still, I figured Mr. and Mrs. Shelton knew what they were doing. They had a reputation as the best defense attorneys around, and they didn't earn that name for no reason.

Another thing that happened that caused a stir in the community was the death of Mr. David Moreland, Hank's father. He apparently died in his sleep, and his girlfriend at the time was arrested for taking his Rolex watch before leaving the house after waking next to a dead man. Thinking of spending the night sleeping beside a corpse gave me the creeps, and I wondered what kind of person would steal a watch from a dead man. Later, when I asked Mrs. Dawson that question, she answered, "Easy. The same kind of person who would steal a watch from a live one."

The day the trial began, I didn't go to school. I knew nobody would care, but I also had a subpoena from the Sheltons, compelling me to be there. The trial itself was being held in a courthouse annex in Denton, only about a mile or so from my house.

I was scheduled to be a witness for the defense, so I didn't need to be there at the start of the trial since the defense went last, but I was there anyway. I wanted to be there for Hank, and in my preparation with Mr. and Mrs. Shelton, they thought it would look good if I was sitting behind Hank in the courtroom.

That was when I found out Mr. Metz might want me sequestered. Mr. Shelton said either side could request a witness not be allowed to be in the courtroom during the trial. Still, they wanted me behind Hank, but not at the start of the trial. On that day, they wanted me seated behind the prosecution's table. This increased the likelihood Mr. Metz would allow me to remain in the courtroom. The Sheltons said it would also serve the prosecution if the jury saw them as allowing me to be there. Mrs. Shelton said it was 50-50 that they would want me sequestered, so I kept my fingers crossed that I would be allowed to stay. According to her, if Mr. Metz wanted me out of the courtroom, they could do nothing to keep me there. "Objections are generally not made in those situations because they'd be overruled anyway," she said. "But keep in mind that it goes both ways. We can request it for a prosecution witness, too."

The trial began in mid-March, and Jerry gave me time off to attend. I wasn't in court for jury selection, but when we went in for the trial to start, I saw the jury for the first time. I didn't recognize any of them and found out later they had all been chosen from addresses in Wharton, since everyone in Denton was considered too close to the case and the people involved.

The judge didn't come into the courtroom until nearly ten o'clock that morning. After the jury was seated, each attorney was asked for opening comments.

Prior to the start of the trial, however, the judge noticed I was in the courtroom and asked the prosecutor if he wanted me sequestered. I was seated four or five rows behind the prosecution's table. Mr. Metz looked at me, raised his eyebrows and said, "That won't be necessary, Your Honor. He knows what will be said, and it might help him accept what happened if he hears the truth." I hated that he'd called a lie the truth, but I still rejoiced inside. I would sit behind the defense table, where I would feel more comfortable, after lunch.

Mr. Joshua Metz was a tall man with stern eyes. I saw him smile only once the entire trial. He wore a three-piece suit of light blue, with a red tie. His shirt was so white it seemed to glow, but he looked angry all the time. His brow seemed permanently pinched as if he were always thinking hard about something. If he did browbeat me, he would indeed look like a bully.

Mr. Metz rose and addressed the jury, explaining what the prosecution intended to prove, which was that the defendant, Mr. Henry Pittman, had taken indecent liberties with a minor. He said the prosecution would introduce witnesses who would place the victim with Mr. Pittman alone for hours at a time in the broken-down school bus Mr. Pittman lived in, and they would produce witnesses who would claim to have witnessed a disgusting interaction between Mr. Pittman and the victim. He told the jurors that a man who was in a cell with the accused would testify that Mr. Pittman admitted his actions out of regret, a lie I'd not heard before. I felt strange being referred to as "the victim" like that. I wasn't a victim at all.

Next, Mrs. Shelton stood. She would be giving the opening and closing arguments, something she explained had a psychological edge since because she was a woman. The belief was that a woman would normally be so disgusted by the charges she wouldn't stand in defense of someone who had done the things Hank was charged with.

She addressed the jury and was the total opposite of Mr. Metz, who sounded more like a teacher giving a lecture. Mrs. Shelton was friendly and talked to the jury the way she might talk to her best friend. I watched the jurors as she spoke to them, and I could tell they liked her, perhaps for no other reason than she was less stern than Mr. Metz. She said the actions the defendant was charged with had been fabricated out of gossip. She talked about gossips with lewd thoughts and juveniles whose word couldn't be trusted. Mr. Metz objected twice to her opening, saying she was testifying, but the judge overruled him both times. She closed with the news that the so-called victim was not going to testify for the prosecution, but for the defense, and that the young man understood the meaning of swearing an oath to tell the truth. She said that contrary to the prosecution's depiction of the relationship as one of disgusting acts, it was really one of a young boy in need of guidance and an older man willing to give that guidance out of love, but not the kind of love the defendant was charged with providing.

By the time she was finished, it was nearly noon, and the judge called a recess for lunch. I wanted to talk to Hank or the Sheltons, but as I walked toward them, Mrs. Shelton shook her head slightly, indicating I should not approach them right then. I was unhappy about this but could do nothing about it. I left the courthouse and went home for lunch. The first witness for the prosecution would be called at 1:30, which gave me a little over an hour for lunch before I had to be back in the courthouse annex, this time seated behind the defense table.

I took my seat just a few minutes before the first witness was called. Hank turned toward me and said the first things he had said to me in months. "We're gonna win this." He had a lot of confidence. Either that or he was just trying to ease my anxiety. I hoped he was right. I looked forward to having coffee with him again.

Court was called into session, and Mr. Metz was told to bring in his first witness.

Mr. Metz called Mrs. Polk as his first witness. She strode up to the stand and was sworn in. She wore a dress I'd never seen before. It looked like something she would wear to church. Normally, she was a bit haphazard in her dress and wore no makeup other than lipstick. Now she looked like Denton's most upstanding citizen. I couldn't help picturing her sitting in Kirby's, almost too drunk to walk, and I wondered if I would be able to speak of that image when I testified.

After giving her name and address, the questions began.

"Mrs. Polk, thank you for being here today. I know your work at the school is important to you and the community," Mr. Metz said. I wondered why he would say something like that since plenty of people could take over when she was absent from work.

"Thank you," she said. "But I see this as an even bigger duty."

"Mrs. Polk, do you know Jack Turner, the victim of Mr. Pittman's crime?"

Mr. Shelton was on his feet. "Objection, Your Honor. Until Mr. Metz proves guilt, the defendant is presumed innocent of any crimes."

"Sorry, Your Honor. I'll rephrase," Mr. Metz said, asking the question again, inserting *alleged* with mocking emphasis.

"Yes, I do. He's a student at Denton School where I work."

"Were you ever in a situation in which you worried about him?"

"Several times. Yes."

"Could you tell us about a time you worried about his welfare?"

I wondered why Mr. Metz didn't just come out and ask when she suspected I was being abused, but Mr. Shelton later told me he was trying to make it appear she worried about me a lot over various things.

"It was last summer. I was strolling down to

the Seaside Restaurant near the docks. I was going there to have coffee with a friend, and I noticed Jack going into the dilapidated eye-sore of a school bus down there with an older man."

"Is that older man in the courtroom?"

"Yes, he's the defendant, Henry Pittman."

"Go on," Mr. Metz said. "You say you saw them entering the bus?"

"Yes. I wondered about it at the time. I mean, Jack was just twelve, and Mr. Pittman is in his fifties. The bus door closed and I decided to keep an eye out to see how long they were in there. I chose a table at Seaside that allowed me to watch the bus. I ordered my coffee and my friend arrived. She ordered coffee as well, and I told her about what I saw and how suspicious it all looked. I mean, what in the world would a grown man be doing with a young boy in a bus with all the windows covered?"

"You noticed the windows were covered?" Mr. Metz asked.

"Yes. It was one of the biggest things that bothered me about it. Nobody could see inside that bus, and anything could be going on in there."

"Okay, go on," Mr. Metz said.

"Well, my friend Hilda said, 'Maybe they're having fun.' But she said "fun" in a way that suggested a lot more than playing Monopoly or something. Anyway, I told her that was exactly what I was thinking. By this time, they had been in there for over a half hour. I said to Hilda, 'What else could they be doing in there for so long?' and she agreed."

"And how long was it before they came out of the bus?"

"They were in there for over an hour!" she said, suggesting that being alone together proved we were up to no good. Her gaze swept the jury as if they were already on her side. By the looks of them, they were.

"Was there another time you thought Mr. Pittman was doing things he shouldn't be doing with Jack?" Mr. Metz asked.

"Yes! I began to make sure I was at the Seaside every morning just to watch and see. It seemed every day they were going inside that bus to be alone together, or Jack would arrive and go in. Each time they were in there for at least a half hour, usually more."

I resented how she characterized how we were going into the bus to be alone, rather than to just be indoors out of the sun. She was seeing us either as I arrived to have coffee and talk with Hank, or when we'd been outside working or something and went in for something to eat or drink.

"Did you ever speak to Mr. Pittman about any of this?"

"As a matter of fact, I did," Mrs. Polk said. "One night I was walking past Kirby's and saw him through the front window inside drinking a beer. I decided it was high time someone said something to him about what he was doing. Let him know he wasn't getting away with it like he thought. I spoke to him about it, and he said for me to mind my own business. I could see the fear in his eyes, though. I scared him plenty because he knew he'd be in court soon trying to defend his actions." I knew she was lying, unless she was referring to that time when she spoke to Hank when she was drunk. I noticed, though, she didn't tell the jury she was drunk.

"And what happened then?" Mr. Metz asked.

"Well, they were still meeting with each other. Jack would stop by in the mornings, and they'd be inside for a long time, at least a half hour."

"At what point did you decide to go to the police?"

"When I realized letting him know that I knew what was going on wasn't going to make him stop. I marched myself right down to the police station and told them what I'd been seeing. And they were plenty concerned, believe you, me!"

"Thank you, Mrs. Polk. I'm sure we all get the picture." Mr. Metz sat in his seat, glancing at the Sheltons and saying, "Your witness."

Mrs. Shelton rose and walked to the small lectern where the attorneys would stand to question witnesses. She thanked Mrs. Polk for being there as well, but that's where the pleasantries ended.

"Mrs. Polk," Mrs. Shelton said, glancing at her legal pad, "in all these times you were watching the bus while Mr. Pittman and Jack were inside, did you ever see them doing anything illegal or immoral?"

"What do you mean?" Mrs. Polk asked.

"I mean, did you ever see anything such as Mr. Pittman touching Jack inappropriately? Did you see them doing any of the things you suspected they were doing inside the bus?"

"Of course not," she said, "the bus's windows were covered so nobody could see in. I said that before."

"So, you never actually saw a crime being committed, is that right?"

"Well, what else were they doing in there?" Mrs. Polk asked.

"Perhaps the same thing you were doing? Having a cup or two of coffee and talking like friends?"

"Jack was just twelve years old. Why on earth would that man want to spend that much time talking to him? He recognized that Jack was a needy child and took advantage of it."

"Are you a mind reader, Mrs. Polk?"

Mr. Metz started to stand and object, but Mrs. Polk answered before he could. "Don't be ridiculous. Of course not."

"Well, you certainly seem to be acting as if you

are. You claim to know what was going on in Mr. Pittman's mind."

"I know what was going on in that bus!"

"Mrs. Polk, you have accused Mr. Pittman of a heinous crime. Don't you think you should have had something more than easily explained suspicions before going to the police?"

"Hank wasn't doing anything to stop what was going on! Someone had to stop him!" Mrs. Polk's face was turning a bright red.

"Hank?" Mrs. Shelton said. "So, you knew him well enough that you called him by the name his friends call him?"

Mrs. Polk froze on the stand, seeming to turn into a statue.

"I've known him for a while, yes," she finally said.

"For a long time, actually, correct?"

"Well, yes," Mrs. Polk said. I decided Mrs. Shelton knew something, but I didn't know what it was.

"Isn't it true that you once dated Mr. Pittman? Hank, as you call him?"

"Did Hank tell you that?" Mrs. Polk said.

"I'll ask the questions, if you don't mind, Mrs. Polk. Shall I repeat the question?"

"No, that won't be necessary."

"So what is your answer? And may I remind you that you're under oath?"

Mrs. Polk glanced over at Mr. Metz, who was sitting forward in his chair. This was evidently news to him as well, and he didn't like it. For a moment, Mrs. Polk remained silent.

"Mrs. Polk?" Mrs. Shelton prodded.

"Yes, we dated for a while," Mrs. Polk answered, though it was clear she didn't want to. I wondered why she wouldn't have realized Hank would mention that to his attorneys, though I wasn't sure how that would affect her testimony.

"Isn't it true you wanted more of a relationship with Mr. Pittman?" Mrs. Shelton asked before correcting herself. "Hank?"

"That's my business!" said Mrs. Polk.

"No, Mrs. Polk, I'm afraid if you come into court leveling charges against a man who spurned you, it becomes the court's business," Mrs. Shelton said. I couldn't see Mrs. Shelton's face, but from behind, her posture suggested anger, as if fed up with Mrs. Polk and her accusations.

"He didn't *spurn* me!" said Mrs. Polk.

"How many times did the two of you go out?"

"Twice," came the answer.

"Why only twice?"

At that moment, I heard the doors to the courtroom open, and I turned to look, mostly because of the recognition on Mrs. Polk's face upon seeing who it was. An older woman about Mrs. Polk's age was entering and took a seat several rows behind me on the aisle. I looked back at Mrs. Polk. Her formerly red face was now pale.

"Mrs. Polk?" Mrs. Shelton said, once again trying to prompt an answer.

"What?" she said, sounding out of breath.

"Why did you and Mr. Pittman—I mean Hank—go out only twice?"

"He said he didn't want to see me again," she said, her voice low.

"Did you tell any of your friends at the time about the fact the two of you were dating, and your hopes regarding the possible outcome of that relationship?" Mrs. Shelton turned and glanced at the woman who had entered earlier. I turned to look at her again. She was staring at Mrs. Polk, her face grim.

Mrs. Polk seemed to deflate on the stand. She said something, but I couldn't hear her, and I didn't think anyone else could either.

"I'm sorry. Could you speak up?" Mrs. Shelton prompted. I could tell she was enjoying this as much as I was.

"I said, yes. Yes, I did."

"And what did you tell your friends?"

Mrs. Polk stared at Mrs. Shelton with utter hatred. Mrs. Shelton's posture didn't change. She could have been waiting for a table at the Seaside.

"I said I wanted to marry him."

"Isn't it true that after Mr. Pittman broke off

the relationship—if you could call two dates a relationship—that you contacted him numerous times asking him to reconsider?"

Mrs. Polk didn't say anything. She just nodded.

"You'll have to speak your answer, Mrs. Polk. The court reporter can't write down gestures," Mrs. Shelton said.

"Yes."

"And isn't it true you've been stalking Mr. Pittman, waiting for an opportunity to present something to the world that would make it seem you aren't the reason for the breakup? If Mr. Pittman liked young boys, he was the one with the problem, not you? Isn't that the truth, Mrs. Polk?"

"No!" she said. "*That* is not the truth!"

"Are you saying you didn't call at least one friend and say that now you had proof you weren't the problem? That he stopped dating you because you weren't a young boy?"

Mrs. Polk glanced out at the lady who had walked into the courtroom earlier, and I guess she decided enough was enough. She needed to find a way to get off the witness stand. Denying the accusation would only extend her embarrassment.

"Okay! So I wanted to marry him. What does that prove? I'm a widow. I'm allowed to remarry. But it's the truth! I know he molested that boy. He said I was crazy, but now we know, don't we?"

Mrs. Shelton turned to the judge before taking

her seat and said, "I'm finished with this witness, Your Honor."

The judge frowned at Mrs. Polk and said, "The witness is excused."

I grinned as Mrs. Polk left the stand and marched out of the courtroom. She didn't look at me at all. I had never known Hank had dated her, but now she looked to all the world like a vengeful woman, which I suppose she was.

## 20

Mr. Metz brought Officer Hicks to the stand next. After being sworn in, he sat back looking as if he owned the world. I wasn't sure what the jury was seeing, but I saw a bad cop who thought he was better than everyone else. When he was asked to state his full name and address for the record, several jurors tittered at the mention of his first name, Dagwood, causing him to blush. I didn't know if he was embarrassed, angry, or both. He obviously didn't appreciate the laughter. He sat back and tried to look important.

Mr. Metz started by asking if he was one of the arresting officers in the case. Officer Hicks said he was. Then Mr. Metz asked about the arrest. Officer Hicks related the details of the arrest, emphasizing that "the subject was drinking in Kirby's, a local bar he was known to frequent."

"Was Mr. Pittman surprised at the charges?" Mr. Metz asked.

"It didn't look like it," Officer Hicks answered. "In fact, he kind of acted like "well, you caught me.""

Mr. Shelton rose, "Objection, Your Honor. Calls for conclusion. How could he know what my client was thinking?"

"I've arrested lots of people, Judge," Hicks said, "and I know—"

Mr. Shelton interrupted him. "Your Honor! Could you prevent the witness from doing the prosecutor's job by arguing legal points he has no expertise in?"

The judge looked at the witness and said, "Officer Hicks, if I want your input, I will ask for it. The objection is sustained. Jury will disregard the witness's conclusions about what the defendant was thinking."

"Officer Hicks, have you ever arrested someone on these charges before?"

"Once, when I was a policeman in Wharton."

"Was the man found guilty of those charges?"

"Yes."

"Was the victim male or female?"

"Male."

"Did the victim of the man you arrested back then ever admit to what the man did to him?" Mr. Metz asked.

"No, he didn't. The department's psychiatrist said it was because—"

Again, Mr. Shelton was on his feet, interrupting Officer Hicks. "Objection! Hearsay, Your Honor!"

Again, the judge sustained the objection.

Mr. Metz went to his table and lifted a thick book, holding it up for all to see. "Your Honor, I have here a textbook titled *The Role of Denial* by a noted psychiatrist, Dr. Leland Cosgrove, who is also a professor of psychiatry at Duke University. I submit it as State's exhibit A and wish a portion to be read into the record."

Mr. Shelton said, "May we approach the bench, Your Honor?" The judge nodded and waved them up. The Sheltons and Mr. Metz stepped up to the judge's bench and had a brief discussion. A few minutes later, they returned to their tables, and the judge announced the textbook would be allowed.

Mr. Metz asked, "Approach the witness, Your Honor?" The judge waved him up and Mr. Metz handed the opened book to Officer Hicks.

"Would you read the highlighted section, Officer Hicks?"

Hicks blushed before struggling to read the information Mr. Metz wanted entered into the record. "It is . . . sig-ni-fi-cant . . . that victims occasionally deny their own role in being . . . victimized. This stems from the fact that to admit they were victimized often leads to self-doubt and feelings of emotional—" He glanced at Mr. Metz before looking back at the book.

Squinting at the next word, obviously trying to figure out what it was, he quickly realized he had no idea and held the book up to the judge. Judge Franklin peered through his bifocals, scowled at Officer Hicks, and said, "inadequacy."

Officer Hicks continued as if nothing had happened, "inadequacy. They fear that the . . . victim-ization . . . will result in becoming lifelong victims of the . . . ma-ni-pu-lations . . . of others."

Mr. Metz sighed and took the book from Officer Hicks before handing it to Mr. Shelton, who passed it to Mrs. Shelton. She began poring over it while Mr. Metz continued his questions, paying no attention to the Shelton's.

"Is it your opinion as a member of the law enforcement community that victims of crimes sometimes deny they are victims?"

"Yeah, it happens more often than people think," said Officer Hicks.

"And would you say that the victims you have encountered were more likely or less likely to deny being a victim the more embarrassing the activity was that they were victims of?" asked Mr. Metz.

"Oh, more likely."

"Did Jack Turner, the victim in this case, admit to being victimized by Mr. Pittman when he was brought in for questioning?"

"No, he denied it completely. Still does." Officer Hicks looked at me. "I feel sorry for the kid."

I shook my head in disbelief.

Mr. Metz sat in his chair, and turning to Mr. and Mrs. Shelton, said, "Your witness."

Mr. Shelton stood. "Good afternoon, Officer Hicks. Thank you for being here today. Are you acquainted with the alleged victim, Jack Turner?"

"Sure. I've seen him around."

"Have you ever shown any animosity towards him?"

"What d'ya mean?"

"I mean, have you ever shown you either dislike or don't trust him?"

Officer Hicks's face showed he knew where this line of questioning was leading. "No."

"Really?" Mr. Shelton said, acting surprised at the answer. "Did you investigate a reported car theft at the home of Mrs. Mary Jane Dawson where Jack Turner was working as a gardener?"

"Yeah."

"While there, did you suggest to Mrs. Dawson that Jack might have something to do with the car's disappearance?"

"It turns out he didn't," Officer Hicks said.

"Yes, I know," Mr. Shelton said. "I believe it turned out that for the twenty-four hours between the time Mrs. Dawson spoke to you initially and her remembering where she left it that the car had sat parked on the street in front of the police station, correct?"

Some members of the jury chuckled, but a few laughed outright, not attempting to hide their reaction to such incompetence. Officer Hicks turned red again while the judge banged his gavel and asked for quiet, while Officer Hicks glared at Mr. Shelton.

"Yeah," he said, his tone suggesting he was not happy that where the car had been found had been made public.

"But I repeat, did you initially suggest to Mrs. Dawson that Jack may have something to do with her car's disappearance?"

"Well, he'd just been hired to do her lawn and garden work. It would only be natural to suspect he may have had something to do with it." Officer Hicks glanced my way and turned back.

"What was Mrs. Dawson's reaction to your suspicions?"

Officer Hicks squirmed in his chair some before saying, "She didn't agree with me."

"And it turned out she was correct and you were wrong, is that right?"

The answer had been made clear already, but it seemed that Mr. Shelton was pouring salt on the wound by reminding everyone of where the car had been.

"Yeah, that's right." His squirming in his seat made it obvious Officer Hicks wanted to move on to another topic.

"And early last fall, did you investigate a shoplifting incident at Moreland docks in which Jack was involved as the employee reporting the shoplifting?"

Mr. Metz rose. "Your Honor, I have to object to this entire line of questioning. What does this have to do with the case?"

Mr. Shelton spoke up in response. "Your Honor, Mr. Metz established that the witness feels sorry for Jack Turner, and the witness seemed to suggest in his answers that he likes Jack. We disagree and believe his feelings are influencing his testimony. Mr. Metz opened this door. We're just walking through it."

"He has a point, Josh," said the judge. "Overruled."

"Thank you, Your Honor," Mr. Shelton said and repeated the question.

"Yeah, he reported an *alleged* incident of shoplifting," he said before adding, "which proved not to be true!" Officer Hicks glared at me, seeming to accuse me of filing a false report or perhaps stealing the rods and reels myself.

Mrs. Shelton stopped poring over the textbook that Mr. Metz had introduced as evidence to look up when Officer Hicks said that last part, and she smiled. I realized why she liked the officer's last statement. His entire demeanor suggested hatred. She glanced at me and smiled before turning to Hank and whispering something, which made Hank chuckle. Officer Hicks was watching and noticed the exchange.

"Did your response to the shoplifting end up with Jerry Moreland, the shop's owner, calling the police department yet again about the same incident and getting a detective to come investigate what you had dismissed as unworthy of investigation?"

"Well, first of all, I said the shoplifting proved not to be true, so according to your own words earlier, it's only *alleged*. Second, yeah, they did call and waste the time of one of our busiest detectives with their claims my brother and his friend—who will both be testifying against Mr. Pittman—stole two rods and reels."

His anger was starting to get the better of him, and I wondered if this was what Mr. Shelton wanted. He certainly didn't need one of Denton's cops angry at him. I was evidence of that. Still, he kept needling Officer Hicks as if trying to make him mad.

"Your brother, then, was one of the *alleged* shoplifters?"

Later, Mr. Shelton told me he couldn't bring up the point that Carl Hicks was one of the people I had accused of shoplifting because, as Officer Hicks had said, the shoplifting had never been proved. He was delighted that Hicks himself had mentioned it.

"Yeah. Jack has it in for him because of the testimony he plans to give to hang your client and because of a fight that happened between him and my brother last summer when my brother beat him up."

"That would be the time Jack undercut your brother's price for cleaning fish?"

"Yeah. That's the time."

"The same incident in which your brother, who is bigger and a year older than Jack, enlisted the assistance of six other older boys to beat up Jack?"

"Objection, Your Honor!" Mr. Metz said, rising from his seat.

"Withdrawn," Mr. Shelton said.

I looked at the jury, and their demeanor had changed. They obviously didn't like Officer Hicks, and they were already set up to dislike Carl.

"We're through with this witness," Mr. Shelton said, and Officer Hicks was dismissed.

I again took pleasure in watching one of the prosecution's witnesses walk out of the courtroom angry and humiliated. He glanced at me as if promising revenge and stomped toward the exit. When he reached it, he grabbed the door handle and swung the door open so hard it slammed against the door-stop on the wall, startling everyone in the courtroom.

Mr. Metz called the detective who had questioned me to the stand and asked about my interrogation where I refused to say anything against Hank. The detective basically told exactly what happened. Then, Mr. Metz asked the detective if he had encountered victims unwilling to admit they were sexually assaulted, and he said he had. The Sheltons had no questions for him.

The next witness surprised me. It wasn't anyone I knew. The bailiff called out his name, Vincent Morgan, and a short, wiry man strode to the stand. He had tattoos on his forearms and almost no chin. His black hair fell down his neck in waves. His eyes seemed too large for his face, and I was reminded of a villain I'd seen in a movie.

Once he was sworn in and stated his name and address for the record, Mr. Metz started right in.

"Mr. Morgan, are you acquainted with the defendant?"

"A little."

"And how do you know him?"

"We was cellmates at the county lockup for a spell."

"Did you ever engage in a conversation with the defendant?"

"Sure did. He was a real talker. Talked too much in fact. I was wantin' to get some shut-eye and he was still talkin'."

"And what did he talk about?" Mr. Metz asked.

"What he done to that boy mostly. He seemed proud of it. Wanted to brag about it, 's how it seemed to me. I just wanted him to shut up. It was sick stuff."

"And what, exactly did he say?" Mr. Metz, said.

At that point, the judge stopped the proceedings.

"Mr. Metz, do you intend to have your witness give details about what he claims Mr. Pittman told him?"

"Yes, Your Honor. We believe the jury needs to hear exactly what Mr. Pittman is accused of doing."

Mr. Shelton rose, his face set in a frown. "Your Honor, we wish to once again object to this as prejudicial."

"So noted, but once again your objection is overruled. However, I am inclined to clear the courtroom of minors."

Mr. Shelton looked around at me, smiled oddly, and turned back to the judge. I wasn't sure what he was thinking.

"We agree, Your Honor. I don't think Jack or any child should be forced to listen to this, even if it's fiction."

"Objection, Your Honor," Mr. Metz said. "Defense shouldn't attempt to prejudice the jury by referring to Mr. Morgan's testimony as fiction."

"Sustained. Do you have an objection to clearing the court of any minors, Mr. Metz?" the judge said.

"No, Your Honor. We heartily agree, in fact. Mr. Morgan's testimony is likely to become rather detailed." Mr. Metz was tapped on the arm by his assistant and leaned down to listen.

I looked around. I was the only minor there, and I thought it was silly for them to behave as if dozens of us were scattered around the courtroom. I also thought it strange that if these things were supposedly done to me, why would they be trying to protect me from the details. Apparently, this had occurred to Mr. Metz's assistant because Mr. Metz, after listening to his assistant, said, "Then again, Your Honor, Jack was there when it happened."

Mr. Shelton spoke up. "Excuse me, Your Honor. I believe we're in this courtroom to make that determination. It's the defense's contention nothing happened at all and this is just the result of vindictiveness by a few people."

"We know your contention," Mr. Metz said, and the judge banged his gavel as a murmur started among the spectators.

"Counsel will address the bench instead of each other," he said. Looking directly at me, he said, "Young man, I'm afraid we're going to have to ask you to leave until Mr. Morgan's description of what he says he was told by Mr. Pittman is finished."

I stood to leave but stopped. Turning back to the judge, I asked, "Can I come back when he's finished with all the dirty talk?" A smattering of laughter rippled through the courtroom.

"Yes," the judge said, smiling at me. "I'll even have the deputy in back get you if you like."

"That would be fine. Thank you," I said. I could tell that Mr. and Mrs. Shelton wanted me out for this part of the trial for their own reasons, and I was happy to comply with their wishes.

I sat alone outside the courtroom for nearly a half hour, rehashing what had gone on so far in my mind. Finally, the deputy who was stationed at the back of the courtroom stuck his head out and said, "Judge Franklin says you can come back in now."

When I entered and took my seat, Mr. Shelton was cross-examining Mr. Morgan. He seemed well into his questioning, so I figured he had finished with any of the questions regarding the man's lies about what Hank said to him.

"Mr. Morgan, you say you were in jail with Mr. Pittman?"

"Yep."

"On what charge?"

"Drunk and disorderly."

"And this was your first night in the jail following that arrest?"

"Sure was."

"How much did you have to drink?"

"A lot."

"Did you go to court on those charges?"

"Yep."

"Were you found guilty?"

"I was, but the disorderly part was trumped up charges."

"Did they do a blood alcohol reading on you the night in question?"

"Yeah, they did. I was drunk. I don't deny that. It's the disorderly part that ain't right."

"Okay, fair enough," Mr. Shelton said. "And do you recall your blood alcohol reading?"

"Nope. It was pretty high though. I'd been celebratin' my divorce." Again, he laughed, a high-pitched giggle that irritated me. I could tell the jurors didn't like his laugh either. Some of them squirmed uncomfortably.

"Would you be surprised to learn you blew a .19, just a shade less than double the amount needed to be charged with public drunkenness?"

"Nope, not a bit." He grinned at the jury, as if they all enjoyed getting that drunk. They just stared back at him.

"Are you also aware that when a person is that intoxicated, he has a distorted perception of his surroundings and the events taking place?"

"What?" he asked. It was obvious from the look on his face he had not understood what Mr. Shelton said.

"In other words, you were so drunk you would have trouble carrying on a coherent conversation."

"Co—" Mr. Morgan said, trying to understand what Mr. Shelton meant by *coherent*.

"Coherent. It means you would have had trouble understanding everything that was said to you by anyone. In fact, I have your arrest record for that night." Mr. Shelton looked at the judge. "Your Honor, we would like to enter this arrest record into evidence as defense exhibit A."

He handed the paper to Mr. Metz who looked at it and handed it back, a glum look on his face. "No objections," Mr. Metz said.

Mr. Shelton brought a copy to the judge, who looked at it and said, "Continue."

"Mr. Morgan, your arrest record states, 'The prisoner kept falling over so that he had to be seated to avoid injuring himself. He made several attempts to stand, falling over twice. He was handcuffed to his seat to prevent injury.' Do you recall any of that?"

Mr. Morgan looked at Mr. Shelton, a puzzled look on his face. "Not exactly."

"Do you honestly expect us to believe you were able to have a detailed conversation with Mr. Pittman and remember it well enough to come in here and swear to its accuracy? Are you sure you didn't dream this took place? Are you even certain that a conversation took place between the two of you at all?"

"Yeah, we talked. He told me about what he did."

Mr. Shelton changed tactics. "Mr. Morgan, have you ever been a witness for the prosecution in a trial before?"

Mr. Morgan considered Mr. Shelton with suspicion, and his eyes narrowed until he was almost squinting at him. "Maybe."

"It's a simple question. Either you have or you haven't. Which is it?"

I suppose guessing Mr. Shelton had proof, he admitted it. "Yeah." He wasn't behaving as smugly as he had before, and his irritating giggles were gone.

"Were you ever offered anything in return for that testimony?"

He looked at Mr. Metz, who was ignoring him. I guess the prosecutor was seeing his case go up in smoke.

"No," Mr. Morgan answered, but even I could tell he was lying.

"How many times have you testified in a trial for the prosecution prior to today?" Mr. Shelton asked.

"Don't remember," he said, which was odd for someone who apparently remembered an entire conversation he'd had when he was dead drunk.

"I have that information right here," Mr.

Shelton said, picking up a piece of paper and looking at it as if he didn't know exactly what was written there. "Three times, Mr. Morgan. This makes four. I just thought I'd mention it in case it ever comes up in a trial again when you're testifying for the prosecution."

"Objection," Mr. Metz said, but I could tell his heart wasn't in it.

"Sustained. The jury will disregard everything after 'this makes four,'" Judge Franklin said.

"We're through with this witness, Your Honor," Mr. Shelton said, shaking his head as he sat, as if disappointed this was the best Mr. Metz could do. Then he leaned over to whisper something to Hank.

I wondered if Mr. Metz had been aware of Mr. Morgan's past court testimony, or even his arrest record for that night, and I decided the state attorney's office was about as incompetent as Officer Hicks. They'd brought a case to trial without any other evidence so far than the say-so of a spurned woman, the accusations of a vindictive and angry policeman, and a professional jailhouse snitch. I wondered what the testimony of Tommy and Carl would bring.

As it turned out, I wouldn't know until the next day, though. The judge called a recess until the following morning. I wanted to talk to Hank but knew the Sheltons wouldn't let me, so I just caught his eye and gave him a thumbs-up and a smile. I wouldn't be surprised if the state withdrew the charges by the next morning.

21

As I walked home, I thought about all that had happened. Mrs. Shelton had spoken to me before I left and told me the case wasn't over yet, and I should not get overconfident. Still, I didn't think it could have gone better and told her so. She said, "It went well, but I've seen juries convict despite days like this for the prosecution."

When I arrived home, I found some hot dogs in the refrigerator and fixed myself two of them. I had to pinch off some mold on the buns, but that was fine. At least the wieners were fresh. After I ate, I went outside and fed Bones, sitting with him and petting him while he ate. It would be a warm, clear night, so I decided to sleep outside with him. I went inside to get a pillow and the sleeping bag Hank gave me for Christmas. Bones wagged his tail, and I sat beside him and started telling him what happened that day in court.

Sunset was getting later so it was still light when I saw Lee and Roger walking down the street. I called them over. They knew I was at the trial while they were in school and wanted to know what happened. They had been at the park throwing a football around and were headed home.

"It's been a great day for Hank," I said. "The Sheltons made the prosecution witnesses look like idiots." I told them all about the day and they smiled, especially at the part where Mrs. Polk was made to look like she was getting back at Hank for dumping her after only two dates.

"They're pretty good lawyers," Roger said. "My dad said they're the best."

"Yeah," I said. "But Mrs. Shelton told me not to get my hopes up, but I can't help but do that. I mean, it went so great today."

Lee said, "I came by to let you know some of my folks' friends came over to our house last night. They asked me about you, saying they felt bad for you and what Hank did to you. I told them Hank didn't do anything, but they looked like they didn't believe me. They said sometimes kids won't say what happened to them."

"Well, I'd tell you guys if he ever did anything like that to me," I said. Hank loved me like the grandfather I never had, and Mrs. Dawson was like a grandmother to me.

"Well, I just wanted to tell you what they said. They think he's guilty as sin," Lee said.

I looked over at Roger, who looked worried. "What about you?" I asked. "Have you heard anything?"

"Well, I was in Grayson's the other day, and I saw Mrs. Woodruff in there talking to Mrs. Polk. I hid behind a display and listened. Mrs. Polk was going on about how Hank would finally get what he deserves, but what would you expect?"

We chatted a little more and they left to go home after dusk turned into night. I lay down in my sleeping bag beside Bones and was soon asleep. My wind-up alarm clock went off at seven the next morning. Although I had slept outside, I thought it was my best night's sleep in a while.

I went inside, where I took a bath and dressed in my newest clothes, the ones Mrs. Dawson had given me for Christmas. After feeding Bones, I fixed myself some coffee and ate some cereal. Finally, I started walking to the courthouse. I hoped I would be able to testify today. After what happened yesterday, I was starting to look forward to it.

As I arrived, I saw that the parking lot was filling. That had not been the case yesterday, and I wondered if news had spread about the trial, and people were curious to see what might happen today. I hoped this was good news for Hank as far as public opinion went. Of course, public opinion didn't change the jury's decisions.

When I walked into the courtroom, I nearly fell over. It wasn't packed yet, but it was certainly getting there. I looked at the defense table and saw the Sheltons there with Hank. As I approached, I saw that the Sheltons had put a legal pad with the word "RESERVED" on the top sheet in a seat behind them. I smiled at that, and Mrs. Shelton grinned at me. "Can't lose our lucky charm!" she said. I took my seat and waited for the second day of Hank's trial to start.

A man came out through a door behind the judge's bench and walked over to the Sheltons. He leaned down and said something I couldn't hear. Mr. Shelton smiled and looked at Mrs. Shelton, saying, "Shall I handle this, or should you?" I wondered what it was they needed to handle. From the look on their faces, they were happy about this and seemed to expect it, and I wondered if the DA was dropping the charges after all.

"You go. I'll stay here with Jack," she said.

Mr. Shelton said something to Hank and they both stood to go into the judge's chambers located behind the bench. I leaned forward to the edge of my seat and asked Mrs. Shelton if she could tell me what was going on.

"We think Mr. Metz is making an offer," she said.

"What kind of offer?"

"Not sure yet. That's what Chuck and Hank are going to find out. My guess is he's offering to reduce the charges, but we won't take a deal. The offer, though, means he's desperate."

While this sounded good, it wasn't what I wanted to happen. I wanted the charges dropped completely.

When Mr. Shelton and Hank returned, they weren't as happy as they were when they'd left. Mr. Shelton, in fact, looked downright upset.

"What is it?" she asked.

"Surprise witness," Mr. Shelton said. I'd seen enough courtroom dramas on TV to know what that meant. A witness for the prosecution had come forward at the last minute to testify against Hank. This wasn't supposed to be allowed, but it happened anyway. "We have twenty-four hours to depose him and prepare our cross."

"Who is it?" Mrs. Shelton asked.

"That's the worst part. It's Hank's older brother, Ted."

I had been leaning in and listening to this and disappointment washed over me. Why would Hank's own brother come forward to testify against him?

"What does he have to say?" I asked.

I looked at Hank, as did his attorneys, waiting for an answer. Hank glanced at me and said to Mr. and Mrs. Shelton, "I'd rather talk about this in private." I knew what he was saying and it crushed me to hear him say it. He didn't want to say whatever it was in front of me.

"The judge is going to grant a continuance until tomorrow to allow us to depose Ted Moreland," Mr. Shelton said.

At that moment, the bailiff entered the courtroom and said, "All rise," and announced the court was in session.

"Be seated," the judge said, and we did. I looked around. Only a few people in the room knew what was about to happen. They'd all come to witness the spectacle, but today they would be disappointed. The trial wasn't going to resume until tomorrow.

"Mr. Metz, you may call your next witness," the judge said.

"The state calls Mr. Theodore Moreland."

An audible gasp ran through the room. The people were obviously shocked that the defendant's brother was testifying for the prosecution. Mr. Shelton stood as if on cue.

"Your Honor, because this witness did not come forward until last night, and we were not informed about him until just a few minutes ago, this is not a witness we were prepared for. We request time to depose the witness in order to prepare a cross-examination."

"Mr. Shelton, I'll give you twenty-four hours. We'll re-convene tomorrow morning at nine." The entire proceeding had a rehearsed quality since it had been done only to get it on the record.

With the bang of the judge's gavel, the day's proceedings were over. I decided my life was over. I still couldn't get over the fact that Hank's own brother had come forward to testify against him. I couldn't even picture a situation that would lead me to testify in court against my brother, and he had more or less abandoned me. He'd been sent to Vietnam, and I wasn't even sure he was alive. Yet here was Hank's brother doing something I could not imagine myself doing.

I left the courtroom in tears, doing my best to hide the fact I was crying. I was thirteen and should be too old to cry at such things, but I couldn't help it.

I walked home and changed out of my best clothes before going down to the docks to talk to Jerry. I wanted to talk to him and see if he knew what this was all about. When I arrived, Jerry was sitting outside in a rocker, drinking a beer and staring out at the Gulf beyond the pass where Denton Bay and the Gulf of Mexico met.

Sitting in the next rocker, I said, "Do you know what your brother Ted is going to say?"

"I have an idea," Jerry said. He sounded as unhappy as I was, and I could tell it was more than an idea. He knew exactly what would be said the next morning in court.

"What?"

"Not sure I should tell you. Hank doesn't want you to know about it."

"I don't care," I said. "I'll be in court tomorrow, and I don't want to hear whatever it is for the first time in front of more than a hundred people."

Jerry thought about that and sighed heavily. "You have a point, I suppose."

"Then tell me."

Jerry continued to stare at the water. The beautiful turquoise-green water reflected the sun, its beauty in contrast to our moods. He took a large swallow of his beer without looking at me and said, "Our wonderful father, may he roast in Hell, was exactly what Hank is accused of being. He did things to my sisters and Hank. I've no idea why he didn't do anything to Ted or me, but he didn't." Jerry turned to me. "And that's not some psychological talk about how people can't admit things like that to anyone. Frankly, I'd rather not be admitting any of this at all. Why Ted is going to is beyond me." I wondered if Ted would be telling this story if his father hadn't died.

"How do you know about this?" I asked.

"Ted caught them together and told me about it when I was older."

"So, what does this have to do with Hank and me?"

"Evidence suggests that people who are abused grow up to be abusers themselves."

"That doesn't mean anything!" I said. "Everybody's different."

"I know, but Josh Metz knows it can help sway a jury if Hank was a victim of abuse."

I sat there thinking about this for a while before it hit me that this was the reason David Moreland's daughters hated him so much. He'd abused them. I thought about how that explained a lot of things I hadn't understood until then.

Rising from my seat, I said, "Well, thanks for telling me. I guess I'll see you tomorrow."

He raised his beer to me as I walked off. Unlike yesterday, when I was looking forward to the start of trial the next day, I dreaded it. I could only hope that Ted's testimony wouldn't do too much damage to Hank's case.

I didn't sleep as well as I had the night before, and the morning felt like a dead body draped over me. I fed Bones but skipped breakfast myself.

Petting him after he finished wolfing down his food, I set off for the courthouse.

The courtroom was packed even fuller than it was the day before. It seemed everyone in town was there to hear what Hank's brother had to say. As I entered, I heard someone say, "If your brother is testifying against you, you have to be guilty." I hoped the jury didn't think that.

I saw that the Sheltons had once again kept my seat for me. I stepped up to them and took my seat. I suppose I looked rather glum because Mrs. Shelton said, "Don't worry. We've scored a lot of points so far with the jury, and we've lined up a rebuttal witness."

I smiled at her just because she was so nice, not so much because her words reassured me. I lived in worry about what would happen to Hank. If he'd done what they accused him of doing, I would be fine with him going to jail, but he hadn't, and I blamed myself because I'd not said something sooner about Mrs. Polk.

When court was called into session, the judge instructed Mr. Metz to call his next witness. Mr. Metz stood and said, "State calls Mr. Theodore Moreland to the stand."

Mr. Ted Moreland looked like an older version of Hank, except Ted was going bald and he had no facial hair. He was also a bit heavier around the middle. Mr. Metz went straight to the point.

"Mr. Moreland, what is your relationship to the defendant?"

"I'm his older brother."

Mr. Metz looked at the jury as if to make sure

they heard that. "Are you aware of anything that happened to the defendant that might have some bearing on this case?"

"Yes," Ted Moreland said.

"And what would that be?"

Mr. Metz sat back and allowed his witness to tell his tale. He didn't relate any graphic details, but he said he had caught his father molesting Hank and his sisters. He said his father threatened him if he ever told. Following a collective gasp by the spectators, as well as the jury, the courtroom grew so quiet I could hear my heartbeat.

Mr. Metz allowed the silence to continue for a moment until he said, "But your father recently passed away, correct?"

"Yes."

Mr. Metz turned to Judge Franklin. "Your Honor, if it please the court, I would like to enter another statement from the textbook by Dr. Cosgrove that was previously accepted as the words of an expert in the field of psychiatry."

"Mr. Shelton?" asked the judge to make sure the defense had no objections.

"No objection, Your Honor."

Mr. Metz took the book to Mr. Ted Moreland and handed it to him, opened to a page. "Would you read the highlighted material, Mr. Moreland?"

Ted Moreland leaned back in his chair and put on his bifocals. "It should be noted that a person who is abused as a child has a much higher chance of becoming an abuser than the rest of the population (see Chart 9.2, page 224). This is due to what can be termed learned behavior. The abused child often learns that being abused is part of growing up, so he is inclined to continue the cycle of abuse once he becomes an adult, despite knowing by then that such actions are wrong."

"What does that mean to you, Mr. Moreland?" Mr. Metz asked.

"Someone who's abused as a child is more likely to abuse someone as an adult."

"Thank you, Mr. Moreland." Mr. Metz turned to the Sheltons. "Your witness."

Mrs. Shelton stood and said, "Mr. Moreland, were you abused as a child?"

"No."

"Why do you think that's so?"

"I don't know. Lucky, I guess."

"What about your youngest brother, Jerry. Was he abused, to your knowledge?"

"No. He's here in the courtroom and could tell you the same thing. We talked about our father's special problem, as we called it, and Jerry told me he had no idea it was going on."

"So just Hank and your sisters were abused?"

"That's right."

"Are you aware of your sisters' viewpoints on child abuse?"

Ted Moreland fidgeted slightly in his seat, before saying, "Yes."

"And what is that viewpoint?"

"Objection," Mr. Metz said. "Hearsay."

"Your Honor, we would be happy to subpoena both sisters. One could be here tomorrow for us to put on the stand."

Mr. Metz considered this briefly before saying, "Objection is withdrawn, Your Honor. No need to bring them into court." He apparently realized for some reason that having a sister testify would be worse than whatever Ted Moreland could say as hearsay.

"Witness will answer," said the judge.

"They are against it. Both my sisters are extremely careful with their children, making sure about who is allowed to be alone with them."

"Would you say the idea of abuse is abhorrent to them?"

Ted Moreland considered the question and said, "Yes."

"Yet, they suffered the same abuse the defendant did, is that correct?"

"Yes."

"And to your knowledge, has either of your sisters abused a child, either her own or someone else's?"

"No. Definitely not."

"Yet, you think your brother is capable of

committing this terrible crime?"

"I—I'm not sure of that. I just thought when I heard about what he'd been charged with it might be a case of the sins of the father passing down to his son."

"Do you have any solid evidence that the defendant ever did anything to a child?"

"No."

"The defendant had a son and a daughter who were killed in an auto accident, correct?"

"Yes."

"When his children were alive, were you ever suspicious that he might be abusing one of them?"

"No."

Mrs. Shelton suddenly changed direction as if her next question was still about Hank's children. "Mr. Moreland, you own quite a bit of property in Denton, is that true?"

"Objection, Your Honor," Mr. Metz said. "How is that relevant?"

"I will show relevance, Your Honor, if I am allowed this question and one more."

"I'll allow it," the judge said, "but be sure you show it."

"I will, Your Honor," Mrs. Shelton said before repeating the question.

"Yes, I do." I could tell Ted Moreland had no idea where this was going, and neither did I. His brow wrinkled as if he was trying to figure it out.

"Is the prosecuting attorney in the process of purchasing seventy-five acres of that land?"

"Objection!" Mr. Metz shouted as he shot to his feet. "That has nothing to do with these proceedings!" Mr. Metz's face was nearly purple with anger.

Mrs. Shelton spoke over the end of Mr. Metz's outburst. "I was just trying to find out why a man who supposedly loves his brother would so casually besmirch his character, Your Honor." She sounded totally innocent, as if she had no idea this would cause such an angry objection from Mr. Metz.

"Sustained!" said the judge, rapping his gavel for a full ten seconds to restore order. "Unless you can show direct evidence that this testimony is part of a deal to purchase land, that is!" Mrs. Shelton looked at the judge, who said, "Well, do you?"

"No, Your Honor."

"Jury will disregard any questions pertaining to land owned by the witness!" the judge said, eyeing Mrs. Shelton, his face pinched in a scowl. "You know better than that, Trisha! You try something like that again, and I'll find you in contempt, not to mention asking if the prosecutor wants me to declare a mistrial."

"My apologies, Your Honor," she said, looking apologetic. "We're finished with Mr. Theodore Moreland."

Ted Moreland stepped down from the witness

stand and left the courtroom, his own face turning red. I noticed that neither he nor Hank looked at each other.

The judge cleared his throat and said, "Call your next witness, Mr. Metz."

"State calls Mr. Thomas Gordon."

Mrs. Shelton stood. "Your Honor, we would like for Mr. Carl Hicks to be sequestered outside the courtroom during Mr. Gordon's testimony."

"So ordered," said the judge, and Carl, looking angry, was escorted out. As she had explained before, objections to such a request were almost never granted, so Mr. Metz didn't even try.

Tommy Gordon strode up the aisle to the witness stand, dressed in a suit that didn't fit him well. He took the oath, but I wondered how much it meant to him. He wasn't a Christian. In fact, he had bragged once how he didn't believe in God at all, so to swear to tell the truth "so help me God" meant nothing.

After taking a seat and giving his name and address, he sat forward in his chair as if hanging on every word Mr. Metz said.

"Mr. Gordon, were you a witness to something that might have some bearing on this case?"

"Yessir, I was."

"Would you tell us about this incident you witnessed?"

"Well, me and Carl Hicks was walking up in

Panther Dunes one time, and we spotted Jack Turner and Hank Pittman skinny-dippin' in Helmer's Creek. We didn't know they was naked at first, but when they come out, we could see they didn't have a stitch on. Anyway, Hank goes up to Jack and, well, started messin' with him. You know, like touchin' him in private areas. Then, well, they did somethin' else." He stopped, and I had the idea this pause was rehearsed.

"You saw them both?"

"Yeah."

"Go on," Mr. Metz said, a confused look on his face for some reason. I focused on Tommy and how he was testifying. He seemed reluctant to say anything that might offend people, which wasn't like him at all. I figured he had been coached on what to say and how to say it. If he tried to keep from being too detailed, he would be seen as a clean-cut kid trying to do the right thing. I longed to tell the jury what a fake performance this was.

I noticed Hank lean over and whisper in Mr. Shelton's ear. Mr. Shelton's face spread into a grin. I didn't know what Hank had said, but Mr. Shelton seemed to love it. He whispered to Hank, and Hank shook his head. Then Mr. Shelton leaned over and whispered to Mrs. Shelton. Her smile beamed.

"Well, uh, he had Jack, um—" Tommy said.

"What did you see the defendant force Jack to do?" Mr. Metz asked.

"Objection to the use of the word 'force,'" Mr. Shelton said.

"Sustained," the judge said. "Rephrase, Mr. Metz."

Mr. Metz said, "What did the defendant do regarding Jack?"

"Well, it didn't look all that forced anyway, but he had Jack, well, he had Jack take him in his mouth."

"Jack performed oral sex on the defendant?"

"Yeah."

I was surprised nobody had asked that I be sequestered for Tommy's testimony, but of course I said nothing. I supposed that Mr. Metz had decided, as he'd said before, that I'd been there and knew what had gone on.

Mr. Metz smiled as he sat. Glancing at the jury, he said to the Sheltons, "Your witness."

Mr. Shelton rose and stepped to the podium to question Tommy. He showed a spring in his step that didn't match the damage Tommy's testimony had done to the defense. "Mr. Gordon, about how far were you and your friend from the defendant and Jack Turner when you saw them swimming?"

Tommy thought for a moment before he responded. "I'd say maybe fifty or sixty foot."

"And you say both the defendant and Jack had taken off all their clothes to swim naked, is that correct?"

Tommy glanced at Mr. Metz before saying, "Yeah. So?"

"Did you see the defendant's backside?"

"His backside?" Tommy asked. "You mean his butt?"

People in the courtroom chuckled before Mr. Shelton smiled and said, "Yes, did you see the defendant's butt?"

"Yeah, I saw it," he said, sounding sure of himself.

"Did you notice anything unusual about it?"

Tommy shrugged. "I didn't pay much attention to it. I mean, it was a guy." Chuckles floated throughout the courtroom again. Tommy shifted in his seat and blushed, and I could tell this line of questioning was making him uncomfortable. Judge Franklin tapped his gavel, and the courtroom grew quiet again.

Mr. Shelton, who had laughed at the comment as well, said, "I understand, but you see, the defendant has something very noticeable in regards to his backside—his butt. You were only fifty feet away and should have seen it. Did you notice it?"

I glanced at Mr. Metz and could see he was wondering where this was going as well. He looked ready to object, but he seemed to be having trouble coming up with a viable reason. He leaned over to speak with his associate, but the associate just shrugged.

Tommy seemed to make a decision and said, "No. I didn't notice it. Like I said, I don't look at guys' butts." This time no chuckles resulted from his words, just tension in the room.

"But you say you did notice he was naked from the waist down and that you saw his backside, or do you want to change your testimony that the defendant was naked?"

"No, he was naked," Tommy said. I wasn't aware of the trap that was being laid, but I could tell one was waiting for him. Tommy looked as if he could tell the same thing, even as dense as he was.

"Yet, you have a clear recognition of seeing his 'butt,' but you didn't notice anything?"

"Objection!" Mr. Metz said, as if thrilled to have a chance to stop this line of questioning, if only for a moment. "Asked and answered."

"Sustained. Move on," the judge said to Mr. Shelton.

Mr. Shelton said, "The defendant, Mr. Pittman, was in the infantry during World War II. He received severe wounds to his 'butt' when he was fighting for our country."

"Objection, Your Honor! Counsel's testifying," Mr. Metz called out from his seat.

"Your Honor, we only today learned that the witness claims to have seen the defendant skinny-dipping. In his deposition, that information was left out. However, we will be happy to provide photographs to be taken during the lunch recess, or the defendant can 'moon' the jury."

"No need for sarcasm, Chuck. You can provide photographic evidence after the lunch break," Judge Franklin said.

Mr. Shelton turned back to Tommy. "So, how is it you saw the defendant's backside yet do not recall seeing what the defendant assures me is a rather gruesome scar due to the fact his left buttock is completely gone?" Mr. Shelton said.

Challenged, Tommy grew red in the face and growled, "I don't know! Maybe there was some trees in the way or somethin'. I don't remember. But they was naked together."

I glanced at the jury, and at least several looked as though they doubted that.

"If trees were in the line of your sight, how could you see Jack performing oral sex?"

"I did!" said Tommy, almost snarling. "We did! You can ask Carl yourself! He was with me."

"I intend to," Mr. Shelton said. Looking at the judge, he said, "We're through with this witness, Your Honor, but may I ask that he not be allowed to see his friend Carl Hicks prior to Carl's testimony? I believe he is the only remaining witness for the prosecution."

Judge Franklin suggested it would be a good time for the lunch break, saying they should stop early to allow Mr. Shelton to get the pictures he needed. Mr. Shelton asked that Carl Hicks be sequestered where nobody could talk to him prior to his taking the stand, even offering to buy Carl's lunch so it could be brought in.

When the judge granted his request, saying the court could afford Carl's lunch, Mr. Metz stood and said, "That won't be necessary, Your Honor. We don't plan to call Mr. Hicks to the stand. The State rests."

Stunned silence filled the courtroom. Everyone stood as the jury was led out and the judge returned to his chambers behind the bench. When Mr. Metz sat back down, he looked drained of energy. I didn't blame him. Tommy's little addition to his deposition had destroyed his case.

22

I was finally allowed to accompany Hank and the Sheltons to lunch. We went to the Seaside *Restaurant*. I had never been inside, let alone eaten there. I looked at the prices and was trying to find the least expensive dish they served, knowing I couldn't afford to eat there.

"What're you going to have, Jack?" Mrs. Shelton asked.

"I was thinking I'd have a grilled cheese sandwich," I said.

She smiled at me and said, "Order what you want, Jack. We're buying."

I loved her smile. It was the most genuine smile I'd ever seen. It lit up her entire face and made her look as though whoever she was talking to was the most important person in the world.

I grinned at her and looked back at the menu. I wouldn't get the most expensive thing on the menu, but I could do better than grilled cheese. Finally, I settled on a fried flounder sandwich with fries and coleslaw. Lee was always talking about how good the flounder sandwiches were at Seaside, and this was my chance to find out. My mouth watered to think of my lunch.

After we ordered, we talked about the case. I was so excited about what had happened that morning, I was nearly coming out of my seat.

"We're going to win, aren't we?" I asked, unable to contain my glee.

Mr. Shelton looked at me and said, "Don't count your chickens before they hatch, Jack." With that, he recounted four cases he was aware of where the jury's verdict was a complete surprise to both sides. I listened carefully, wondering if something like that could happen to Hank.

"I'm not sure about some of the jurors," he continued. "If one of them has a strong personality and is determined to convict, he can persuade the rest to go along."

I looked around the table in disbelief. "You mean after all that evidence that Hank didn't do anything, they might still find him guilty?" This just didn't make sense to me.

"What evidence has proven he didn't do it?" Mr. Shelton said. "All we've really been able to do is question the motives of the witnesses. That's not proof that he didn't do anything."

"But he didn't!" I protested. I noticed several people at the restaurant glancing my way because I was getting too loud. I lowered my voice and repeated, "But he didn't."

Mr. Shelton smiled at me, but it wasn't like Mrs. Shelton's smiles. This one was sadder, as if something bothered him. "I agree with you, but this is all a case of one side saying one thing happened, and another saying something else. Neither side has any rock-solid evidence to support their side of the story."

I considered that and realized he was right. He'd already told me months before that juries are strange beings, like some kind of space alien made up of human brains. Each juror brings his or her life into the jury box. He explained that if any of the jurors had been molested, they would bring that experience with them into the jury room and could decide to convict before the first witness had been called. I asked him at the time if he wouldn't weed those people out of the jury, and he had said he would try, but that jurors tended to hide things like that.

Now, I said to him, "You did more than question Tommy's motives, though. You proved he was lying."

"Maybe, and maybe not," Mr. Shelton said. "He did bring up the idea maybe tree branches were in the way of his seeing the scars, and a juror hell-bent on conviction will take that and run with it. Believe me, I never trust the outcome until the verdict is in." He gave me that same sad smile. "And I know it hurts not to hope too much, but you shouldn't trust the outcome either. It only sets you up for more pain and anger and the bitterness that can follow."

The room seemed to be closing in on me. I had been so sure the trial was going to end in an acquittal, but now I knew it might not, despite how well things had gone for us.

Our lunches arrived, and I found I couldn't eat it. I took a few bites, but I was no longer hungry. What Mr. Shelton had said had upset me that much.

"Now look," Mrs. Shelton said, scolding Mr. Shelton. "You've ruined his appetite."

"I'm sorry. I didn't mean to," Mr. Shelton said, "but he has to be prepared for any verdict. You know that."

"Yes, I know it, but it could have waited until after lunch." After that, Mrs. Shelton tried to get me interested in my meal, but I just wasn't hungry anymore. Finally, she asked for a doggie bag for the food, and Hank took it to his refrigerator when we stopped to get a Polaroid picture of his buttocks.

As we returned to the courthouse, Mr. Shelton asked me if I was nervous about testifying.

"No. I can't wait, in fact," I said.

"Good. Just remember, no matter what Mr. Metz says, he's just trying to break you. Under no circumstances should you show anger or even irritation."

"I won't." That would be easy. I was used to staying calm with my parents when they were drunk. Having someone sober yelling at me would be easy by comparison.

"I'm hoping he'll go after you with everything he has. I've seen it before, and even though he knows it's not a good look for the jury, he continues to do it in his zeal to get a conviction. Joshua Metz has eyes on moving up the political ladder, and a good record of convictions is a prosecutor's way of building rungs."

Mrs. Shelton turned around to look at me and smiled her warm smile. "You'll do fine, Jack. I think by the time this is over, you will sway at least a few jurors in your favor."

We entered the courtroom and took our seats. When court was called to order, Judge Franklin said, "Mr. Shelton, do you have the photographs?"

"We do, Your Honor. May we approach?" The judge waved them forward, and Mr. Shelton gave some photos to Mr. Metz, who looked at them without emotion. The judge looked over his own set.

"Any objections, Mr. Metz?" the judge asked.

"No, Your Honor," Mr. Metz replied, still looking at the photos.

The judge looked at his pictures and handed them to the bailiff, who handed them to the first juror. He looked at them and started passing them to the other jurors. The judge allowed them time to look at the pictures before turning to Mr. Shelton.

The judge said, "The photographs will be entered as defense exhibit B. Are you ready to present your defense, Mr. Shelton?"

"We are, Your Honor. Defense calls Mrs. Mary Jane Dawson to the stand."

Mrs. Dawson strolled forward. I noticed her arm was bent at the elbow as if she were carrying Yogi, and I suddenly realized she'd always done that. I was surprised I hadn't noticed it before. Either she was too used to carrying the dog or pretending to do so made her more comfortable.

After she was sworn in and had given her name and address for the record, Mrs. Shelton stepped to the podium and said, "Mrs. Dawson, thank you for being here today. You are acquainted with the defendant?"

"Yes, we're friends."

"Just friends?" Mrs. Shelton said. I wondered

why she was doing that and when I asked later, she told me she was preventing Mr. Metz from implying they had a romantic relationship.

"Yes."

"Are you also acquainted with Jack Turner?"

"Yes, he worked for me last summer as a gardener and general handyman." She looked at me and smiled. "I would recommend him highly."

I smiled back. I thought about how I would recommend her as an employer as well.

"Did you find him to be honest and truthful?"

"Absolutely. I left a few dollars in cash and some coins lying on my kitchen table the second or third day he worked for me, just to see if he would take any. The coins were scattered, quite a few of them in fact. I wanted him to think I might not know how much money was there, but I knew the amount to the penny. The money sat there for three days, and he never touched it. I would count it each evening to make sure, and he never took one cent."

I remembered that and thought at the time she was awfully careless with her money. It had never occurred to me to take any, nor was I aware she was testing my honesty. I'd done some illegal things in my life, such as helping myself temporarily to Dan Russell's rowboat the time I found Bones, but I never did anything that could possibly hurt someone, and I counted stealing among them. Dan's boat was just borrowing without permission since we'd never considered keeping it. I had shoplifted a few times, but I'd had a good reason.

"Since you know him as well as you do, do you believe his statement to the police that the defendant never touched him in any inappropriate way?" Mrs. Shelton asked.

"I believe him because he's an honest young man. Furthermore, I know Hank, and the idea he would touch a child that way is utterly ridiculous."

"Did you ever witness any interactions between Jack and Officer Hicks of the Denton Police Department?"

Her face grew stern. "Yes." She sounded annoyed.

"Would you tell us about that?"

She explained how Officer Hicks first suspected me of having something to do with her car's disappearance, mentioning again where the car was found and how it ended up there. Then she mentioned his rough treatment of me when the detective was at her house questioning her about the car. She finished with, "I told Jack at the time he should watch out for Officer Hicks because the policeman seemed to have an enormous dislike of Jack for some reason."

"Would you be surprised to learn that Officer Hicks testified he was sad for Jack?"

Mrs. Dawson scowled. "Yes, I would. If he did, it's a pack of lies. Believe me. He doesn't like Jack in the least. He was even suspicious that Hank took my car when I reported it missing. The idea!"

"Your witness," Mrs. Shelton said to Mr. Metz, offering her warmest smile to the jury.

Mr. Metz rose and stood at the podium. "Mrs. Dawson, how many years ago did you first meet Jack Turner?"

"It was just last summer."

"So, you've known him only a few short months?"

"Yes," Mrs. Dawson said, her scowl intensifying at the line of questioning.

"Yet you claim to know him to be completely honest?"

"Yes."

"Did he ever tell you about how he found his dog?" Mr. Metz said.

"Yes."

"Did he tell you he and two friends stole a rowboat to get to Sugar Isle that day?"

"He told me he *borrowed* a rowboat."

"Did he *borrow* it with the owner's permission?"

"I don't know, but he didn't keep that man's row boat either because he is aware *that* would be stealing."

"Yet, that doesn't seem to be the actions of someone who is as honest as you claim Jack Turner is, does it?"

"You may see it as dishonest. I don't. I see it as a trio of twelve-year-old boys on an adventure."

Mr. Metz left it at that and asked, "Are you aware this honest young man was caught shoplifting at Grayson's Market two years ago?"

This surprised Mrs. Dawson. She leaned back upon hearing this. "No."

"Yes, he was caught taking a package of baloney without paying for it."

I wondered where he'd heard that information. I had been caught taking it, but it was because I hadn't eaten in two days when my parents had not come home from a party they'd attended one weekend.

Mrs. Dawson seemed to already come to that conclusion. "Perhaps he was hungry. His mother and father aren't exactly candidates for 'Parents of the Year.' If he were stealing what a child would normally steal, I would think he'd have taken a candy bar, not baloney."

Mr. Shelton, who had not heard of my one shoplifting episode, looked back at me and I nodded toward Mrs. Dawson, indicating it was exactly what she'd said it was.

I was also glad my parents weren't at the trial. They didn't even want to talk with me about it when I made it home in the evenings. If they had been there, they would not have appreciated Mrs. Dawson's comment about their poor parenting.

They might have even caused a scene in court. As it was, the jury and several spectators in the gallery looked at me. I hated the pity in their eyes. I'd prefer anger to pity any day.

"Perhaps, but stealing is still stealing," Mr. Metz said, and I was reminded of Mr. Shelton's comment that prejudice was still prejudice. It made me realize that sometimes degrees of things like stealing and prejudice existed. Nothing was always the same wherever it was found.

"And a starving child is still a starving child," Mrs. Dawson said. Her voice was firm.

"Last summer, Jack was arrested for stealing a different car, wasn't he?"

"Well, he was with a boy who stole the car," she said. Her voice had a twinge of reluctance.

"And they took a couple of girls to a pool hall in Wharton, is that correct?"

"I didn't talk to Jack much about that. I was disapp—" She stopped suddenly, realizing Mr. Metz had led her into a trap.

"You were disappointed in him?" Mr. Metz asked.

"Yes. But all children make mistakes. He messed up and admitted it."

"Was he employed by you at the time?" Mr. Metz asked.

"Yes."

"Why wasn't he at work?"

Mrs. Dawson looked at the purse in her lap, glanced at me as if to say she was sorry, and said, "He didn't come to work that day."

"Isn't it true he played hooky from work? Didn't you expect him to show up, but he didn't?"

"Yes."

"And instead of being at work, this honest person went joy-riding with a friend and two girls in a stolen car. Is that correct?"

Mrs. Dawson tried to avoid addressing that I had skipped work. Instead, she said, "He told me he didn't know it was a stolen car. You'll have to ask him about that."

"I'm sure I will," Mr. Metz replied, allowing what he'd said to stand on its own without Mrs. Dawson's admission.

Mr. Metz must have figured he'd done enough damage to me and my honesty. "The state is finished with this witness," he said, and Mrs. Dawson stepped down and took her seat in the gallery several rows behind me. She ignored Mr. Metz as she passed.

"Your next witness?" the judge asked.

Mrs. Shelton said, "The defense calls Dr. Leland Cosgrove."

A dapper, middle-aged man stepped up and took the stand. I didn't know him, but I knew who he was. He was the author of the textbook Mr. Metz had entered into evidence to explain why Hank was somehow predisposed to do what he was accused of doing to me as well as to discredit my insistence that Hank never did anything to me.

Mr. Metz stood. "Objection. We were not informed of this witness until this morning."

Mr. Shelton stood and said, "We are willing to keep our questions limited only to what Mr. Metz himself entered into the record, Your Honor. Dr. Cosgrove is a rebuttal witness, and as the author of the very textbook Mr. Metz cited, we only wish to get his complete opinion on the matter Mr. Metz used the textbook to explain."

Judge Franklin looked at Mr. Metz and said, "You entered the textbook into evidence, Josh. The defense has a right to explore the assertions you used the textbook to support. Objection overruled. Proceed."

Mrs. Shelton said, "Dr. Cosgrove, you are aware of the testimony your textbook was used to support?"

"Yes."

"In the text you say that a child who is abused is more likely to become an abuser. What percentage of those abused children, according to your years of study, become abusers as adults?"

"Maybe one-third of them."

"So, you're saying that two out of every three children who are abused do not become abusers themselves?"

"That is correct."

"What did your findings indicate as to the most likely reason for that?" Mrs. Shelton said.

"Those who do not become abusers usually were repulsed by any idea of abusing a child. They had suffered such abuse and knew how wrong it was to do something like that. They tended to be completely disgusted by the idea. The ones who do become abusers generally have other factors involved, such as a lack of a support system to help them deal with the abuse."

Mrs. Shelton looked toward the jury, and I knew she must be smiling at them.

"Dr. Cosgrove, you also mention in your textbook, and this was also entered into the record, that children often lie about the abuse. What percentage of children have you found in your studies will do that?"

"What I found was that if asked, the child will admit to the abuse in most cases. I did find that children will occasionally deny the abuse, and those children are generally afraid of the outcomes of admission. I found that the admission rate when victims were pressed was around seventy percent."

"You say the following in your textbook: 'It is significant that victims occasionally deny their own role in being victimized. This stems from the fact that to admit that they were victimized often leads to self-doubt and feelings of emotional inadequacy.

They fear that victimization will result in becoming lifelong victims of the manipulations of others.' So, what you are saying is that occasionally, as used in your book, is about thirty percent of the time, would that be correct?"

"Yes, that would be correct."

Mrs. Shelton turned to Mr. Metz. "Your witness, Mr. Metz." She turned to the jury and I again realized she was smiling at them because several of them smiled back. Despite what Mr. Shelton had said about getting my hopes up, I thought this was a very good sign. I hadn't noticed any of them smiling at Mr. Metz.

Mr. Metz stepped to the podium and asked, "Dr. Cosgrove, is it possible that the defendant is a part of the one-third of abused children who grow up to be abusers?"

"Yes."

"And is it equally possible that the victim in this case, Jack Turner, is part of the thirty percent who deny being abused?

"Yes, it's possible."

"Thank you," said Mr. Metz. "We're done with Dr. Cosgrove, Your Honor."

"Witness is excused," Judge Franklin said, and Dr. Cosgrove stepped down and left the courtroom. The judge looked at the defense table. "Call your next witness."

Mr. Shelton rose, cleared his throat, and said,

"Defense calls Jack Turner." The room suddenly grew quiet when my name was announced, and I blushed, despite wanting to testify.

As I stood, I felt every eye in the room on me. I walked to the witness stand and took my seat. Before the trial began, the attorneys and judge had already hashed out in a hearing weeks ago that I knew the difference between the truth and a lie, so I could testify.

"Would you state your name and address for the record," Mr. Shelton said.

"Jonathan George Turner, 128 Driftwood Road, Denton."

"Before we get to other matters, would you explain why you stole the baloney?"

"I was hungry. My mom and dad had gone to a party on Friday and hadn't left me anything to eat. On Sunday I decided to steal some baloney. I wanted to steal some mustard and bread, but I knew I'd get caught if I did. I was caught anyway. Now my parents make sure that I have enough food to eat if they leave."

"You make it sound as if they leave often."

"No, not really. It's only happened a few times since that time when I was ten."

"Do they leave you for long?"

"Just a couple of days." We had not gone over this in the preparation, and I wondered why Mr. Shelton was asking about this. I was anxious to get to the part where Hank didn't do anything to me. What did my parents have to do with any of this?

"And could you tell us about the incident when you were caught with a friend and two girls in a stolen car?"

"I just wanted a day off and decided to go to the beach. I met a friend there who was talking to these two girls. They were sisters, and my friend said he had a car. I knew it wasn't his, but we went into Wharton together. I should have said something, but I didn't want to look like a jerk or something, so I didn't. We were at a local pool hall where my friend likes to hang out. He's good at it and likes to play. We were there for a while and when we left, the police pulled up and stopped us from leaving.

"I know I shouldn't have done that, and I learned a lesson from it. I didn't know the car was stolen, but I knew it wasn't his." I shrugged. "I messed up."

"It's nice to see you're smart enough to learn from your mistakes," Mr. Shelton said. Later, I realized that by getting me to tell my side of the story, it would make anything Mr. Metz did regarding that time with Mark Hales seem more like bullying me. As it turned out, he didn't ask me anything about it, and I figured it must have been because Mr. Shelton had me tell my side of it before he had a chance.

"Okay, I think we're satisfied that you had no other choice to steal the baloney and wouldn't steal just to take something that didn't belong to you. And we now know you learned your lesson regarding hanging out with guys you probably should avoid.

"Now, let's get to the reason we're all here today. Would you tell us how you met the defendant?" Mr. Shelton went to his seat and sat. He'd told me he would do this. He wanted all the attention to be on me. I saw Mrs. Shelton smile at me, and I smiled back before beginning.

I told the court about finding Bones and needing to make money, explaining how I had been beaten up by Tommy, Carl, and the other guys at the docks. I told everyone about Hank offering to help me out by giving me work. I even mentioned how he'd said he wasn't interested in me doing anything "odd," as he'd put it. Next, I shared how he helped me get the job with Mrs. Dawson, allowing me to keep Bones and get him the medical care he needed. I talked about how we would have coffee together every morning, and that's all we were doing inside the bus.

I told the jury about going skinny-dipping, including why I took off my shorts instead of swimming in them and how Hank barely even looked at me. I swore to everyone he was dressed the entire time and that Tommy had lied on the stand. I explained about finding the job with Jerry at the docks and how Tommy and Carl had stolen the rods and reels but gotten away with it. I mentioned how Carl's older brother had chosen not to look into it and how the guys had their stories all straight by the time a real policeman showed up to investigate. When I came to the part about how Tommy had stolen the lure and I hadn't said anything out of fear, I realized everyone in the courtroom was staring at me. They seemed fascinated by my story.

"I ended up buying an identical lure from Jerry the next day with my own money and putting it back on the shelf when he wasn't looking. I felt terrible for allowing Tommy to steal the lure, and it was the only way I could think of to make sure it wasn't Jerry's loss while still being able to keep my job. I was afraid if I told Jerry the truth, that I hadn't stopped Tommy or said anything about it, I'd be fired. Part of me knew I deserved to lose my job, but I vowed never to let Tommy or anyone else steal from Jerry again, but it happened anyway."

"Tell us about your dog," Mr. Shelton said.

"He's great. I've been able to fatten him up and he's fine now, even after Tommy tried to poison him. All I have is what Tommy said to me as proof he did it, but he admitted it to me. But I don't have any witnesses, so it's his word against mine, but he said he did it. I'm kind of worried he might do it again because that's what he said he'd do.

"But I'm happy I have Bones, and I'm happy I saved him. He's smart, and when I'm sitting with him, he puts his head in my lap. He deserves to live and be happy. I deserve to be happy too." I looked at Hank. "Hank told me that. More than once in fact." I looked at Judge Franklin, who was looking at me. I said to him, "He's been nothing but good to me. He doesn't deserve this."

I looked at Mr. Shelton. Then I noticed again how everyone in the packed courtroom was looking at me, completely silent.

Mr. Shelton cleared his throat and said, "One more question from me, Jack. How have you been sleeping since Hank was arrested?"

"Not good," I said. "I have trouble getting to sleep, and sometimes I wake up in the middle of the night and can't get back to sleep."

"Why do you think that is?"

"I'm worried that Hank will end up going to prison for something he didn't do."

"Thank you, Jack. That's all from me." Turning to Mr. Metz, he said, "Your witness."

Mr. Metz jumped from his seat and stepped to the podium. He did not look happy at all. In fact, he looked angry. I wasn't sure why until he spoke.

"That was a very good tale, Jack. You practically had me believing it, too."

My back stiffened as I prepared for his attack. I remembered Mr. Shelton's words that no matter what he did or said, I was not to get angry. He'd even said doing that would hurt our case so much that Hank could get convicted if the jury saw me get mad at Mr. Metz.

"That's okay you feel that way. I didn't expect you to believe me. It's your job not to believe what I said."

He appeared stunned for a moment, then recovered. "Jack, are you aware that lying on the stand while under oath is a crime? That committing perjury, which is what that's called, could land you in jail?"

Judge Franklin looked at Mr. and Mrs. Shelton and asked if they wanted to object. Apparently, Mr. Metz had crossed a line I wasn't aware of, but Mr. Shelton said, "No objection, Your Honor."

Judge Franklin's brow furrowed, showing how puzzled he was about that answer. He sat back and said, "In that case, you need to answer Mr. Metz although I will tell you that perjury for a young man your age would not necessarily land you in jail, though harsh punishment could result." Next, he looked at Mr. Metz and said, "You might want to temper your threats just a bit, Josh."

"Sorry, Your Honor."

I answered Mr. Metz. "I know what a lie is. I've been hearing them all my life from people who think they're helping me. I'm told in school everyone is equal, but then I watch as people get treated unfairly because they don't have money. I sat and listened to your witnesses lie. Yes, sir. I know what a lie is."

"Are you being impudent?" Mr. Metz asked. "Are you purposely being disrespectful?"

"No sir. I'm just doing what I said I'd do."

Mr. Metz looked at the Sheltons as if they had made me promise to do something rude. Unspoken accusations showed in his eyes.

He glared back at me. "And just what is it you said you would do?" His tone suggested he had me now. The truth is I hadn't meant to make him angry or anything else with my answer. I was just being honest.

"I swore to tell the whole truth."

He looked stunned again for a moment before pausing and regaining his momentum. He nearly shouted, "Well, I don't think you are!"

I just shrugged and said, "I know."

"Frankly, I would like for you to finally tell us the truth and nothing but the truth! Hank Pittman molested you, didn't he?"

"No, sir."

"He made you do disgusting things to him, didn't he?"

"No, sir."

"You're going to stick to that . . . *story*?"

"I don't know of anything else to say," I said, and I didn't.

I could actually see him give up. He let out a long breath and said, "No more questions." It was the quietest thing he'd said while I was on the stand.

Mr. Shelton had warned me Mr. Metz would get ugly with me, and he had, though it hadn't gone on for as long as I thought it would. Mr. Metz knew if he was going to get a conviction, he would have to make me change my story, but part of me wondered if he actually wanted the conviction in the first place. He had been presented with a report of a crime being committed, and he had been forced to try the case. It wasn't his fault that his witnesses were as reliable as a stopped watch.

Mrs. Shelton rose and said, "The defense rests, Your Honor."

She sat in her chair and beamed at me, and I could see tears in her eyes. She didn't have to tell me she thought I did well.

Judge Franklin said, "We'll begin the day tomorrow with closing arguments before allowing the jury to begin deliberations." He warned the jury not to discuss the case with each other or anyone else, which he'd done each day of the trial even though everyone knew they would talk about it. Finally, the jury members were taken back to the jury room to collect their belongings before leaving the courthouse.

Tomorrow, we would find out Hank's fate. I prayed we had done enough to cut through any

Charles Tabb

prejudices of the jury. I knew if they were an honest group, they would acquit. I didn't like to think about what might happen if they weren't.

## 23

When I arrived home, I ate a tuna sandwich for dinner and went to my room to read and wait until my parents went to sleep. When I heard their snores, I rose and went out to get Bones. I needed company that night and it was threatening rain. The wind was whipping the trees and thunder rolled in from the distance. I brought Bones into my room, setting my alarm clock to wake me at six.

I was too keyed up to sleep, though. My mind skittered around the events of the past few days, refusing to let go long enough for sleep to take me. I lay there, staring at the ceiling and petting Bones as streaks of lightning popped outside, sending ghostly shadows through my room.

I imagined the jurors in their own beds. Were they having trouble sleeping, too? What were they thinking about? How many had already made up their minds, and of those, how many were voting guilty? Were any of them undecided? Were any willing to just go along with the majority just to get it over with? And what were the majority thinking?

All these questions and what seemed a million more tumbled through my head and scattered to haunt me. Suddenly, my room was filled with laughing skeletons, some pointing at me as they laughed crazily, some advancing on me where I lay.

A loud noise made me sit up in bed, gasping. My room was empty, Bones alert by my side, and I realized the noise had been thunder and the skeletons had been a dream. I'd drifted off despite my worries. I heaved a sigh and relaxed as reality pushed the terror of the dream away only to be replaced by the real terror of tomorrow. That fear had even invaded my sleep, refusing to let me rest.

The rain had been pouring for a while, and I wondered what it would be like to take a flashlight outside, find some twigs, and let them careen down the street rapids to see how many made it to the underground pipes that led to the Gulf. When that would happen, I always wondered what became of the twigs that made it that far without getting hung up on the islands of debris, adding to the obstacle rather than avoiding it. I wondered how many debris piles gathered in the gutters. Did any of the twigs make it far enough to drift with the tides and float in the Gulf?

When I was five-years-old and first started playing this game with the twigs, I pretended they were alive, that they had an awareness of their surroundings. I was now thirteen and still did that, indulging my imagination. They were just small sticks of wood that had been a part of something bigger, a tree or a bush, but it was more fun to imagine them alive, choosing the debris pile over sailing the massive Gulf of Mexico. That was why I always left them stuck in the web of sticks and grass when that happened. If they had chosen that, who was I to force them to continue the journey to the Gulf?

Rising from my bed, I turned off my alarm and dressed in cut-off jeans but no shirt. Grabbing my flashlight, I took Bones outside with me. The rain poured and I looked at Bones, who was looking at me. I could imagine him questioning my sanity.

"Let's go float some twigs," I said, and he followed me as I stepped into the downpour and made my way to the street where water swelled along the curb, splashing and tumbling along. The lightning still flashed in the distance, the thunder growling at us across the miles.

Finding a few twigs along the wet ground, I set one into the water and followed it with the beam of the flashlight as it careened along. It hung up in debris for a moment. Then, as if changing its mind, it swirled around the barrier, spinning slowly as it went around the obstacle. This first twig made it to the drain, having traveled about fifty yards to arrive there. I smiled at the outcome and walked back up the temporary river to drop the next twig.

I dropped over two dozen twigs that night, following each and keeping count how many made it to the waterfall at the drain. Fourteen. It might have been a record for me; I didn't know because I'd never kept count before, but it felt like a lot to me.

The sky was starting to lighten with the approaching sunrise, and I knew I needed to take Bones back to his place in the yard and change into dry clothes. By the time I had dressed and started a pot of coffee, the rain had ended and the sky was shedding the few clouds that remained. I was tired from not sleeping more than the few minutes that had turned into the nightmare, but I was calmer than I had been all night.

I began walking to the courthouse in time to arrive early. On the way, I thought about how my life had changed since finding Bones. I wasn't sure all the changes were for the better, but I couldn't do anything about it now. I'd done my best to save the man who had become my best friend, and the Sheltons would do their best to convince the jurors in their closing statements that Hank was innocent, the victim of overzealous prosecution.

After that, Hank's fate—and by extension mine—were up to twelve people none of us had met until a few days ago.

When I arrived at the courthouse, it was over an hour before time for the trial to continue. I entered and made my way to the courtroom. As I walked through the swinging doors, I was surprised to see I was only the second person there. Mr. Metz was sitting in his chair. His back was to me when I entered, but he heard the doors open and turned to see me. Our eyes locked for a second before he smiled, something that surprised me. I'd not seen him smile once during the trial.

I was wary of him, and I suppose he recognized that.

"It's okay. The questioning phase of the trial is all over."

I walked down the aisle and sat in my seat. He turned toward me and said, "I know what you're thinking. You think of me as the enemy." I nodded. "I'm not, you know."

"He didn't do it. I swear that's the truth."

Mr. Metz turned in his seat to look at me, squinting and cocking his head to one side as if trying to figure something out.

"The police tell me you're afraid of what he said he'd do if you told."

"The police are idiots."

He chuckled. "Not all of them."

"If he did anything, I would say so, no matter what he said he'd do. He wouldn't be able to do anything because he'd be in prison."

Mr. Metz's face changed, and I actually wondered if he was about to tell me he believed me. I was almost certain of it. He opened his mouth to speak, but at that moment the doors to the courtroom swung open and the bailiff walked in. Mr. Metz sighed and turned away from me and went back to his work. I turned in my seat to face the bench and wait for Hank and the Sheltons.

Five minutes later, they walked through the doors. I wanted to share what Mr. Metz had said, but I didn't. Instead, I smiled at Hank and the Sheltons.

"Well, you're here early," Mr. Shelton said as he placed his briefcase on the table and took his seat. Hank sat between the Sheltons and turned to me.

"How're you holding up?" he asked.

"Fine. Couldn't sleep last night, though. I drifted off once, but a nightmare and a clap of thunder woke me up." I didn't say anything about going out in the rain to float twigs.

"How are you holding up?" I asked Hank.

"Just as fine, though I never slept long enough to have a nightmare." He smiled at me.

Mr. Shelton leaned over to say something to Hank, breaking up our greeting.

The courtroom began to fill as we waited for nine o'clock and the judge's entrance. I glanced over at Mr. Metz a few times, but he was never looking my way. I wondered what he had started to say to me. I sat pondering the world of adults. Mr. Shelton had explained a while back how Mr. Metz had to prosecute Hank even though he knew the case had holes in it. I had always thought adults could do what they wanted, but that wasn't true, and for the first time, I wondered what kind of adult I would become.

At five after nine, court was called into session and the final day of proceedings began.

When instructed to begin his summation, Mr. Metz stood, glanced my way, and stepped in front of the jury box.

"I know what you're thinking," he said to the jurors, who were watching his every move as if he might jump into the jury box and attack someone, and I was surprised because he'd said the same thing to me that morning. "You're thinking we haven't presented any physical evidence in this case. No fingerprints to prove the defendant is guilty. No blood found at a crime scene to help make sense of this.

"But this type of crime has no such evidence. This is a case of one of the good citizens of Denton coming forward after witnessing an unusually friendly relationship between an older man and a boy who is today, months later, barely thirteen.

"This is a case in which the two were seen in what they thought were private moments. The defense has called the motives of the witnesses into question, but they have not provided any testimony that this did not happen, with the one exception being the victim himself, whose denials can be easily explained through psychology. Jack Turner is not a bad kid, but his upbringing, as evidenced by the defense's own witness, has been less than exemplary. Who can blame the young boy for seeking some sort of older man who is willing to show him affection?

"The problem, of course, is that the affection went beyond the boundaries we as a society will accept. The defense presented Jack as an honest child; however, his past provides evidence this is not exactly true. He was caught stealing from a local grocery store, and regardless of the reasons, stealing is still stealing. He admits to taking a rowboat belonging to another person without that person's permission, and he was caught with a friend in a stolen car, which had basically been used to go on a date with two girls they'd met only that day. Yes, basically, Jack Turner is an honest boy. But he will do dishonest things if they benefit him.

"Yes, I feel bad for Jack because of the poverty-stricken life he is forced to lead—a life without the proper influence of his parents, who, I might add, have not appeared once in this courtroom during this trial to give their son support. I do not know why they've been absent. Perhaps they don't care. Maybe they believe the defendant is guilty and see no reason to be here to support their son's lies. Again, I don't know the reason for their absence. I will let you draw your own conclusions.

"However, one thing is certain. The witnesses saw what they say they saw. And since that is the case, you have no other choice but to find the defendant guilty on all counts."

He continued for some time, going over the evidence and trying his best to piece together what they say happened with the testimony from his witnesses. I watched the jury while he did this, and none of them gave their thoughts away. I had hoped to see some disbelief, but I didn't.

When he'd presented his summary, he said, "Finally, I want to thank you for your time and attention to this matter. The State of Florida brings fine people like you into courtrooms to make bold decisions. Jurors affect the lives of many people. The decisions that must be made are difficult because we don't want to believe someone could commit heinous crimes such as the ones before you now. But we do know these crimes exist. Many children suffer from the unwanted attention of adults in their lives. You can make sure today that such unwanted attention will not happen to Jack

Turner again, despite his denials. Thank you."

Mr. Metz took his seat, and Mrs. Shelton wheeled her chair over to the jury box. Positioning it so it faced the jury, she sat and took the posture of someone who has stopped by a neighbor's house for coffee and a friendly chat.

"Forgive me, but I'm wearing new shoes today, and my feet are already killing me." The jurors chuckled at this. I don't know if she was telling the truth or not. Still, it seemed just like what it looked like—a good friend stopping by to talk.

"Yes, the prosecuting attorney is right. This is a case where no real evidence exists to convict Hank Pittman. None. I have to say, I actually pity the prosecuting attorney. He came into this trial stuck between a rock and a hard place. He had to try the case because not to do so would raise lots of questions, especially since Mr. Pittman is the son of David Moreland. Even if the defendant chose to drop his last name, he is still a Moreland, a powerful name in this county. The prosecutor took this case, and I know he is smart enough to realize that this is just a case of a vengeful woman making false accusations based upon her observations of Mr. Pittman and Jack Turner being alone together in Mr. Pittman's home.

"I have to ask you to think about something. Have you ever had someone alone with you in your home for two hours? Someone not related to you?

Did you engage in sexual activities with that person? Should we think you did because—my heavens!—you were alone with that person for two hours? Apparently, the chief witness for the prosecution would have us think that.

"Mr. Metz did well with his summation. He managed to cheat the truth a bit, though. He said that an eye witness saw Mr. Pittman engaging in sex with Jack. I'm sorry, but on cross examination, the witness could not identify what to everyone on this jury was the first thing you would notice if you were to see Mr. Pittman naked. His lower back is covered in very noticeable scars, and he is missing one buttock entirely. The witness tried to come up with a reason for not noticing this, but he certainly seemed sure that he saw the area below Mr. Pittman's waist when testifying about the alleged sexual contact. If he could see his back, why not the obvious scars? The answer is as obvious as the wounds suffered by Mr. Pittman as a hero in World War II. He saw neither because what he described never happened. Jack Turner has come forward and told you that he was indeed naked and swimming that day, and I for one understand what it's like to wear wet denim all day when it's hot outside, as it was that day, and I'm willing to bet you do, too.

"Jack's explanation is plausible. I don't know about you, but as I listened to Jack tell his story, I tried to imagine myself deciding whether or not he was telling the truth. I came to the conclusion he was, and it wasn't even close.

"One thing Mr. Metz said is definitely the unvarnished truth. Jack Turner is honest and a good kid. I've come to know him well over these past months, and a more honorable person his age I've never met. It didn't surprise me at all that he never touched the money Mrs. Dawson laid out to test his honesty. Yes, he did shoplift when he was ten, but who among you wouldn't do the same thing if faced with being a hungry ten-year-old after your neglectful parents disappeared for three days? So, he took a package of baloney. Baloney, for Pete's sake! He was hungry. He didn't do it on a dare. He didn't do it for fun. He didn't do it to see if he could get away with it. Yes, stealing is stealing, but when you're ten and your stomach hurts from hunger, you tend to make decisions like stealing some food to stop the hunger pains. He openly expressed regret for the incident involving the stolen car. I believe him when he said he didn't know it was stolen.

"And consider this, ladies and gentlemen. This young boy sought honest work in order to save the life of a starving dog. He knew what it was like to be hungry. He knew what it was like to be neglected. He knew what it was like to be in need of love. Instead of trying to steal food, he risked his safety by undercutting the price to clean fish and making seven boys so angry at him they beat the tar out of him and took the money he earned.

"The man who came along and rescued Jack was doing for him what Jack did for that starving dog. And for his troubles, he now sits before you charged with a terrible crime. I wouldn't be surprised if everyone stopped helping others if this is the price they have to pay.

"The good news is that people like Hank Pittman would do it again, even knowing that price. Hank loves Jack like a son. He does not love him like a lover.

"Do some adults do what Hank is accused of doing? Unfortunately, yes they do, and if a child comes forward and honestly says it happened, no jail is too terrible a place for the person who harmed that child. Jack swears it never happened to him. I have no trouble at all believing him because if Mr. Pittman had done what he's accused of, I would have told him to find another attorney. We don't need his money that badly."

Most of the jury chuckled at that, and I wondered if Mrs. Shelton had said it to break the tension a bit. For the jurors, it was probably like the relief of walking out of a theater after watching a very intense or scary movie. They could breathe normally now. Everything was fine.

"Mr. Metz was also correct when he said he respects the job you have to do. The defense respects that job as well. But this time the job is an easy one. It should be as plain as the scars on the defendant's backside that Hank Pittman did nothing bad to Jack, who loses sleep for fear that you will return a verdict of guilty. He would not do that if he were the victim of abuse. If that were the case, his fear would be that you might set Hank free.

"So, for the sake of all that is holy, set Hank Pittman free. Tell this state they should have more than a vengeful woman's word and the obviously false testimony of a boy who hates Jack Turner to take a good man to trial on such a charge. It would be one thing if Jack didn't want to talk about what did or didn't happen to him, but he's adamant it never happened. Believe him. He's a remarkable young man, and he's not lying. Not even close. Thank you, ladies and gentlemen. I trust you to do the right thing."

Mrs. Shelton wheeled her chair back into place as silence held the room for a moment, much as it had several other times during the trial.

Judge Franklin cleared his throat and charged the jury, telling them if they thought one thing they needed to find the defendant guilty, and if they thought another thing, they should find the defendant not guilty. He used a lot of legal terms and such in his instructions, but in the end the jury was taken back to the jury room to discuss the case and decide on the verdict.

Two hours went by. Why was it taking so long?

I asked Mr. Shelton about it.

"Well, juries should take their time with a verdict."

"But it's obvious he's not guilty," I said.

"It's obvious to you and me, but not necessarily to them. Like I told you, probably one or two walked in the first day thinking he was guilty. Some folks believe that if the police arrest someone, they had to have a good reason to do it. That's not always true, but plenty of people believe it is."

I sat back, praying they would return with a verdict of not guilty.

We went out to lunch again, but I didn't order anything but a coke and some crackers to help my stomach. Hank didn't eat either. Apparently the Sheltons were used to waiting for a jury to make a decision. They each had a full lunch.

When we returned to the courthouse, the jury was still out. Lunch had been ordered in for them, so we prepared ourselves for a long wait.

Finally, just before four o'clock that afternoon, they sent word they had reached a verdict. The length of their deliberations meant some of them had probably been pretty set on a verdict the others didn't agree with, according to the Sheltons.

The verdict probably depended on what the majority thought at the beginning of their deliberations.

Judge Franklin entered as we rose and the jury

was brought in. They looked tired, as if they'd been engaged in hard physical labor, and several refused to even look in our direction. Glares were exchanged by some of the jurors, and I wondered how much anger and hatred had been born in the jury room. The bailiff ambled to the jury foreman, who handed a sheet of paper to him. He slowly walked the paper to the judge. The Honorable George William Franklin III spent an eternity reading the verdicts to each charge to himself before he handed the paper back to the bailiff, who returned it to the jury foreman. Each second was agony.

Finally, Judge Franklin asked, "Mr. Foreman, has the jury reached a verdict?"

*Tick. Tick. Tick.*

The foreman was a tall man in his forties with dark hair, black-framed glasses, and a red bow tie. "We have, Your Honor," he finally said after clearing his throat for a maddeningly long time and pinching the bridge of his nose below his glasses. I looked up at the clock and watched as seconds ticked by, one after another. The bailiff sneezed. The judge looked out at the people in the gallery before turning his gaze to Hank and the Sheltons.

"The defendant will rise," Judge Franklin said. Turning to the foreman, he continued, "On the first count of the state's indictment, contributing to the delinquency of a minor, how do you find?" The room itself seemed to hold its breath.

The foreman looked at the paper in his hand as if he didn't know what might be written there. Seconds continued to tick by. "We find the defendant—" Someone behind me started coughing, interrupting the foreman's announcement of the verdict. He gazed out at the gallery, finally decided to ignore the momentary disturbance, and returned to the paper, once again seeming not to know what was written there as he squinted at the paper. I could hear it rattle in his hands.

"—not guilty," he croaked.

My head swam as I tried to work out the meaning of those simple words, and I remember being happy I was seated to prevent me from falling to the floor. Tears stung my eyes as the sense of the first verdict dawned on me and my heart pounded.

"On the count of taking indecent liberties with a minor, how do you find?" said the judge.

Look. Squint. Read. "We find the defendant not guilty," he said again.

"On the count of sodomy with a minor, how do you find?"

The foreman paused. "We find the defendant not guilty," he finally said.

I couldn't contain myself. Not guilty on all counts! I jumped up and whooped. Judge Franklin banged his gavel several times.

"Young man, I would remind you that you are

in a court of law and will conduct yourself accordingly."

I sat back down, but my face glowed as one big smile.

The next several minutes were a blur, going by as quickly as the previous minutes had crept. A jumble of motion and noise followed as Hank hugged his attorneys, thanking them over and over. We parted at the doors to the courthouse, and I left with Hank. We walked to his bus, my home away from home. He invited me to stay for dinner, and I accepted as long as I could go home and get Bones. He agreed, saying he had to run to the store and buy some steaks anyway.

"Don't forget, though, you have a flounder sandwich in my refrigerator," he said. "You can stop by tomorrow for lunch and have it."

We ate our meal that night with Bones lying on the floor between us, praying for something to drop to the floor. I removed some fat from my steak and dropped it, and Bones pounced on his manna from heaven. Hank did the same with his fat, even though he liked it almost as much as the meat.

I looked at the man who had taken me in when I needed it most even though I didn't know how much I needed him in my life until I feared losing him. I wanted to say so many things, but I couldn't find the words to express them. I was sure he knew them already anyway.

# 24

I stared through my windshield at the house that had never really been a home. The tears had long since dried on my cheeks, and I wondered what I would say at the funeral of the man who had done more to raise me than anyone else. He had nearly sacrificed his freedom for me. For years people would look at me as if wondering if the allegations were true. The question was in their eyes, but thankfully not on their lips. That's the problem with allegations like that. People often refuse to change their original conclusions. Occasionally, Hank and I would talk about what happened and he would admit to the same looks, as well as losing several friends, if that's what he could call someone who so easily abandoned him. After my parents died one night driving home from another drunken party, I moved in with him. By that time he'd broken down and bought a house.

We found out about the jury vote after a couple of jurors were interviewed by the local paper. Of the twelve jurors, three were determined to vote guilty, despite everything we had done. It took the other nine all that time and effort to wear them down enough to change their votes. Nothing about that has changed. Juries still get hung by stubbornness, though that can sometimes be a good thing.

I pulled away from my childhood home and drove to the mortuary where the service would be held prior to burying Hank's ashes in a small plot next to his wife and children. Getting out of the car, I saw Mrs. Dawson and Jerry on the front steps. Mrs. Dawson gave a whoop of delight when she saw me, making her way down the steps and hugging me harder than I thought she could at her age. Jerry smiled and shook my hand. He hadn't changed much in the seventeen years since I left Denton for college and a career, other than his hair had turned gray. Mrs. Dawson had dyed her hair a red so bright it was almost orange, reminding me of Lucille Ball. Her face was more wrinkled, but her smile was still the same one I'd always liked.

Pictures of Hank, including a few of his late wife and children, were everywhere. My favorite was one of the two of us, taken a couple of weeks after the trial. We were sitting in Jerry's store, laughing about something long forgotten.

When it came time for me to speak, I stepped to the front of the room and faced the thirteen others who were there, including the Sheltons and their two sons, along with their families. The Sheltons accounted for nine of the mourners. The sad smiles of those gathered to say good-bye to Hank greeted mine, and I could see tears brimming in both Mrs. Dawson's and Mrs. Shelton's eyes, but the three of us managed to hold it together.

I hadn't prepared anything to say, trusting it would come to me at the proper time. I spoke of how Hank and I formed our friendship and how he had done so much for me. I apologized to him for not coming back sooner, but I'm sure he understood. We spoke by phone often and exchanged greetings and gifts by mail at holidays and birthdays. I talked about everything he meant to me. And I spoke about the horrible night he had earned his silver star for heroism, a story he'd told me a few months after the trial with instructions never to tell anyone else until he was gone. I'd kept my promise.

He had been the victim of an explosion when a soldier who was walking behind him stepped on a land mine, resulting in the eventual loss of Hank's left buttock and quite a bit of flesh on his back. Yet even in immense pain and weakness from blood loss, he managed to save the life of another soldier, who was also wounded but unconscious. He had dragged himself and the other soldier along the ground, clawing his way toward the forest nearly three-hundred yards away where the safety of camouflage waited. He had done what he could to patch up his friend. While hiding there, he managed to kill nine Germans in a firefight. He claimed it was a miracle he and the other man didn't die or get captured at least. The other soldier survived as well. That man had gone on to become a surgeon and worked to save lives himself.

It was the story of how lives are like dominoes in a row. One action has a ripple effect, touching the lives around us, and that thought made me recall the floating twigs of my childhood and the solitary game I had played for the last time in my life during the trial.

We left the mortuary and drove the three miles to the cemetery that sat among moss-draped live oaks not far from the shore of Denton Bay. It was a nice little place, shady under the canopy of trees that surrounded the small cemetery, which covered no more than an acre. The oaks drooped, appearing to be in perpetual mourning for the dead they were destined to watch over. Still, it seemed like a happy place.

I had dinner that night with Jerry and Mrs. Dawson. The Seaside had closed several years before, so we went to the new Captain's Dock on Sugar Isle, which was built on a pier over the water. The food was good, but the restaurant reminded me of the eyesores assaulting the shore.

When we finished, I said my good-byes and drove away, promising to visit again soon but knowing I probably wouldn't. I think they knew it too. As I drove over Denton Bridge, I took a last look at the condominiums and townhouses that covered Sugar Isle like a shroud. Their lights gleamed in the darkness like fake stars. I could see where I found Bones, who had lived until I was a senior in high school. I had spent three days crying over my loss until I realized I hadn't lost anything really. I had only gained.

As I drove to my home in New Orleans, stopping for the night in Pensacola a few hours west of Denton, I thought about all I had gained from knowing Bones and Hank.

And I prayed they had gained something from knowing me.

## *About the Author*

Charles Tabb retired from teaching and now writes full-time. His work has appeared in various literary journals, including *Ariel Chart*, *The Scarlet Leaf Review* and *Fiction on the Web*. He lives near Richmond, Virginia, with his wife Dee, their rescued dog, and Dee's two off-the-track thoroughbred horses. Besides writing, he likes to travel, read, and spend time with family.

Charles is a proud member of the Virginia Writers' Club, The Hanover Writers' Club, and James River Writers. Please visit his webpage at charlestabb.com and follow him on Twitter, @CharlesTabb919.

Made in the USA
Middletown, DE
11 December 2020

27494796R00236